PRAISE FOR LOSING ABSALOM
BY ALEXS D. PATE

"In honest and lyrical prose, Pate explores the American dream, the inner city, the hope and the sorrow of parenthood and the fragility of life." —*Publishers Weekly*

"Convincing . . . powerful . . . a memorable, searing tale of life in the City of Brotherly Love . . . Its value transcends racial or cultural boundaries. Pate's novel is a testament to life as it is lived now." —*Philadelphia Daily News*

"Extraordinary . . . breathtaking . . . gripping and vivid . . . *Losing Absalom* portrays with remarkable insight and sympathy a contemporary African-American family's struggle . . . Pate colors *Losing Absalom* with grace and poignancy, and imbues the novel with an air of immediacy. The calm energy and passion of the narrative make the inevitable final tragedy especially wrenching." —*Indiana Review*

"A tour de force of assurance and metaphorical style . . . Pate has staked out territory in the stratosphere of American writers, and readers should be warned: This is the start of a strong career by this writer."

—*Aesthetics*

continued . . .

"This is the book I needed to read the day my father died. *Losing Absalom* by Alexs Pate opened the door to the African-American home. Many readers will think of their own loved ones who daily confront illness, who struggle to build dreams and survive. *Losing Absalom* might just be as important as Baldwin's *Go Tell It on the Mountain*."

—E. Ethelbert Miller,
African American Resource Center,
Howard University

"*Losing Absalom* is a novel about struggle. On an individual level each character is fighting to find out exactly who they are and how they fit in the world, while on a deeper level they symbolize all African-American people fighting to find the same thing." —*Los Angeles Times Book Review*

"An epic novel that spans a wide range of people and experiences instead of the usual span of continents and time... *Losing Absalom* is a sharply drawn portrait of a black family in crisis that's so chock-full of tasty nuggets of prose and jump-off-the-page characters it's almost too good to be true."

—*The Mac Weekly*

"A moving, poignant story of love, family and community, which unfolds against the deteriorating backdrop of urban America ... masterful, provocative literature."

—*Quarterly Black Review*

LOSING ABSALOM

ALEXS D. PATE

BERKLEY BOOKS, NEW YORK

"song," copyright © 1987, by Lucille Clifton. Reprinted from GOOD WOMAN: POEMS AND A MEMOIR, 1969–1980, by Lucille Clifton, with the permission of BOA Editions, Ltd., 92 Park Ave., Brockport, NY 14420.

Excerpt from "Times Are Gettin' Ill" (Rob Ginyard), reprinted with permission. Copyright © 1988 Protoons, Inc./Hikim Music/ASCAP.

A portion of this book has appeared as a chapbook, *Absalom Falls,* published by the Minnesota Center for Book Arts, 1993.

The original publishers would like to thank the Star Tribune/Cowles Media Company and The McKnight Foundation for major grants that helped make this book possible. Additional assistance was also provided by the following funders: Dayton Hudson Foundation; The Lannan Foundation; and The Andrew W. Mellon Foundation. This activity is made possible in part by a grant provided by the Minnesota State Arts Board, through an appropriation by the Minnesota State Legislature. Major new marketing initiatives have been made possible by the Lila Wallace—Reader's Digest Literary Publishers Marketing Development Program, funded through a grant to the Council of Literary Magazines and Presses.

LOSING ABSALOM

A Berkley Book / published by arrangement with
Coffee House Press

PRINTING HISTORY
First hardcover edition published by
Coffee House Press, Minneapolis, Minnesota, 1994
Berkley edition / August 1995

ISBN: 0-425-15013-5

BERKLEY®
Berkley Books are published by The Berkley Publishing Group,
200 Madison Avenue, New York, New York 10016.
BERKLEY and the "B" design
are trademarks belonging to Berkley Publishing Corporation.

PRINTED IN THE UNITED STATES OF AMERICA

10 9 8 7 6 5 4 3 2

Shouts and Acknowledgments

The energy to write this story, to tell it as well as I could, was generated by so many people, in so many ways. suzanna maria gipsky read the manuscript in each of its many versions—each time with a sharp eye, love, and wonder. I couldn't have done it without her. The friendship and unflinching literary support from Mary Francois Rockcastle buoyed me through the toughest times. David Mura, Judith Katz, J. Otis Powell!, and my homie Ralph Remington gave great gifts: They believed in me.

There once was a group of African American writers, assembled by Charyn Sutton at Temple University, from whom I learned the significance of the literary arts to the survival of African American culture. We called ourselves the Maji Collective and included: Meta Carstarphen, Jerry Fluellen, Dine Watson, Michelle Parkerson, Sam Logue, Gail Brown, and Garland Thompson. We, in turn, were touched by the fire of Askia Muhammad Toure and influenced by Houston A. Baker, Jr.

To the following people I can only say thanks for the love, support and strength: Yvonne Cheek, Earl Irby, Essex Hemphill, Seitu Jones, Soyini Guyton, Meta Carstarphen, Jean Anne Durades, Roderick Thomas, Me-K, Cyprian Lamar Rowe, Cynthia Mayeda, Barrie Jean Borich, Walter Alan Bennett, Kimlar Satterthwaite, Wilfred Smith, Otto Saunders, Wanda Pate, Napoleon Andrews, Patrick Scully, Howard Cherry, Walter Williams, Nikki Billingsly, Dine Watson, Robert Watson, Patricia Hampl, Sue Halloran, Margaret Hasse, Kathy Coskran, Jill Breckenridge, John Slothower, Nancy Rains, James Naiden, Julie Landsman, Susan Sencer, Sandy Benítez, Nora Shapiro, James Spady, Homer Jackson, Don Belton, Sandy Agustin, Carei Thomas, Erica Herrmann, John Killacky, Nate Fields, Pamela Holt, Pamela Fletcher, Norma Anderson, Michelle Helgen, Margie Ligon, Susan Broadhead, Marcela Kingman, Sheila O'Connor, and Willis Bright.

Every writer in every city should have an organization like The Loft to be nurtured by; it was there that this writer's voice bloomed. And, my sincere gratitude goes to Allan Kornblum, editor and publisher, who brought a careful, sensitive eye to this book, as did David Caligiuri.

Finally to my agent, Faith Childs, goes my deepest appreciation and affection.

Gyanni, Alexs and Chekesha . . . I have not forgotten.

For Alexander and Lois Pate

LOSING ABSALOM

song

sons of slaves and
daughters of masters
all come up from the
ocean together

daughters of slaves and
sons of masters
all ride out on the
empty air

brides and hogs and dogs and babies
close their eyes against the sight

bricks and sticks and diamonds witness
a life of death is the death of life

—LUCILLE CLIFTON

O my son Absalom, my son, my son Absalom!
Would God I had died for thee, O Absalom, my son,
my son!

—2 SAMUEL 18.33

Absalom moved like a hummingbird, flitting from place to place, taking what nectar there was to take and then moving on. He had discovered this ability only recently as the clamping, sharp whip of cancer lashed across his left temple.

Absalom was like a living ghost. He was everywhere. And even though it sometimes frightened him, he willingly accepted it, clung to this existence as a way to keep living. Sometimes it was magical, sometimes sad. He could dance on the branches of spruce trees. He could clearly see things take place in his mind that were happening somewhere else, even at a different time. Reality changed as the pain intensified. His mind seemed to take charge and demand diversion. From wallowing screams of pity, through scribbles of fantasy, through recollections of love, through the terror of ending, his mind fluttered like beating wings, slowing only when there was no pain and it was safe to rest. Then Absalom let himself be cradled by shadow and silence.

Absalom had only recently lost the ability to talk to those around him. He no longer controlled his physical movement. Nurses, doctors, aides forced his body to do things. Not him. He resented their control. They determined if he were to lie in the sun or be wheeled into the shade. They covered him if he shivered. They hooked up the contraption that helped him urinate. They emptied it.

To escape them and the fire in his head, Absalom had only to let his mind catch a strand of the air that slowly, awkwardly rolled into his laboring lungs and he would find himself set free.

And now that he was once again ensconced in the operating room, he could feel them inside his head. It was an unusual feeling, as if he had a football helmet on and someone was scraping the outer surface with a coin. Or like being submerged in water while, poolside, people clacked by in high-heeled shoes. Through the thick drape of anesthesia, he felt the metal objects being manipulated in his head.

He fought them. He could not lie there and let them reduce his life to the thing they held under their tunneling fingers.

''Gwen? Where are you? Thought you'd be here by now? You and Sonny should have been here by now.'' Absalom stopped as he realized that they couldn't get to him. The operating room was a place they didn't know. It was a room where even the sun could hide.

In the blinding light Absalom saw his father riding his tractor toward him. He rode right through the North Carolina cornfield, through the white walls, past the crowd of white-coated reapers, and up to Absalom's bedside. "Ab, you slopped those hogs yet?"

"No sir." Absalom was frightened, his body tensed. He couldn't help it. He had never not been afraid of his father.

His father's dark body was burned dry. Thin strings of white ash formed lines in his skin like a map. One of his large hands held the steering wheel, the other an old Bible.

"Relax, son, I ain't gonna hurt you. I know you gonna get to it." His father's voice had a softness that only death could give it. Absalom thought he could smell the gasoline fumes from the tractor's engine. He heard its rumbling. He could see his father trembling in the metal half-moon seat.

His father stared at him. "I thought you was gonna be a preacher, Ab, I truly did. When you was about to be born I coulda swore that God sent me a sign that you was gonna be a preacher."

Absalom had heard his father say this before. But he had never been attracted to the church. He hardly ever went to Sunday service. He found his worship at home. "Me? A preacher? I wouldn't be no good at preachin'."

"You're wrong, Ab. I had a sign. I coulda swore it. Why you think you got the name you got?"

Absalom remembered the story. His father had received a leather-bound Bible as a gift from a friend from Delaware who was passing through North Carolina. The Bible was already old.

According to his father, the fading signature on the first page was penned by the great former slave Absalom Jones. It was he, along with Richard Allen, who led his African American flock out of the Methodist Episcopal church. Those who remained Methodist went with Richard Allen, and those who wanted to worship as Episcopalians, with Absalom Jones.

The Bible had been displayed, opened to the inscription, on the mantle over the hearth of Absalom's young years. Now his father held it out to him. "It ain't too late you know, you can always follow through on your calling."

Absalom stared at the book, its gilded edges faded. Even now he didn't feel holy. There was no calling. "I'm dying, Daddy. Your prayers for me have to be bigger than that book." Absalom knew his father was dead but couldn't make his image go away. He knew that his father had already given the Bible to him and that he, Absalom, had already given it to his daughter, who kept it in her bedroom.

Still his father sat there, smiling. "I told you, Ab, this here book was a sign. Reverend Jones fixed his name right here. And above that he wrote,

*Through the sun and the rain, through everything—
God.''*

Absalom smiled. He watched as the Bible and
then his father and then the tractor disappeared. He
sighed. He moved again. Now he could see his wife
and *his* son coming to him.

Absalom had named the boy Sonny and the
daughter that came four years later Lorraine, who he
insisted everyone call Rainy. He'd gotten the idea
from the inscription in the Bible, ''Through the sun
and the rain.'' Neither of the children had liked their
names, but, in some unexplainable way, Absalom
had felt it was his duty to connect them to his father
and the Bible that had always been there.

He felt them coming to be with him. Like a choir
to concert, he knew they would come: Gwen, Sonny,
Rainy, maybe others. Their voices full up, throaty,
ready to gospel him away.

1

Sonny stood in the Saturday sun, looking up at Mid-town Hospital, which jutted up against the bright August morning like a gleaming silver-white monolith. It was a place where people came for help. A chapel for slipping voices. A place where the waning song was often ushered into silence.

Sonny watched his mother enter the hospital. She was welcomed into the spinning doors and transformed to healing energy as she disappeared into the standing hymn. He stood by the car for a moment, as if he were a chauffeur. He leaned back. Loneliness grabbed him like a drunken lover, digging fingers into his flesh.

A feeling settled into his stomach—a slow, steady, draining emptiness. His smooth paper-bag brown face contorted in response to the sun and the task before him.

Sonny's face was pliant like Absalom's in his prime. In pleasure, a smile could move both earlobes. But under strain, it could roll up like Gwen's crescent dinner rolls. Dreading his role as the son of a dying man, all his distinctive features merged into the frameless picture of a man fighting tears. He slammed the car door shut, cleared his throat, and sighed.

Twenty-four hours earlier, he had been in Minneapolis sitting at his desk on the twelfth floor of a Fortune 500 computer company, a vast building of dark windows that did not open. When the telephone rang, Sonny had been hunched over his computer keyboard, his cedar fingers spreading amber letters across the screen. At work, Sonny was happy and ambitious, and he loved the surge of power that flowed through the company. He was on the rise at Data Central. He was just a manager now but he saw the path to executive status being cleared for him. All he had to do was work for it. Which was what he was doing.

He was beginning to believe what his mother had always told him: that he was special, that he could be a success, and that there was a whole *nother* world on the other side of the ghetto wall. He had found it. Even at this point in his career, he was making more money than Absalom ever had, and he liked it. He liked the corporate life, the wine and expensive lunches. He like the way people treated him when he paraded his designer suits in front of them. He was proof that if a person thought of himself as important, he could become important.

And yet he carried a secret in his heart. He was afraid. There always came a moment in each day when he was frightened. When he really wondered whether he belonged where he was. After all, it was so far away from where he'd come. The shadows of the inner city. The houses that stood body to body, separated only by alleys and avenues. The shake of funk that underscored every movement.

Here he was, a black man on the move. Buried in a life long held away from men like him. A life in which white men, who were no more talented than the brothers he had known on the street, made decisions that affected everything. They were the captains of industry. And he was now sitting at their table. And every time he thought this, he became afraid that one day someone would ask him to leave, to go back home.

He shouldered the façade of having everything together, of being strong and self-assured, even though at certain moments, it was a façade of incredible thinness, like tissue.

Still, he couldn't deny that it was *his* work, *his* press releases that spurred the avalanche of revenue into the company, *his* personal contacts at the country's most influential newspapers that gave his company the kind of exposure it was getting for its new products. Everyone, whether they wanted to admit it or not, knew as much.

There were, of course, many people in the company who looked at Sonny and were gratified, impressed. Here was the product of diversity and affirmative action. Sonny knew they wondered about him and he reveled in it. He could hear them thinking "Who is this black man? Where the hell did he come from?"

Not hell, not hell, but North Philadelphia. A place with as much love as pain. As much gold as tarnish. Though the stone truth was that more people were beaten by the harsh life than should be true. But Sonny wasn't one of them. He had dodged gangs, avoided drugs and the increasing disintegration of life that moved like a long line of dominoes in gentle fall in every major eastern city.

He had broken free, thanks in part to his mother, and climbed aboard the modern underground railroad, otherwise called education. And he knew who he was, an African American man who could be successful in a white world. Now he was on the doorstep, on the verge of money and power.

He viewed his computer screen, perusing his latest creation, a treatise on computer-based education and its capacity to transform inner-city schools. He had specifically asked to work on this project. He had chosen Data Central very carefully. Its chief executive officer believed there was a way to tie profit-making to inner-city needs. The computer-based education product was the company's first attempt. They were offering an entire high school curriculum in an interactive computer program. They would try it first in inner-city schools.

This was how he could contribute. He could use his education and his growing influence in the company to help educate the people he had left behind.

When the telephone rang he was already five minutes late for the weekly staff meeting. He ignored it, hoping his secretary would intercept; but after the third ring he picked up the receiver.

When he heard his mother's voice on the other end he felt tremors in his stomach. "What's wrong? Is there anything wrong?" he said even before hello. He called her often enough for family news. When she called him, it usually meant trouble, and he could tell by her hesitation that this call was no exception.

"Well, ah . . ."

He steadied his jaw, a brown rock thrown from the dirt of his father's North Carolina earth. After five years with the public relations department at Data Central, Sonny had become expert in putting on the right face, showing just the right amount of emotion. Finally it became the way he dealt with his personal life, too.

He felt his mother holding back rivers. It had to be bad. It was a Thursday morning. She would never call him on a workday morning unless it was important. Finally he took a deep breath and plunged into the darkness. "How's everything, Mom?"

"Fine, Sonny, just fine. I was just calling to see how you were."

Right. He knew better. "Oh, I'm doing okay."

"Well, I was just thinking about you today. Thought I'd call." Her voice shook.

Suddenly his father's face flashed in front of his eyes. That was it. "How's Dad?" he asked.

"Well. . . ."

"Is Dad sick?" Sonny felt himself flailing as he scrambled to find a pocket of air amidst the tension.

"Well, we . . . ah . . . we took your dad to the hospital today. They want to do some tests."

"Tests? Tests for what?" Sonny's mind quickly searched through all the casual reports of headaches and earaches over the past year.

"Well . . . they're not sure."

"Not sure about what, Mom? What's wrong?" He wanted to scream at her, "Just tell me. Damn it. Just tell me what the hell is going on." But instead he held it inside just like she did.

"Sonny, I think you better come home as soon as you can."

Sonny knew then his instincts were right. His father had to be very sick. And even though he specifically asked her what was wrong four times, Gwen never said.

At that point he had no more questions. Everything was clear. No, he didn't really want to go back to Philadelphia at that precise moment, but he didn't have a choice. Because no matter how far Sonny had gone, how much money he made, or how far he was from them, he was the son of Absalom and Gwen

Goodman. He would swim into the darkness for them.

He hung up the telephone and began preparing for his trip home. His desk was full of work. Interruptions in the quest for corporate power could be deadly. If he was interested in a vice presidency, this wasn't the best time to leave.

He felt the enamel sparks from his grinding teeth. He slowly slid his chair back, gathered together some papers, put them in a manilla folder and headed into Frank Templeton's office, where the staff meeting was held every Thursday. He walked past the castigating stare of Templeton's secretary, knocked on the door and walked in.

Four of the five people in the room smiled in unison, beginning their welcome. Templeton—a thin, pockmarked man with an ever perfect white flyaway collared shirt, a solid blue tie, and gray pinstripes—sat stiff and looked through him. Sonny took just one step inside the room.

"Sorry I'm late. But . . . I've got a problem at home. Ah, in Philadelphia. My father's sick. I've got to go."

Templeton seemed about to say something but didn't. One by one the other four slowly rose from their chairs. Bouquets of fragrant lilies blew from their mouths. Sonny couldn't hear them. He was focused on Templeton, who began to swell.

"I brought the press releases with me. Here they are." Sonny approached Templeton and placed the folder in front of the man. "I really wanted to be here to make sure everything went smoothly, but we've got a good communications strategy and I've included my personal contact file ... And before I go, I'll get my staff together and make sure they know what to do. I'm sorry, I know this is bad timing ..." Sonny swallowed and tasted only traces of the sterile, heavily starched air. He was conscious of the distance between him and everyone else. No one rushed to touch him.

Templeton surprised Sonny. His stiffness seemed to evaporate. It was as if Templeton had realized, for the first time, that Sonny *had* a father. "It's an emergency?"

Sonny wasn't sure that Templeton had even seen him nod his head because he was quickly scanning the contents of the folder that Sonny had handed him. "Good work, Sonny. I'm sure we can make this go. Can we do anything to help?"

"I think I just need to get going." He thought of the trip ahead and felt his stomach jump. The thought of going to Philadelphia made him nervous. If his parents weren't still there, he'd probably never go back, except on business.

"Of course, don't worry. Our prayers will be with your father and your family." Now Templeton rolled his heavy leather chair back and stood, offering an awkward hand.

Sonny took it, although he couldn't help feeling that Templeton was being too considerate. It wasn't like him. There were too many times, which Sonny had witnessed, that Templeton had completely disregarded the personal needs of his employees.

He stood there a second before he straightened himself and walked out.

Back in his office, Sonny made arrangements to meet with his five-person staff. He couldn't shake his sudden sense of guilt. Templeton was probably disappointed in him. This would likely turn out to be a bad mark on his record. He had seen comers whose careers were derailed by births and illnesses. But he knew it was time for him to go home to his father. There was nothing else for a son to do.

After meeting with his senior staff and getting the plane tickets from his secretary, he grabbed his trench coat and walked down the hall through the maze of mauve partitions to a cluster of cubicles. His mind was already bound for Philadelphia, but he had one more thing to do. He had to tell Allison. He hoped she would be at her desk.

Allison, eight years younger than Sonny, had also come to Minneapolis to work for Data Central. From the beginning, Sonny thought she was beautiful and smart. It didn't take him long to get her assigned to one of his projects, whereupon he had turned on the charm, big time. They were dating in two months. After two years, they were at a crossroads. She was ready to get married. He wasn't sure. Wanted time.

Absalom was a whisper in his ear as he knocked

on the metal strip that outlined her cubicle. Allison was leaning over her desk reading. She turned around and her smile enswirled him. A tall brown woman, her fine Ethiopian eyes spoke words before her mouth did.

"Oh Sonny. Great. I'm glad you stopped by. I've got something to tell you." When she was excited, Allison could be a sunburst.

Sonny didn't break the cast of his face. He couldn't smile. He wanted to. She was so pretty. He wanted to return her excitement. But he couldn't. "I've got something to tell you too."

"What is it, Sonny?" Allison put her energy on hold.

"My mom just called from Philly and thinks I need to come home. My father's not doing too well." Sonny paused as he saw all the play drain from Allison's face.

Allison jumped from her chair and put her thin arms around him. "Did she say what it was?"

"Not really, I just got the message loud and clear. I just wanted to say goodbye. I wish I didn't have to go. I know this isn't the best time for me to be leaving . . ."

Allison pulled her head back so she could see him. Sonny felt her soft hair pull away from his face. "Why not?"

"Well for one thing, you know we're just rolling out the new product and then . . . well, I mean, I just feel like there's something wrong between us and I don't want to leave you with things up in the air.''

"Well, you can't control everything. You didn't pick the time for your father to get sick. You just go and do what you have to do there. I'll be here when you get back. We can deal with everything then.''

"Do you promise? Promise that you'll wait until I get back?'' Sonny put exaggerated drama into the words, then broke a tentative smile. He knew what her response would be.

Allison brought her head to rest in the corner of his neck and shoulder. ''Sonny, you know I don't make promises. I don't promise nobody nothing. You just go and take care of home. Okay?''

Sonny kissed her and held her tightly. Something was definitely wrong. He could feel it. She was pulling away. He wanted to change his plans right then.

But Allison was really pushing. She turned him around with her hands. As if she had read his mind and was forcing him to stay with his first plan. ''Now you go home, pack, get a good night's sleep. Your father needs you.''

Sonny felt his feet moving. Yes. Absalom needed him. Everything else would have to wait. But as he reached the hallway he turned back. ''What was your surprise?''

Allison didn't want to tell him. She had hoped that he'd forgotten. But she couldn't lie. ''Well, I just thought that we should spend a weekend away together. I booked a cabin on the North Shore. I can cancel it. It's not a problem.''

Sonny was stunned. ''What was that about?''

''Nothing. I just thought we needed to get away and talk about things. But it will wait. Now, get going. Everything will be fine.''

That was Friday. This was Saturday and he now stood in the street, in front of the hospital. Data Central, Allison, Frank Templeton all faded into the distance of 1180 miles. Now he struggled with what lay ahead.

His mother had finally gotten enough courage to explain that Absalom had been sick for over six months. That it was cancer and that it was taking Absalom's body apart piece by piece. As they had driven from the airport to the hospital in his father's car, Sonny tried to prepare himself. It was hard to imagine Absalom as anything less than a large-framed man who had once been strong enough to move the washing machine from the kitchen to the basement by himself.

Sonny was afraid to face the man who had been the silent presence in his life. Afraid to see any diminution in the size or the power of Absalom. He knew it would be hard to carry it off without crumbling.

Absalom knew it. Sonny's fear reverberated, found its way to Absalom's heart. He felt sorry for the boy. Even at forty, Sonny was a little boy to his father. Their life together had made it impossible for Ab-

salom to ever be less than a teacher, a guide. The one who cut down vines and cleared paths through the wilds of life. Even a black father, especially a black father in a Jim Crow world, had to sacrifice, hold himself together in the face of a society that never stopped trying to tear him down.

Absalom saw the man he and Gwen had created, molded. He tried to inhale Sonny's success, wanted to feel what it was like to achieve. Somehow, no matter what he had done in his own life, how far he had come from the tobacco fields of North Carolina and his father's cold white-eyed stare, the feeling of accomplishment always evaporated even as he broke his mouth to smile.

Sonny had learned to love his father only after he realized that Absalom had measured his own life by Sonny's achievement. He and his sister were Absalom's only salvation. Even if Sonny were locked in a struggle to make sense of his life, to his father he was already a success. There had been tense times between them, but in Absalom's later years, their relationship had smoothed to a thick-threaded dhurrie that accentuated and highlighted the connection between them.

"You want a ticket, buddy?" The voice reached over Sonny's back. He scrambled to regain himself. He came down from the clouds, out of the sun. He turned around. Through the moving yellow and orange sunspots in front of his eyes, he made out a blue and white car. As the spots dissipated, Sonny saw the face of a white man within the car, sweating through his blue shirt, tapping his nightstick on the dashboard in front of him. His partner, the driver and a black man, stared ahead. The cars behind blared. "Move the car."

Sonny nodded. He peeled himself away from the car and walked around to the driver's side. The cop had gone. He put the car in gear, waited for an opening in the traffic and pulled out, turning left at the next small street, and then quickly into a parking lot.

He thought he recognized the parking lot attendant as a face out of his past. A man from deep down beyond adulthood, past tunneled adolescence, and into the free space of youth. He was dark, deeply creased, pockmarked, gray-haired, and slightly bent over. But when Sonny looked up, the man smiled through him, unrecognizing.

"Hospital?"

"Yes."

"How long?" The man pulled a yellow ticket from a stack and slid it into the jaws of a machine that stamped the time.

Sonny hadn't thought about it before. "I don't know. A few hours, I guess. My father's sick."

"I'll take the keys, son." The man swimming inside a blue short-sleeved shirt with inch-high white sailboats on it opened the door and stood back.

"You'll take care of it?" It was out of his mouth before he knew what he was saying. Self-preservation. Father love. Dad's Caddy. He knew that his father's Cadillac was, next to Gwen, a major love. And if Absalom, by the grace of God, were to ever walk out of that hospital, the car had better be just like he left it.

"Get paid for it. Couldn't be here long if I fucked up people's cars dontchaknow. It's a nice one. Ain't seen this kind of roof on a Cadillac before. Real nice. Yours?"

Sonny lingered, admiring the soft leather of the cranberry Landau roof. "Yeah." It was the first time he had ever driven it. He was aware of the attention he got on the way to the hospital. Even with his mother in the car. Women stopped, people stared. Back in Minnesota he had a Volvo, but after driving his father's car, he felt underprivileged.

"I know a piece of work when I see one." The man slid behind the wheel. He turned the ignition. It started. "Yeah," he sighed. "I got a special place just for this baby. Don't you worry 'bout it, you hear? I'll put it right over there next to mine." The man pointed, sticking his hand towards the front of the car, touching the windshield with his finger.

Sonny followed the direction of the man's arm. He started where the dark-hued skin—dry, wrinkled, and cracked—emerged from the blue shirt. He paused at the point where his finger was creating a grease spot on the window. Then, looking through the smudged windshield, he saw a green 1975 Pontiac Bonneville in a corner stall of the lot. He tried a smile. His face wasn't strong enough. The smile broke free, dangled momentarily on the corner of his mouth and fell off into the asphalt.

Sonny headed in the direction of the hospital. He hadn't been in the city for six years. He hadn't walked the hot summer city streets. He hadn't breathed the smell of the kosher hot dogs, the sauerkraut, the hot pretzels, the falafel, the pizza, the onions. It was all around him. His stomach jumped up and down in a nervous tremble. At the same time, his mouth salivated.

The face of the parking lot attendant hovered before his eyes. He turned around, thought about going back. Maybe he should have said, "I used to live around the way. You know, in North Philly. On Whither Street. Over by 26th and Girard. Did you used to live over there? Did you go the Athletic Center? Did you have a son at Robert Morris Elementary School? Did you play basketball with us? Did you coach Little League? Were you a scout master? Were you always sitting at the bar of the Satin Doll? Did you eat greasy hamburgers at Spady's? Where do I know you from?" But instead he turned toward the place where his father was and picked up his pace.

Midtown Hospital twirled its doors for him. Waved to him. The building promised coolness. A rest from the heat and intensity of downtown Philadelphia, which, after six years in Minnesota, actually felt intense.

The moment he was inside the hospital he knew

immediately that this wasn't a casual passing through. The hushed voices announced gravity. All emotions, all thoughts curled themselves into tight little balls and bounced inside his head. They pinged.

People draped in uniforms buzzed about like flies. The security guards, the Philadelphia police, the nurses, the doctors, the receptionists, the dieticians, the woman behind the gift shop counter, the cafeteria workers, the visitors, the patients, they were all going to or coming from some sickness, some pain. They were all bringing comfort or complication to the delicate process of staying alive.

Sonny sucked in the smell of disinfectant and sickness and plunged into the thick moving air. He swam past all those uniforms. He passed everything that lay in his way. At the elevator he remembered his mother's instructions. Twelfth floor. Right turn, two corridors then left, down the hallway, then right, into Oncology.

Absalom could hear people talking around him. The sentences were short and clipped like those of an overconfident poet. Their meaning did not get through. Absalom felt Sonny coming closer to him.

Sonny, now on the twelfth floor, faltered. Could he face his father? Could he do this? He fell into a soft chair and closed his eyes. He needed a minute to collect himself.

He looked up, jarred by the garbled voice of an older man. The man, his sallow face splotched with melanoma, had skin that hung from his body by invisible threads, as if it were an oversized sheath of latex covering his skeleton. He wore a flowing faded robe.

And yet the man smiled. His cheekbones were like fists. Sonny drew deep. This was what you had to expect in hospitals. This is what sick people looked like. He struggled with the impulse to close his eyes or jump up from his seat and turn away. He silently calmed himself. Rainy had warned him about their father, had tried to prepare Sonny for the physical changes. He could not expect his father to be the same, to have the same breath, the same sound.

Suddenly it felt like ages since he had seen his mother. She had just left him a few minutes ago, but he was aware of the distance between them even though he knew she was just ahead and around the corner, waiting for him.

"Visiting?" The man stared at him, his robe gaped, exposing a frail body with loud, pointed bones that seemed about ready to burst through his skin. When he moved, his latex skin barely noticed.

"Yeah."

"Hope it's not too serious."

"I think it is."

"Sorry." The man looked away, appearing to have lost interest. Sonny couldn't help but look at his feet. They were scaling and almost black, as if the man had been walking on the ashes of a long-extinguished fire. His legs had no muscle and relied solely upon the strength of his bones.

The man turned back and stared into Sonny's face. "There is one important, very good thing to consider, regardless of the situation." The man paused. He touched the top of his head where only the whisper of hair remained. There were sweeping islands of darkened, almost yellowish tan spots that spilled over into his face.

"Something good, eh?" Sonny steadied himself and faced him.

"That's what I said, young man. You can cry, you can pray, you can curse God, but when it's all said and done, there isn't much you can do about whatever is happening to the person you came here to see. Except live your own life. You can do that."

Sonny smiled. The tension in his shoulders rolled down his arms and flew away. The man was not dying at this precise moment. What Sonny feared most was facing the reality of death, of seeing it. He didn't want to see his father die. He didn't want to see anything die.

"Mr. Seltzer, it's time for your nap." A short, broad-hipped, dark brown nurse with hair cut close like a man's interrupted them.

"Naps. I'm seventy-four," he said, turning his head to Sonny. "Seventy-four and she's putting me to bed. A few years ago I'd a had her begging to get into the damn bed with me. But now, well . . . now I guess I'll take my nap."

"Take care of yourself." Sonny pushed his back into the chair.

"I will, there isn't much I can do otherwise." The man struggled to put one foot in front of the other as he leaned into the nurse. She smiled at Sonny and turned away. The man went a few steps and then stopped. He turned back toward Sonny. "By the way. Be thankful you're a visitor. You get to go home."

Sonny smiled. "I'll remember that."

Absalom could see Sonny sitting there alone, eyes closed and in silence. He wanted to talk to him. That was the thing. He couldn't get over the frustration of silence. But he could see him. Tall, stocky like he had once been, skin the color of an autumn leaf, burnished and deep. That was his son.

Finally Sonny pulled himself out of the chair and entered the Oncology department. Immediately the air around him changed. In the other corridors there was careless movement. People almost strolled about. In this space everything was serious. There was ominous machinery in the shape of animals everywhere. Electronic eyes blinked. Artificial vitality strobed. Things palpitated. All sound, though, was dampened by heavy spirit. The visitors looked sad. In the rooms, the patients were enswirled in tubes and blinking lights.

He walked up to the nurses' station. "I'm looking for Absalom Goodman." He could see the ABSALOM GOODMAN clipboard on the wall. One of the women standing there stared at him a moment. She broke a smile.

"You must be Sonny Goodman."

"Yes, that's right."

"Both your mother and father have told us about you. I feel like I know you." Sonny didn't know what to do with the unexpected greeting. She must have seen his fear, there was no way she could have missed it.

"Did you just get into town?" If she had seen it, she didn't reveal it.

"Yes." Sonny stared back. She had dark, almost olive-colored skin. Her long black hair and excavating eyes hinted at Mediterranean heritage. Italian?

"Well," she met his probe with deflection, "your father's room is just over there. 1248. If there's anything you need, just call. Your mother just asked me if I'd seen you. My name is Angela."

"Thank you," Sonny said as he turned away and gathered his strength.

2

Absalom's baby daughter, Rainy, was afraid too. She felt her father's energy receding like the North Philly sun dropping over Twenty-ninth Street. But instead of rushing out of bed and to the hospital, she sought relief in the slow movement of love.

Dancer's flesh felt like a tangle of soft blackberry vines stringing their way around her. His long strong arms diminished her somehow. Rainy felt something run out of her when he held her so tight. She squinted her eyes as he pressed. She didn't have a name for it, but whatever it was that happened when he encircled her, it didn't increase her sense of existence.

The burning August sun was bursting through the bedroom curtains, showering shards of white yellow light across the room. The two windows on the wall facing the street were separated by a dresser with a large oval mirror. The dresser, an old refurbished piece from the 1950s, had been painted over three times, the last ending in antique white with gold trim and gold handles. Beside the bed was a night table that matched the dresser. On it sat the Bible that Absalom had given her. She dusted it weekly just as she did everything else in the room.

Rainy lifted her head from the curve of Dancer's shoulder, opened her eyes and watched the airborne dust float aimlessly in the midday sunlight. For a moment, she pulled herself up into the aging air of the master bedroom of the old Goodman house. She became a puff of smoke, a particle of dust, a sunbeam.

Intense giddiness greeted her out in space. She hopped about like a woodland nymph, at home among the water lilies. She pushed both of her arms outward in a slow motion, as if she were doing the breast stroke. She zoomed to the highest point of one of the windows, to a space where the curtain and the window separated just enough to let in the light. There she gently treaded air, flitted momentarily and then, when the thrill of anticipation was so intense she could barely stand it, she straddled the column of light and slowly, in excruciating pleasure, slid down, into the belly of the room.

This was her time to sing. To elevate her life out of the North Philadelphia shadows and fling herself fully upon the stage. The footlights showered her in soft blue and golden light. Her aqua sequin

gown glittered in a shapely silhouette. Rainy, now a
star, belted out a dreamsong that held everyone
within the range of her voice. Through the haze of
the lights and the smoke she could see Patti LaBelle
and Gladys Knight, Diana Ross, and Chaka Kahn
sitting in the audience with their mouths open.

Dancer thrust himself into her with such force
that he jolted her out of her dream life. At the instant
that she felt him inside her, she lost her ability to
sing. Then she was only a woman lying under a man
who was desperately "making love" to her. And for
some reason, she liked it. As she moaned into Dancer's ear, her dream dissipated.

She didn't understand the ferocity with which
she enjoyed this feeling or why she needed it, even
though she felt lonely after, even though it was often
bad or boring or both.

Rainy watched the sweat appear on his skin. It
was magical. Suddenly, a drop of water trembled
upon his brow. It arose out of his skin unannounced,
unheralded. She stared up at him. He was grimacing
now. She knew he no longer felt connected to her,
that he no longer understood English. She could say
anything now and he would simply grunt and thrust
and shake and shiver and groan and beg and whim-
per and go limp.

But she didn't want to waste time playing with
him. She wanted what he wanted. She wanted that
sweat to mean something. She wanted to match the
life of sunbeams and airborne dust. She wanted in-

tensity. Passion. She wanted it now too, just as much as he did.

Dancer opened his eyes. Even wide-awake they were sleepy eyes. Now, under the full threat of orgasm, they were heavy, almost droopy. His hair, long and chemically curled, cradled his head in dark brown.

"Damn, baby. Damn. Don't stop."

Stop? How could she stop? This was her life too. She was in it to win, just as he was. "Slow down Danny, slow down baby." If he would just ease up, then she could relax a little more. She could slowly release the tension that was building inside her, hold him tighter. She could explore her fear. Maybe, if it would grow slowly, building step by step to a crescendo, then maybe she would be able to cry.

Rainy needed to cry, she knew that, but she was afraid. When Dancer was done singing this song, she would have to get dressed and go to the hospital.

So she held on. Rising above him. Whispering his name. Hoping he would take forever to come. Wishing he would become a gush of fresh air. She hoped for so much. Then, as she looked into his face, she realized it would soon end. He was sliding further into the place where his body spoke a language only he understood. Rainy had experienced it many times before. He always left before she wanted to let him go.

And in an instant their connection was broken and with the slow fall of breath and movement,

Rainy mentally began preparing for her visit to the hospital. But trying to prepare herself was silly, really; nothing ever softened the picture. Nothing, except not looking at her father, relieved the impact cancer had had on him. Each new trip to the hospital was more difficult. She found herself measuring his life by the amount of weight he had lost.

She jumped from the bed and started toward the bathroom. In the bathtub, Dancer rolled off Rainy's skin, mixed with the soapy water, and ran his course, into the drain. She thought briefly about joining him there, but decided instead to lift her sleek, black body out of the white tub and get ready to go to the hospital. Her stomach was beginning to tighten, even the sex had not helped. She hadn't come anyway. The only reason she had wanted to do it in the first place was to see if Dancer could take her away, build a veil between her and the future. He had failed.

She stared into the mirror on the medicine cabinet that hung over the white toilet and finished putting on her makeup. Her soft brown features, clear lustrous skin, sharp eyes, and full lips made her feel good for a brief moment. She took great pride in the way she looked. Sometimes, as she worked the lotions and oils into her face, she would compare herself to famous women, women with honey satin skin like Lena Horne, grand, sophisticated. One day she would set her own standard of beauty. People would say her voice was nearly as silky as her skin.

Rainy heard the doorbell but decided to ignore

it. Dancer could see to it. She figured it was Half-Dead anyway. That was one of the major drawbacks of being with Dancer: his friends, especially Half-Dead. She could accept Dancer's roughness, his pre-occupation with making money—they both had hopes of being great. She thought he could be a tal-ented photographer. There was something in his eyes that told her stories. She waited for those stories to develop into art. But for the moment all they had were fantasies and people like Half-Dead. Rainy de-cided to rush through her dressing and get down-stairs.

Having exploded into Rainy, Dancer now curled up into a ball. He sought the space in which nothing happened. On the inside of his eyelids a series of images flashed like a slide show. There was his dream house. There was his dream car. There was his dream wardrobe. There he sat at an expensive restaurant.

But downstairs, standing on the four-step stoop at the front door, a tall man, so dark he appeared purple in the high sun of late morning, depressed the doorbell and disrupted Dancer's dream. It clunked once on the way in and again on the way out. The doorbell had lost its chime long ago. Now it sounded like a child's xylophone with keys that were too loose.

He heard Rainy in the bathroom, the falling wa-ter creating enough noise to shield her from the doorbell. Dancer, not wanting to move, cursed. He had wanted to stay in bed until Rainy left. That was the way you made love. If you had to do something after, then what was the point?

He heard the doorbell again, wondering why Rainy hadn't had it fixed. He slid out of bed, found a pair of pants and a gray sleeveless sweatshirt.

The bell sounded again as he reached the top of the steps. He stopped there, momentarily disoriented. Back home in Mississippi there had been no stairs to climb; everything happened in three rooms. And there had been no bathroom. He smiled. People talked about the New South, but for Dancer there would only be one South. The South that made him feel dirty. The South that told him he was dumb and that he stank. Never again. Still, sometimes it was as if he had never left. In a flash of panic he would suddenly be back in Mississippi, hungry and lonely, even in a small room with six other children. He shook off this feeling and slowly started down the stairs.

There were two front doors. The outer aluminum storm door was locked, as was the wooden door, so visitors had to stand on the stoop until someone let them in.

Absalom now found himself at the front door standing next to the tall dark-skinned man who had rang the doorbell. Absalom had a vague recollection of the young man but couldn't place him. Already his memory was drifting. But one thing he knew: the man didn't belong in this house. This was Absalom's house. This was his territory, his world. For most of his adult life, the 2500 block of Whither Street with its porchless houses had been his universe.

When Dancer reached the thick wooden inner door he looked through the window. He unlocked both doors and stepped aside. Half-Dead came in. Half-Dead walked in a kind of strolling stumble that exaggerated his forward movement. Sometimes people would simply stand back and watch him walk. A slightly built man, Half-Dead began curving forward a little above the waist, so that by the time your eyes reached his head, he appeared to be nearly falling over. His profile resembled a ski.

Walking past Dancer to the sofa, Half-Dead filled the room. He brought all of the dirt and ugliness that was scattered about the North Philly neighborhood with him. It stuck to his shoes, clung to his clothes. Once inside the small house, it was released into the air, an alteration of the atmosphere that would remain until Half-Dead left.

"What's up, home?" Dancer spoke to the back of Half-Dead's cap, a dirty, tan Kangol that always shadowed his face.

Half-Dead had not gotten his name because he had been shot three times, or because he had been beaten up and left for dead too many times to count. It was because he was slow. He had never played stickball with the guys, never played football, never done anything that required speed. In fact, if quick movements were required, Half-Dead was in trouble. That was one reason he had been beaten up so many times.

"We got trouble, my brother. We got serious trouble." Half-Dead settled into the black leather sofa, which made a sound like that of a quick rain shower as it resisted his weight, slight though it was.

"Well, come on, man, give it up. I can't deal with it, if you won't give it up." Dancer pulled open the drawer under the lamp table next to the sofa Dead sat on. He took from it a pack of Salem cigarettes.

"The word is that Buck Teeth is moving in." Dead spoke with a shaking lip. There was a small amount of white slime gathering in the corner of his mouth. He stopped, unwrapped his huge tongue and wiped his lips with it. They glistened. "Yo, man, Buck Teeth is gonna try to bust in on our turf."

Dancer sat back, lit his cigarette, took a long draw, and blew the smoke out. So that was it. He had felt something changing. He hadn't been able to put his finger on it. For a hot minute he thought it had something to do with his relationship with Rainy. Now he knew. Half-Dead was a reliable source of information and stone loyal. He was a little crazy and had a hair-trigger flash point, but Dead would do anything for Dancer.

"Word up, Dead, man. I knew something was up. Now we know. Okay, so the motherfucka is gonna try to come in here and steal our shit." Dancer showed his confidence for Half-Dead. He couldn't show the least sign of weakness. Half-Dead depended on Dancer's bravado and energy. But thinking about BuckTeeth Rodney made Dancer very nervous.

"Ain't nothing but a party man. I ain't worried about it." Half-Dead took his cap off and rubbed his large thin hand over the outline of hair on his head.

"Yeah, things might get kind of rough though." Dancer, forgetting his decision to appear confident, thought about the implications of a violent, encroaching competitor.

"Hey Dance, if the motherfucka gonna come round here trying to take our business, then we gonna have to deal with it. If he don't start nothing, won't be nothing. Know what I'm sayin'?"

"Yeah, I'm with that too, Dead, but we gotta try to keep this thing cool."

"We could bust his ass you know, and dust him off real quick. I could get some of the dudes from down—" Half-Dead stopped abruptly as he saw Rainy's legs hit the first step. He looked up at her, unconsciously trying to see up her dress, his mouth stuck in the open position.

Dancer felt some of the air clear as Rainy neared the bottom of the steps. She was beautiful. Tall, graceful, an air of importance preceded her. "How's my baby?"

"What were you two talking about?"

"How you doin' Rainy? You sure are one fine

woman,'' Half-Dead said, although even Rainy didn't see his lips move.

She stared at Dancer. ''What were y'all talking about?''

Half-Dead, almost in a trance, began, ''I just found out that—''

''You're a dumb-ass,'' Dancer interrupted, looking at Half-Dead, who unconsciously covered his mouth with his hand. He could tell from Dancer's tone that this time, at least, he had moved too quickly. ''Nothing, sugar. We wasn't talking about nothing important.''

Rainy looked around the room. She saw all the junk that Half-Dead had brought in with him. She walked to the front window and saw the violence gathered in the corner of the windowsill. She turned around, looked directly at Dancer and said, ''He's not the dumb-ass, Dancer. If you don't tell me what's going on, you're the dumb-ass. Because you know I'm going to find out.''

''What makes you so sure something is up anyway?'' Dancer still had a smile on his face.

''It's up to you, Dancer, if you don't want to tell me, well . . .''

''Okay.'' He paused, searching for the right way to put it. ''According to Dead, the word on the vine is that BuckTeeth Rodney is looking to move into this area. If it's true—''

''It's true, home,'' Half-Dead broke in.

''Well, you know, it could get very nasty around

here if he starts throwing down." Dancer looked at Half-Dead as he spoke. He consciously squinted his eyes to increase the fierceness he knew he could project.

Rainy felt the knot in her stomach tighten. They had managed to keep things quiet for so long. "Is it happening now?" she asked and held her breath.

"Naw," Half-Dead said and crossed his long legs. "The word is, he's just thinkin' 'bout it right now. But you know the way that goes." Half-Dead brought both hands into the air, like a preacher. "He could decide to move on in anytime. We just have to be ready."

"Don't y'all do a damn thing till I get back." She picked up her Gucci purse and pulled the shoulder strap over her thin arms. "Dancer, I'm not playing. Nothing. Don't you make a move until I get back and we have a chance to talk about this. Promise me."

Dancer shot a glance at Half-Dead. A smile creased Dead's face. Dancer broadened his own. The air crackled with the smacking of palms of acknowledgment. It was a parade of respect for Rainy's beauty and control. They understood that she meant business.

"We won't do a goddamn thing. Ain't that right, homeboy?"

Half-Dead was full of smiles. "Straight up."

She walked over to where Dancer sat in the black leather Lazy Boy. He got up. "Listen Rainy,

I hope things work out at the hospital. If you need me, just call. I love you baby.''

"Love you too.'' The words moved from her mouth in a swirl. "Take care.'' After they were spoken, the words became a splash of her scent, which remained in the space she had occupied. In leaving, she had left something, and what she left behind began chasing the traces of ugliness brought in by Half-Dead.

Amid the silent swirl of this pursuit, Half-Dead and Dancer sat staring at each other.

"That's one tough lady you got, man.''

"I know. Why you think I'm still here?'' Dancer got up and walked from the living room, through the dining room, the breakfast room, and into the kitchen. It was a small house with a lot of rooms. The kitchen was just big enough to cook in, the breakfast room just large enough for a small dining area and a refrigerator. The dining room was dominated by a large dark wood table with many thick coatings of varnish, surrounded by six chairs.

He hollered back at Half-Dead, "She ain't like no other sister I ever been with, man.'' He opened a cupboard and pulled out a cookie canister. He reached his hand in the jar and pulled out a small bag. On his way back to Half-Dead he stopped at the refrigerator and pulled out two cans of beer.

In the dining room he stopped again at a break-front that was part of the reconditioned dining set, to pick up his pipe. Dancer paused, looked around him, and said, "This is a super-sweet deal. We can't let nothing mess this up."

"I heard that," Half-Dead said with emphasis, realizing that it would be a couple of hours before he would gather everything he brought with him and leave the house on Whither Street.

Soon, the smoke became a new ceiling. It hovered there, two feet above the men. But above this layer of smoke, the history of the Goodman family and the house on Whither Street was lived and relived in an endless attempt to provide context. Absalom carried Gwen over the threshold and later pulled himself through her legs here. Sonny and Rainy were born here. The house had been their refuge, their shelter from the violence of oppressors and the frustrations of the oppressed. They sought their freedom within.

"You gonna hog the goddamn pipe, homeboy?" Half-Dead spoke, unconsciously drawing in the sweet cloud of smoke pushing from Dancer's mouth.

"Hey man, hold up. We got this thing under control," Dancer said as he passed the pipe across the room.

Up and down Whither Street, cars were parked end to end, nearly touching each other on both sides of the street. Each house took its place alongside the next, sharing common walls, the same cement, the same alley—fusing the values of a community.

If one family had roaches, the entire side of the

street, and probably the whole block of houses, would become infested. You could only tell one house from another by the way it was painted on the outside. Unembellished or unpainted, the red brick exteriors visually blended one house into another. Every few houses, however, an owner would detail the mortar between the bricks with white paint or break tradition completely and, ignoring the mortar lines, paint the entire façade a bright pansy pink or soft seashore blue-green. Absalom had always convinced Gwen that a plain red brick exterior was the wisest choice. There was no reason to be flamboyant.

He and his neighbors had made the block a working middle-class oasis surrounded by less stable, deteriorating neighborhoods. Unlike many North Philadelphia neighborhoods, the houses on Whither Street were owned by people who lived in them. Absalom could stand on the front step of his house and list each family on the block.

In 1948, when they moved to Whither Street, Absalom and Gwen had been one of the first African American families to live on the block. The neighborhood had been an Old World enclave with blocks of Lithuanians, Poles, and Germans. The stores were owned mostly by Jews. Gwen and Absalom had had to brave the stares and chilliness, the fear and the isolation. But as more black families moved in and the whites left, they reformed the neighborhood into a barrier against the worst of inner-city life, believing in their ability to control their own destiny. They took it seriously. There had never been a time when the streets weren't clean or the small houses neatly kept. Absalom, Gwen, and their neighbors had managed, for the most part, to save Whither Street from sinking into the soft ground of utter poverty and urban tension. They had accomplished it in the only way it could have been done. They worked. They worked all the time. And in exchange they were able to walk to the corner store for bread, essentially safe from the growing threat around them.

Absalom could see and feel the change the 1980s brought, and finally admitted that they could no longer fight the conditions that were creeping through the dense neighborhood. Most of the children of the people who lived around him were out of work. It seemed like jobs had become a privilege and those who were denied began to create new ways to make money. Desperation grew and flowered. Cars were stolen, houses were broken into. Slowly, it was the hardworking people like himself who were victimized by the folks around them, people whom he loved, people he knew or whose parents he knew. And in the end, the community began to break into pieces. The old guard began to flee the heat. Absalom and Gwen were among the first to leave.

Really, it was Gwen who pushed the idea of abandoning their North Philadelphia neighborhood. When they had moved in she never expected to be there thirty years later. She had had dreams, too. She wanted a lawn and a garden. After all, they had both come to Philadelphia from North Carolina, both from farms.

Gwen wanted two things. To have fertile soil around her and to have the chance sometimes to feel grand. Two distinct and disparate desires. One rising like a peanut flower out of her father's peanut field and the other out of the flickering image of television's Dinah Shore.

Absalom remembered sitting on the couch in the living room, staring at Gwen, feeling his stomach quiver, the day before they were to meet a realtor who would show them a new life, in a new place. "Whatever we do, Gwen, I don't want to have to sell this house."

"I know, Ab, I don't either. But we got to get out of this neighborhood. They're startin' to break into everybody's house." Gwen was determined to move. Her involvement in neighborhood activities had only solidified her will to leave.

He had stared at her for a long time, trying to determine if their moving was a flight from some unwritten, unspoken responsibility. "You sure it's the right thing, now? I want you to be sure."

"I'm sure, Ab. We've got to go."

Absalom felt that conversation and everything else that had ever happened in the Whither Street house every time he came back. In a way, this was the only place he could truly be himself. He loved this house.

But Rainy had not been taking care. He could feel it. It wasn't the appearance of the house, it was more like a spiritual void had opened. He loved Rainy but felt her searching through the rubble of her reality for some magic that would save her. Absalom had noted and warned Rainy about her tendency to fall in love with men who had problems. Their problems always seemed to drag her away from herself, confusing her. Absalom could see her pouting at him. She had fearlessly confronted him after he ventured forth with his observation and warning.

"Daddy, I am, regardless of what you might think, very capable of choosing my own boyfriends. You have to learn to let me make up my own mind. If I get hurt, I get hurt."

"But I'm your father. I don't want to see you get hurt. If you get hurt, I get hurt." Absalom realized the futility of the discussion and left her alone. She would have to learn to protect herself.

If the Whither Street house had a voice, it would have been a slow moan, a creak, or a shudder. It had knowledge. But now, flecking chips of its memory fell into unused corners and were eventually swept away.

The house was the sum of those who had lived within it. It *was* them. It absorbed their spirits without complaint. It existed to hold their dreams, aspirations, and pain.

But houses are not immune to the ravages of

their inhabitants and the natural consequences of time. Everything deteriorates. Paint chips and falls away, wood splinters, plaster flakes off in large chunks. In a slow-motion ballet, parts of a house move slightly and unexpectedly. This was happening to the house on Whither Street. But the deterioration was not entirely material; a spiritual deterioration was happening at the same time. Everything was falling apart.

In an earlier time, when Absalom and Gwen were young, the house was always filled with music and animated color. They were both children of Africans, children of slaves. Absalom was like a little boy, had boundless energy. Gwen was proud. Although the house was small, and didn't have a lawn or a porch, it was theirs. For Gwen it was just the beginning—she had big plans. They borrowed money for new furniture and adorned the house, quietly confident that it was the sharpest on the block. And when Sonny and Rainy were born the house zapped and popped like the July Fourth fireworks display at the Liberty Bell.

But that was the past. Things were very different now that Gwen and Absalom had been gone for more than five years. A house can only be as good as the people that live in it. It is a servant.

Absalom heard the moans of the Whither Street house and understood them. He knew that things weren't well. And now, now there was Dancer.

3

Sonny needed a hand to help brace him for what was ahead. He knew that the man he loved and had lived with for nearly half of his life would not look the same. He took a deep breath and entered Room 1248. But, as soon as he was in the room, his eyes quickly shuttled to his mother. She sat there, on a chair, as if in a trance, staring at an empty, perfectly made-up bed. His father wasn't there.

"Where's Dad?" Sonny stood frozen. How long had it taken him to get there? Was he too late?

"He's not back from surgery." Gwen Goodman looked at her son. When he left home, she had been sorry to see him go. He did something to her. For her. His presence made her feel stronger. For years, she had secretly worried that he would never pull himself free of the spider web hold of North Philly.

Even though she hadn't ever talked about it,

Gwen knew very well that on each corner of their dense neighborhood was a living danger. During the sixties, when Sonny was a teenager, street gangs ruled the intersections. Their members were called cornerboys. There was Twenty-fourth and Whither, known as the "2-4 ws." There were the "2-4 RS" on Rednor Street. And the most feared, "2-8," which had extended its turf in so many directions it no longer used its Oxford Street identity. In the 1960s, 2-8 was the power in the hood.

And Gwen knew that every time she sent Sonny out for food or cigarettes, when she used to smoke, or when he was outside playing, that he had to maneuver the best he could around the constant wars that raged on the corners.

In those days it wasn't about drugs. It was about territory. If you lived on Whither you didn't belong on Rednor. And if you were a boy and you couldn't manage to make enough friends for safe passage, you could easily leave the living world on your journey.

Gwen remembered how Sonny always stuck close to home. He spent his share of time on the corner of Twenty-sixth and Whither with his friends. But they weren't gang members. Mostly boys who played basketball and imitated the Miracles and Temptations until they had to go in. As far as she knew, he had never been a gang member. Still, she saw the tension and the pressure that was around him.

She knew it wasn't the same as growing up in the country, like she had. Gwen had come of age in the small farming community of Newton Grove, North Carolina. And from the moment she picked up her first *Life* magazine, she wanted to move north. Newton Grove wasn't big enough, lively enough. Gwen wanted what the women in the magazines had: a manor and servants.

And in 1946, at twenty-three, one year after her father died, she packed her things and moved north. Her sister had moved to Philadelphia the year before and had cleared a path. Her dreams of society aside, the primary lure was opportunity. With the war industry still in full gear, fueled by new speculations of conflict in Korea and elsewhere, there were plenty of jobs. Gwen found work quickly at the shipyard, working on an assembly line for the navy.

Her first apartment was in a dark, narrow brownstone in North Philly. A cousin from Goldsboro lived in the building and had arranged everything. For the next thirty-four years she lived in North Philadelphia. From 1948 on, she lived with Absalom, on Whither Street, not more than three miles from where she had first set down her suitcase. North Philly became the backdrop to her life.

She watched Sonny intently. He was very uncomfortable, sweating profusely. His suit was beginning to pucker. She hoped he'd be okay, but all of her prayers were for Absalom. Every ounce of emotion, of optimism, of everything she had, had become a legion of soldiers marshaled under Absalom's command. They would fight to the bitter end.

Gwen thought about Absalom and the war they had been waging for his life. They had talked about it openly. Indeed, they had had strategy sessions in which they focused on using their combined energy to stop the growth of the cancer. Gwen was convinced that this was the only way to fight the disease. The doctors seemed to lack confidence in their ability to confront it. She would not wait around passively while Absalom deteriorated. If life was this way, she would adjust.

During the past year her soldiers had provided backup support for his soldiers. In the beginning, this imaginary attempt to heal Absalom seemed to work. Their spirits and his health kicked up a notch. But the enemy, a cancerous growth that fought for the occupation of his brain, continued to widen its field of engagement. It fought on multiple fronts. It defied military logic. And yet, the most devastating thing about the enemy was its persistence. Small defeats did not weaken its ability to rebuild its strength. Gwen looked at Sonny and slowly gave herself, in pieces, over to tears. She was very tired.

Sonny saw her eyes crystallize. He swallowed hard, slowly walked to her, bent down and kissed her on the cheek. Her chocolate-nougat brown skin savaged by winds, worry, and the intensity of life felt cool under the thin coating of cosmetic powder. The weight of her hands sank into his chest. He felt her fingers caress his spine. And slowly his feet disappeared into the floor. He shuddered once and collapsed into a pool of brown water.

He looked into his mother's eyes and saw everything that she had not said to him up to that moment. She was not the type of woman to talk much about the past. Nearly everything happened in the present. And the present was primarily positive. His mother hardly ever played the heavy harp. He walked into her eyes, felt his own reflection and understood that she needed him.

"Has anyone said when he's coming back?"

"No, they just said we should wait here." As Gwen talked, she exhaled a body full of air. "Nothing we can do, I guess, but sit here and wait."

She focused on Sonny. He was heavier now than he was two years ago when she had visited him in Minneapolis. But he was still tall and handsome. She often wondered how he had managed to remain a bachelor for so long. She thought he was more attractive than Absalom was in his prime. Sonny had Absalom's cool, penetrating brown eyes that could explode with a smile, but the rest of his facial features were softened by Gwen's beaming exuberance just beneath his skin.

"Where's Rainy?"

"I don't know. She was supposed to be here by now. But that girl moves so fast, always got so much going on that you can't fully count on her. Do you know what I mean?"

"Yes, Mom." Sonny relaxed. He knew his mother was just warming up. She had picked him up at the airport and had begun to fill in the details on everything. How sick his father was. How Rainy was doing. What kind of hospital they were dealing with. The longer he was with her, the more information he would get. His mother loved to talk and Rainy was her favorite topic.

Gwen had a well of patience for Rainy, confident that Rainy would eventually become something special, just as she thought Sonny had. And to Rainy's credit, she tried to realize her mother's expectation. But something always seemed to go wrong. Rainy's dreams were constantly being put back. Sometimes it was a man who stood in her way, sometimes it was herself.

The way Gwen saw it, Rainy's main problem was laziness—she just didn't work hard enough. If Rainy wanted to be a singer, then Gwen expected her to take singing lessons. But Rainy refused, believing that her connections would give her the ultimate big break. Now, at thirty-six, it seemed unlikely that she would ever pull her life together. Rainy, like so many around her, completely believed that it wasn't hard work that led to success, but people. Who you knew. What contacts you had.

Even though Gwen could see how confused Rainy was, she could never say anything negative. Gwen just listened patiently to everything Rainy had to say, all of her pipe dreams and fantasies, and hoped that things would turn out right.

"But she's getting much better. Much better. Since she's been going out with her new boyfriend, she's been slowing herself down a little." Gwen's words were always clear and well paced. There was little Southern sound in her voice; she had tried to leave that back in North Carolina. When she was tired or angry it would find its way in anyway.

Sonny sat back in the chair and crossed his legs while his mother's words filled the hospital room and transformed it into a parlor with plush over-stuffed brocade chairs. He had always loved to hear her talk—he could still see himself, a little boy, listening to her read Mother Goose.

"Who's this new boyfriend?" Sonny asked.

"Some guy she met at the community center. He's real nice, though. I like him. He's smart." Gwen wiggled her body, pulling the material of the beige cotton dress downward. The wiggling was not graceful, but it straightened her dress. "He's smart like you."

Sonny had never heard her say anything positive about any of Rainy's boyfriends, ever. He was shocked. He just stared. This was big news. As smart as his mother thought he was?

Absalom groaned.

"Where did she meet him?" He was going in no particular direction, but he instinctively began a search for the critical weakness. It was inevitable. Sonny believed that all men had an essential, critical weakness that other men could identify with swift precision. It could be a core of coldness in a warm peaceful exterior, a fear, a streak of terror carefully woven into the fabric of bravado, or, worst of all, a dark cynicism carefully tucked away in a hopeful body. To Sonny, the men that Rainy chose, while smooth as Godiva chocolate, were in fact weaker than most.

"She met him in a class she was taking. Some kind of photography class. He treats her real good, too." Gwen knew what Sonny was up to and she wanted him to know that she was on Rainy's side this time. She didn't want to encourage Sonny's habit of picking on Rainy's boyfriends.

When he was younger, still hanging out on the corner of Twenty-sixth and Whither with his friends, Sonny had learned not to trust the smooth ones. In fact, he had come to believe that any sign of smoothness was a telltale danger sign. The Rooster sign.

Rooster, one of Sonny's friends when he was sixteen, was every parent's dream of a best friend for a young boy. He smiled, he was polite. He had surpassed even his television mentor, the character Eddie Haskell from *Leave It to Beaver*, who personified the art of parental deception. Rooster did it better. Absalom and Gwen never suspected he was an accomplished rogue. When things went wrong, no one ever thought about Rooster Jackson, the skinny kid with long, thick hair and an unending smile.

For a while, Rooster and Sonny spent a lot of time together. Away from adults, Rooster was a quicksilver shoplifter, never once getting caught. He would steal leather coats, tennis shoes, watches, jewelry—nearly anything in a department store. Sometimes he'd take the trolley, the subway, and a bus all the way to the Northeast, stand in front of a white school and rob students as they went home.

"Why are you doing this, man? Why are you always trying to get over on people?" Sonny remembered asking.

"How you think we gonna survive this shit, man?" Rooster talked fast. "Anyway, I do it 'cause I can. That's what power is."

Hanging out with Rooster was exhilarating and challenged Sonny daily on the choices he had to make. Sometimes, late on a warm summer night, sitting on the steps in front of Sonny's house, Rooster would make elaborate plans. In the multileveled sounds of night in the city, Rooster and Sonny's conversation created a world beyond the passing cars, the laughing girls, the watchful parents.

"Yeah, Sonny, we could follow the guy who picks up all the money from the PTC. Somebody picks up all that money, from every bus, every subway station, even the el. Man, think how much money that is. I could get a gun—just to scare him, you know—and we could find that guy who collects all that money and we could get in the wind man.

Maybe go to Mexico or France or someplace where they can't get us."

Sonny always saw how easily they could be caught. Not Rooster. His success as a shoplifter had inflated an already healthy ego to monstrous proportions.

"Sonny man, I could steal the gold out of old man Benson's mouth without him knowin' it."

"But you're gonna get busted, Rooster."

"They can't bust the Rooster. I'm too cool man. Too cool. Smooth as silk. Soft as butter." Rooster's teeth glistened. "Anyway, you're not perfect. What about the peaches you always steal from Peachy's?"

"I quit that stuff, Rooster, you know that. And you should too. I can't be hanging out with you if you keep this up. It ain't right, man. Your life shouldn't be about ripping off people."

"Yeah, right. Whatever you say, man." Rooster turned his white eyes on Sonny.

Sonny stared back. He didn't care if Rooster didn't like it. Rooster was going in the wrong direction. He knew it. Rooster knew it. He couldn't just sit by and let it happen. That's not what friendship meant—going along. "Count me out, man. Just count me the fuck out. You can't live your whole life shoplifting."

"I'm not, man. Check it out. One day I'm gonna do the big one. I'm gonna get me a bank or something like that."

Sonny shook his head and stepped into a distance between them. They lost contact with each other. A year later Sonny went on to college, leaving Rooster in the grip of North Philly. Six months later, he heard that Rooster had been shot trying to rob a bank in Cheltenham. The adults in the neighborhood were completely shocked and would have sworn that he couldn't have done such a thing. Although paralyzed from the waist down, Rooster still lived in the neighborhood, his smoothness now confined by reality. Rooster's fate had scared Sonny, had caused him to create a mythology about the man.

Sonny distrusted most men. The smoother the talk, the more dangerous he thought them to be. He called it the Rooster sign. He watched for it. He listened for it. He had been close to one. He knew.

"What's he do?"

"Oh, he's a photographer. A very good one too."

"Really?"

"Oh yes. He's a very bright young man. He's very good for Rainy. He's what she's been needing."

Sonny smiled to himself. Just a little more time and information and he'd know exactly what was up. "Sounds great."

"I really think he is. He's a real gentleman. You don't find too many eligible colored men like him." Sonny thought she was laying it on pretty thick. He hadn't even met the guy yet and he was starting to hear crowing.

"What's his name?"

Sonny was watching as his mother averted her eyes and began looking at the floor. He wasn't sure what it meant. In the pause of action, he too looked around the room. He noticed the white sheets and white towels that seemed to be lying everywhere. The small television hanging high over his shoulder reflected a blank screen. Suddenly, he realized that his mother had been perfectly silent for too long.

"You don't know his name?"

"Well, ah . . . I guess I know it."

"Mom, what are you saying? You make this guy sound like he's Jesse Jackson or somebody." He paused to catch his breath and to help her absorb his point. "You don't even know his name?" This was definitely strange.

"Now, I told you." His mother didn't appreciate the attitude. "I do know his name. It's Danny." Gwen opened her purse and hunted for a small package of Kleenex. She felt the perspiration rising to the surface. When she found them, she pulled one tissue out and quickly dabbed her nose. "I think."

"You think? Mom, why do I get the impression you're not being honest with me? First you tell me how great this guy is but when I ask you what his name is you act like there's a brick sticking in your throat." Sonny's smile was full.

Gwen fidgeted. "Well, you know that Rainy. She can't just find a nice boy named George or Willie or even Sampson. That would be too much like right. She had to go and get somebody named Dancer. I know the boy's name. It's Dancer.'' Gwen was looking for another tissue.

"Dancer?'' Sonny paused and looked out the hospital room window. It was a strange building. It was built with a large cortile. The rooms on the outer side of the building faced the streets, the ones on the inner side faced the courtyard and atrium. So as he looked out the window he saw a series of lifeless flags of imaginary countries. Below, a McDonald's peddled sodium burgers.

"You're kidding.'' A stunted laugh zipped out of his mouth and ran quickly around the room. He leaned forward with a large cantaloupe smile. "Could you please tell me what kind of name is Dancer? That must be a nickname, right?''

"I don't know, Sonny, he's not my son. I can't keep up with everybody and their names. Anyway, what's the big deal?''

"Dancer just doesn't sound like a real name.''

"Well, as far as I know, it is. Besides, you don't have a lot of room to question people's names. Sonny ain't exactly the commonest name in the world.''

"Well, listen to you. You're the one who gave it to me.''

"Don't you go putting that on me. I didn't give you a name like Sonny. Your father did that to you.'' Gwen chuckled. Her body, seeking comfort, sank deeper into the chair. "I like it now though. It's bright."

"It's bright all right. People think I'm Italian or something."

"Just who are you making fun of?" Gwen was smiling, but Sonny could feel the world's rotation slow to a roll.

"I'm not making fun of anybody. I'm just saying, like I've been saying for forty years, I don't know why you gave me a name like Sonny."

"And I'm telling you, just like I been telling you for the last forty years, that I didn't give you the damn name." Gwen was now focused fully on Sonny. The profanity was out of her mouth so quickly she hadn't had time to reel it in before it broke into the air. "So don't get on my last nerve 'bout no name, boy. Anyway, you know your father gave you that name. And you know why. It ain't like I begged him to name you Sonny."

While his mother was talking, Sonny took a son's step back. He saw his mother sitting before his father's empty hospital bed, tense and edgy, and it made him sad. Sonny turned and looked out over the courtyard, twelve stories below. The south wing of the hospital faced him with its pattern of darkened square indentations. Within that darkness, Sonny imagined, so many people lay, shrouded in a thin hope, struggling for their own voice, singers in recline.

Not Absalom. He would not wait for them to give

up on him. Instead he held his own song high above
everyone. He encouraged Sonny. Nudged him on. He
didn't understand why Gwen liked Dancer so much.
She was not usually so easily fooled. But Absalom
also knew that Gwen worried about Rainy's chances
of getting married as the years passed, and Dancer
was the most serious of all of Rainy's recent boy-
friends.

"Did they say anything about how long we'd
have to wait?" Sonny didn't turn to face his mother.

"Well, no. They said he'd be along in a short
while. They wanted to take another look at him.
Maybe there was something they missed or
something."

Sonny was thinking that he didn't want his
father to die before he had a chance to talk to him.

Suddenly the door to the room opened. Sonny's
heart stopped. He saw his mother's reflection in the
window. He saw the fire of expectation lick the rims
of her eyes. As much as he wanted to see his father,
he was also afraid to see what he might look like.
But he could tell that she wasn't. She was almost
smiling with anticipation. As he watched the resolve
ripple in his mother's eyes, Sonny realized that he
was watching a deep, long-thriving, wildly real bond
between two people who had lived through the dark
evolution of modern racism. He watched the proof
of love reflected in the hospital window—a small,
hesitant smile, flickering.

He turned to face the door and saw a sharp mahogany brown leg pierce the air. He smelled the brilliance of Rainy entering the room. Four years younger than Sonny, Rainy overshadowed everyone when she walked into a room. It took every ounce of their mother's energy for her to wrestle back control.

"Rainy. Where have you been? We've been waiting for you for the last hour." Gwen didn't give Rainy a chance to answer. "I'm telling you, I don't know where your head is. Here we are, your father is sick, and you're out hopping around somewhere."

"Hopping around? Mother, your daughter does not hop around. For your information, I was at home." Rainy looked around and broke into a wide grin. "Sonny, baby. I thought you were coming in later on tonight."

"The only flight I could get left this morning." Sonny moved, his arms involuntarily outstretched, his eyes focused on his beautiful sister.

"It's a good thing someone cares enough to get out of bed and come to the hospital to see your father." Gwen opened her purse. Suddenly she felt crowded in the small white room. She wanted to get up and leave the room. She wanted to be somewhere else for a few minutes. Instead she fumbled around in her purse as her two children hugged.

"I'm glad you came back," Rainy said into Sonny's ear. "She needs you."

"And we both need you, Rainy. How are you?"

"I'm fine. But where's Dad?"

Absalom smiled. Altogether they amounted to pure energy. As a whole they helped him understand his life. He liked for them to hug, to touch each other. That was what a family was for.

Gwen closed her purse with a snap and pushed her hair backward and into place. "They said they wanted to take him into the operating room one last time to make sure there wasn't something else they could do."

"Oh God. Whenever these butchers start testing and experimenting you never know what they're going to do."

"Rainy, please." Gwen grabbed Rainy's hand. "Let's think positive."

"I am positive, Mom. But they haven't done a damn thing for Dad since he's been here. I just don't understand why they can't do something for him."

"They're trying, sweetheart. They're trying." Gwen stood up and walked over to Sonny, dragging Rainy with her. They all stood facing the door, looking over the neat empty bed, staring into space.

Sonny held himself down. The waiting was getting to him. He had a deep urge to walk through the window and exit up through the transparent atrium roof. He had a deep urge to dissipate into nothingness.

Rainy was the first to break the connection between mother and children. "I couldn't sleep last night. I don't want him to die. I wish there was something I could do." The light blue silk Anne

Klein she wore fit her perfectly. Her black brown skin, unblemished, immaculate, glistened in the harshness of the hospital light. She softened the room. She sat on the bed.

Sonny felt the pain stoking deep. Rainy was close to letting go. He looked at her eyes, fell inside, and had to scramble to escape her growing sense of loneliness.

Gwen headed back to her seat, Sonny stared, and Rainy kept talking. "What can we do? They've got him away in some room somewhere." She paused for a long time. "Where is he, Mom?" Her impatience with her mother was now clear.

Absalom fought the force that catapulted him away. He held on, gripping the vision of life tightly. He tried to be there with them. He wanted to comfort them. And yet, he was again cast aloft, free, and into the blackness.

"Well, when I got here, they were taking him out. I didn't know what to say. They said that they wanted to run some more tests. The nurse said the doctor wanted to take another look at the cancer to be sure they didn't want to operate. She told me I should just wait here." Gwen tried to control an intense and instinctive desire to panic.

"Mom," Rainy cut into the last sentence, "these people will tell you anything. You're just an ignorant nigger to them. They think they can tell you anything and you'll just go along with the program." Rainy looked to Sonny for support.

"Girl, I don't know who you think you're talking to. Who do you think has kept these doctors and these nurses on their toes? Why do you think they even gonna take the time to look at him again? They could just let him go, praise God, but they haven't. We're still fighting."

Sonny watched his mother and was amazed. She wasn't crying, her eyes weren't even moist. They were almost steely. This *was* war and she was the general.

"So don't you try to tell me I'm not taking care of my husband. And anyway, where were you when they took him away? Where were you? With that boyfriend of yours? You sure weren't here."

Rainy stared at her mother. She thought about countering but instead relaxed her jaw muscles. "I'm sorry, Mom. I'm just upset, that's all."

Sonny put his arm around his sister. "We're all upset. How could we not be?" He kissed her cheek. "I've missed you. How've you been?"

"I've been okay. This is pretty hard to take, though." Rainy sighed. "But I missed you too."

"Why didn't somebody tell me it was this bad? I can't believe no one said anything." Sonny relaxed his arm just a bit.

He heard Rainy sigh. "We didn't think it was that bad, and we didn't want to worry you."

Gwen looked at Sonny, her eyes rimmed with sadness. "I didn't really know, Sonny. I thought he was going to get better."

Sonny reached for her hand. "It's okay, Mom. Don't worry about it. We're all here now." Her face softened. He wanted to change the mood. It really didn't matter now. All they could do now was wait. "So, who is this boyfriend, Rainy?" Sonny pushed himself away from her, his teeth flashing.

"What do you mean?" Rainy stared at him, trying to discern what he was getting at.

"Just what I said. I've already heard more about this guy than any boyfriend you've had in five years." He loved his sister but didn't know how to talk to her. He didn't know how to say, I think you're fucking your life up, why don't you try a different approach.

"He's a nice guy, Sonny. He really is. He and mother get along extremely well, don't you?" Rainy had brushed away the blood from her mother's attack. She was strong again. She cut her eyes to Sonny. She had specifically chosen her blue suit for him. He was the corporate executive. She knew he couldn't help but associate expensive clothes with being happy, successful.

Gwen began to agree, "Yes we do, I—"

"Wait a minute. Rainy, what is this dude's name?"

"Dancer. Why?"

Sonny opened his mouth to show his white teeth. "Well," he said, stretching his soft shoulder muscles, "I never heard of a man with the name of Dancer."

"Well you have now." Rainy was smiling at Gwen. They seemed at peace with each other. Buddies.

"What's he do for a living, Rainy?" The words almost strutted out of Sonny's mouth.

"He's trying to get into photography."

"Trying?" Sonny knew he had Rainy on the run, momentarily.

"Yes, trying." Rainy pulled her pride, her knowledge of struggle, up through her throat. Then, she intensified it and aimed it at Sonny. It spewed out of her like a river. "I shouldn't have to tell you, Sonny, how hard it is for a black man to make it in this world. Especially as a photographer, an artist, not a corporate handkerchief head."

"Handkerchief head?" Sonny was deeply wounded. "Everybody who works for a corporation is not an Uncle Tom or whatever you want to call it. I do important work." Frank Templeton's face flashed in his mind. He wondered whether the press package had gotten out okay.

"Sure you do, Sonny, if you don't care about destroying the environment or ripping people off." Rainy smiled at him flatly, her lips pulled tightly at the corners of her mouth.

"He's a bright young man, Sonny, he really is." Gwen wanted to support Rainy. She couldn't help it. She was her mother.

Sonny heard his mother but he was staring at Rainy. "I work hard and every day I have to deal with white men who think I'm not good enough, so don't bring that stuff to me. You act like it's an honorable thing not to be college educated and working for somebody.'' Sonny paused. He realized he was getting into bad territory for Rainy and Gwen. He looked at his mother. "I'm waiting for someone to tell me how he makes a living."

"That's none of your business." Rainy spit the words out. It was tight in the room. She got off the bed and walked into the hall. She stood in the doorway, facing Sonny.

Gwen looked past Sonny and out into the courtyard air. The glow of McDonald's reached all the way up to the twelfth floor.

"Come on Rainy, I'm just asking, that's all. Okay, so where does he live? Is he another one of your West Philly pretty boys? You know, light skin, curly hair." Sonny was losing his enthusiasm, but he was curious. He hadn't gotten one clear answer about Dancer from either Gwen or Rainy. Now he felt his mother shrink, curl into a compressed small ball and wedge herself into the corner of the plastic chair.

Rainy's facial features began to smear. She made a gurgling, muffled noise.

Still, Sonny persisted. "Well? Where is he from?"

Rainy pulled her face together. She smoothed the areas that had melted and reformed them. "He was born in Mississippi and grew up in North Philly, just like you. And right now, right now, he's living with me.''

"I see." Sonny's mouth froze.

"He's a nice boy, Sonny. Since Ab has been sick, he's come over and helped me around the new house." Gwen looked directly into her son's eyes. Even though she was tired, even as she waited to see her sick husband, Gwen could find the lightness hidden in a room. "Anyway, what difference does it make? He loves him some Rainy. She's had worse, that's for sure. At least Dancer treats her good."

Angela, the nurse, peeked her head into the room and asked, "Is everything okay?"

Gwen stopped talking and looked up at her. "Where's my husband?"

"I just spoke to the doctors, Mrs. Goodman. He'll be back here shortly. Dr. Mamen will talk with you when they bring your husband back."

"Thank you," Gwen said.

About Dancer, Sonny figured acquiescence best. Rainy walked back into the room and up to Sonny. "Sonny, don't go getting protective about me. I know what I'm doing."

"Well, what are you doing? Where are you working these days?"

Rainy was used to the rough treatment. It was a family habit. Everyone always gravitated to her with the questions. "Where are you working?" "Who are you going out with?" "Where did you find these friends?" "When are you going to make something of yourself?'' Sonny was the primary culprit. No matter what the condition of his life, he could always make himself larger, more stable, more respectable by drawing distinctions between them.

He had no respect for her aspirations. Her desire to sing, to be in show business, was meaningless to him. He wanted her to have a job. ''Where are you working?'' No matter how long they hadn't seen each other, it was never very long before he asked that question.

Gwen leaned back in her chair. She was tired of hearing her children bicker in the same space where so many other important questions waited. ''Dear God,'' Gwen said and brought everything to a standstill. ''Where is my husband?'' This time her electrical system shorted and she convulsed into tears. In a flash, Rainy and Sonny were beside her. The pain was like cinder blocks that had been plastered over the doorway. They were trapped there until someone or something rescued them.

4

Absalom felt the wheels rolling under his body. He was being moved again. He liked the shaking rumble under his butt. It was a familiar feeling. For nearly all of his working life he had been a truck driver for Sy Bonansky's bakery.

In the early hours of the breaking day, Absalom would load up his truck with trays of pumpernickel, challah, and other breads, donuts, cakes, and pies. There were six Bonansky outlets, not including the bakery itself. During the day, he maneuvered his truck throughout the city, in the snow, and in the soft asphalt summer to bring fresh baked goods to Bonansky's customers, most of whom were Jewish. After he delivered to the bakery outlets, there was another set of deliveries to independent stores. Altogether he wasn't finished until about noon.

As tired and sleepy as he felt driving to work at

3:45 in the morning, Absalom loved the time just before dawn. The shadows of the city were in retreat, fading into the bricks and cement as he drove along. And no matter what season it was, that time was the coolest, the quietest the city could ever be.

It was strange how the streets in this city of neighborhoods appeared so similar before people began moving around in them. In the waning darkness, the streets were empty shells, washed-out blood and earth colors against a blue-black background. But as the day progressed and people walked out into the world, each neighborhood became a pounding heart.

South Philly clamored with dark-eyed Italians, Spring Garden with Puerto Rican smiles, 52nd Street with the slick clothes and the sound of jazz, Fishtown and Frankford with weathered skins and T-shirts rolled up with Marlboros at the shoulder. Or the Northeast, where fleeing inner-city Jews had landed.

And in North Philly where the bakery was built, the family-owned business was now just one of the many white islands still floating in the African American sea that surrounded them.

But before dawn, each neighborhood was nothing but concrete and bricks, corner stores and churches, bars and parks. It was the lilt of language and the sweat of culture that defined them.

Absalom wasn't as comfortable on the streets during the day as he was early in the morning. With his truck filled with the smell of fresh baked bread,

Absalom was welcomed wherever he went.

Every morning when Absalom arrived at the bakery, Sy Bonansky would be sitting on the loading dock with a cup of coffee in his hands. Sy nearly always wore the uniform of the bakers—white T-shirt, white baker's pants, and white tennis shoes— even though he had never baked a single cupcake. A bit overweight, with a paunch that put a downward pressure on his pants, he was tall, as was Absalom. His thinning hair was nearly all white.

When Sy was at the University of Pennsylvania he was considered handsome, but time and food had destroyed the few angled contours his face had once had.

Sy had inherited the bakery from his father, who had built it. Sy was twenty-two when his father announced to family and friends that it was he and not either of his two brothers who would ascend the floured throne. Sy had felt the heat from the star that had risen above him. But he had learned the business standing by his father's side, and he worked hard to prove that his father had made the right decision.

"Absalom, my best driver. I cannot have a good day until you get here." Sy greeted him every day with the same salutation. And then he would play-fully slap Absalom on his back and ask about his family. And every day Absalom would cart the trays of bagels, pastries, and bread from the kitchen to the loading dock and then into the truck. Sy would lit-erally follow Absalom's every movement, no matter how many times Absalom had to go back and forth from the kitchen to the dock, or even into the back of the truck.

Sometimes this agitated Absalom. He couldn't believe that Sy didn't have better things to do. Sometimes he wanted to ask him, "What the hell do you keep following me around for?" But he never did. He did, however, on occasion abruptly stop walking, turn around, and stare at Sy. Inevitably, Sy would be in mid-stride, his puffy face frozen in curiosity.

"What? What's the matter, Ab?"

Absalom would just stare at him. Not menacingly. He wasn't angry. He just wanted to know why Sy followed him around all the time. Absalom had his suspicions. At first he thought that Sy was worried that he might be stealing food. But there was no reason to do that. There was more than enough surplus at the end of a run. Absalom always brought food home.

After a while, Absalom came to realize that Sy wasn't trying to catch him doing anything wrong. Sy was curious. That's what it was. He had never known a black man before. Never listened to a black man talk about his wife and family. Sy had never even had a conversation with a black man until he met Absalom. And from the first day that Absalom had come to work at Bonansky's as a kitchen helper, Sy had liked him.

He liked the fact that Absalom was so quiet. He

never joined in the kitchen banter. Never got into flour fights. Whenever things moved to the raucous, Absalom found a way to disappear. Sy learned later that Absalom never "played around" with white men. Having grown up in the South, Absalom could work with white men but wasn't able to feel relaxed around them. In fact, Absalom found it very difficult to let his guard down, unless the subject was sports, especially prize fighting. If the talk turned to boxing, then Absalom's nostrils would expand like little brown bellows. His face would widen to hold the growing smile. Absalom loved the art of fighting and could and would hold his own in any discussion.

One day as Sy was coming into the kitchen he overheard Absalom talking about Cassius Clay. "Naw, Henry,"—Absalom was going through the motions of sweeping, but he was looking directly at one of the bakers—"if you think Cassius Clay is full of hot air you don't know nothing about fighting. That boy is so fast, he puts so many punches upside the other guy's head that his body just short-circuits. Boom boom boom booom booom." Absalom dropped the broom and jabbed his hand into the air. "And then he's out of there."

As Absalom finished his sentence he looked up and saw Sy. He gulped. But Sy was smiling. He had never heard Absalom say so many words at one time. And that somehow solidified his need to know the man better. It had almost become an obsession. And so Sy had made it a routine to drink his first cup of coffee with Absalom. To get to know his family. To try to understand him. At some point Sy realized that he was really trying to see if a black man was the same as a white man. If the stories and the feelings were the same. Along the way he had come to like Absalom.

There were times when Sy's attention was actually pleasant. Absalom loved to talk about his family, anyway. Sometimes Absalom looked forward to their conversations.

He had been working for Sy for eleven years when their conversations reached a new level. He remembered the day it happened because it was two days after Martin Luther King Jr. was assassinated. Two days after angry crowds had set fire to stores on Columbia Avenue.

"What's going on in this country, Ab? Colored people burning down stores. Their own homes. Why would a man burn down his own home?" Sy sipped his coffee. Over the years, his voice had disintegrated into gravel.

"A man would have to be pretty angry to do that, Sy." Absalom was stacking trays of rye bread in the truck.

"I've never been that angry," Sy said. "But burn my own house down? I've worked like a damn dog to get that goddamn house. Vera'd kill my ass anyway if I did something like that." He paused and considered his wife standing in her robe bathed in the glow of flickering flames. "What about you?

You ever been that mad?''

"I don't know, Sy. I don't know."

"I'm talking about your own house. Okay, so you're upset. It's terrible what's going on. It really is. I know about it. My family didn't have it so good, you know. So I understand. I give every year to the NAACP you know. I've been doing that for at least five years. So I put my money where my mouth is. But set fire to your home? That's crazy. What do you say, Ab, that's crazy, ain't it?''

"It depends on how you look at it. Me, I wouldn't do it. Gwen and I kind of like our house. But I guess if you don't think you got nothing then maybe. . . . I don't know why people do things. I just try to do what I'm supposed to do." Absalom thought about what was going on throughout the country. Tension walked the Main Streets. Anger and fear flowered everywhere.

"That's what I mean. I couldn't see you running around the streets like a crazy person. Burning things down.''

Absalom turned away and picked up another tray. He was not incapable of anger. He could explode. Deep inside him there was the potential to step outside his quiet life, strip away the warm smile and the soft voice to reveal just another enraged black man. That rage was there. But it was held in check by good fortune. He had nearly everything he had ever hoped for.

He was making good money, owned his own

house, was married to a woman he loved, and was the father of two children. This was already more than many people had. And yet there was so much that was completely out of his reach. The pictures that flashed on the television of families with new cars, new appliances, roach-free kitchens, and nice green lawns were well beyond his grasp. Even then, Absalom knew there were many things he would never experience, never have. He worked too hard to not be angry about that.

In the beginning, when he left his father's farm to join the army, when he came to Philadelphia to work, when he met Gwen, Absalom believed in the promise of America. He wanted what he deserved for being a hardworking American.

It wasn't race as much as it was economics. Yes, he knew very well that there were white people out there who would hurt him. But most of his interactions with them came from the cab of his truck or when he was delivering food to them. Besides, he wasn't angry at them. His anger was for something or somebody he couldn't identify but which stood between him and a sense of self-completion. Was he just one of hundreds of thousands of working slaves?

"Did you see the news last night?" Sy leaned back into the wall.

"Yeah, I saw it." Absalom knew what was coming next.

"It was shocking, Ab. There were kids out there carrying televisions on their backs. Washing machines. Vacuum cleaners. People just carting what they wanted out of the store. They just busted up the windows and took what they could carry. I couldn't believe it. Why would they hurt the merchants in their own neighborhoods? Some of these people . . . the only reason they are still in the city is because they care about their customers. And what do they get? They get their windows broken and their goods stolen. Those mobs are just criminals. What kind of world is this? I ask you."

Absalom had not only seen the news, but he had driven through the riot-torn area on his way home from work. He had seen the people with new couches on their backs wobbling their way back home. And he had wondered about it. He felt no desire to join them but he understood it. And until Sy had mentioned it, Absalom had already erased those images from his mind. He had a job to do. Hours to put in. He had learned to leave the pain of his people at home. He had to face white people all the time. He knew no way to hold that pain and do his job at the same time.

And now he was fighting the desire to end his conversation with Sy and get to his deliveries. "It's always been a crazy world."

"How come they won't work, Ab? Like you? How come more of them aren't like you?"

"Like me? What do you mean, Sy? Colored people been working like dogs all our lives. Everybody I know who can find a job has got one. And still it don't seem like nothing changes. How many colored drivers you think there are in this city, Sy? I don't know another colored man who drives a truck. Loaders, yeah, but drivers? Those people are taking that stuff and burning those buildings because they're tired, Sy. Just plain wore out. All those televisions and record players and furniture is stuff they can't get. They see it all around them but they can't get it. What do you expect?''

Sy looked up at Absalom, who was now standing over him. Absalom's smile was gone. For a second, Sy's body tensed. ''I know it's not in fashion these days, but hell, Ab, Rome wasn't built in a day, you know. Your people have come a long way. A little patience and some hard work. I mean, there are too many examples of colored folks getting ahead these days. It just takes . . .''

''Time.'' Absalom had heard enough. ''Sy, you know I served in Korea.''

''I know, but—''

''There wasn't no buts then, Sy. They shipped my ass right over there. They took my colored butt, no questions asked. But if I want to be treated like a man, I got to have patience. I got to work hard. Where does it say you got to work hard to be a man, Sy? Where?''

Sy could find no words. He'd never gotten that close to this Absalom. This Absalom was almost trembling with anger. This Absalom made him feel uncomfortable.

Absalom didn't want to fight with Sy, not at 4:30 in the morning and not about race, but he wouldn't let Sy put black people down. "Listen," he said softly, "I got to be getting out of here, Sy, or else I'll be another colored man without a job."

"Absalom, I can see you're upset with me. Maybe I deserve it or maybe you're just more of a hothead than I thought, but you're still my best employee and as long as I'm alive and you want to be here, you've got a job."

Absalom turned his head toward the loaded truck. What Sy had said almost made him feel happy. And yet he couldn't let Sy see it. To make his point, Absalom punctuated the moment by slamming the rolling back door of the truck closed. He tried his best not to see skin color. He tried not to be angry. He tried to work hard enough to become somebody Gwen could be proud of. That was all he knew.

Sy's body jumped when the truck door crashed down. "Come on, Ab, I didn't mean no harm. You know how I feel about you and your family. I know you're a good man. I just don't understand why everybody's so angry at those of us who are trying to stay down here."

Absalom sighed. Sy never knew when to quit. "The only thing, Sy, is that most of the white people who have businesses down here," Absalom headed for the cab of the truck, "go home somewhere out in the suburbs. They don't have to put up with what

we put up with down here no more. It's like everybody's saying just be good and everything will work
out. But it's not happening that way, and you know
it. Now somebody kills our leader. What do you expect people to do? They're tired. That's all. Folks is
just tired.''

Absalom climbed into the truck and headed out
into the morning with his head cradled in the smell
of warm bread.

And now the wheels of the hospital trolley shuttled Absalom through heavy doors that opened like
castle gates as he approached. He opened his eyes
just long enough to see the pictures of open fields
and flowers and abstract shapes hanging on the wall
as they pushed him through the halls. And then he
felt the wind under his body and the movement of
space.

5

The billow of smoke rolled over his head, down his back, anointed his body with its tart, sweet smell. Some ribbons of the smoke twined themselves in his hair, they hid there, sought protection from gusts of fresh air. Dancer's hair was black, brilliantly black, so black it reflected light. His hair had been freshly curled and styled, yet it revealed Dancer's haste in answering the front door. Long, loose, languid, coiled locks, ever glistening, covered his head. Dancer unconsciously shook his head, in a jerking motion, chasing the smoke and the smell of Rainy.

He sat back in the leather Lazy Boy rocking chair. An ottoman magically extended under his feet. The music from his stereo was soft and soulful. A blue Luther Vandross singing for someone's love made the mellowness real. Half-Dead, sitting on the couch perpendicular to Dancer, stretched his long body out, his eyes closed.

Dancer looking at the ceiling, didn't hear Absalom's footsteps as he came down from the bathroom and walked over to the bureau in the dining room, didn't hear him roaming through the old house, noting new cracks in the walls, crumbling plaster, and scarred floors. It was amazing the way houses fell apart. Without relentless upkeep, they slowly crumbled back into the ground, one small piece at a time. Absalom was powerless to stop it. Since he and Gwen had moved out, there had been a steady decline. But now, when Absalom found himself at the Whither Street house, he was mostly sitting at the dining room table, reading the newspaper. He couldn't figure it out and he couldn't change it. He would just be there, sitting quietly, resting, and reading the paper.

If Dancer could have seen him he might have considered it an honor. Rainy certainly would have. But Dancer could not honor what he did not know. And now, under the effect of the thick drug, he felt only the soaring reaches of the top of his head. He felt so completely wide open, nothing could explain it. He wasn't thinking, thinking was impossible. The rock made thinking stupid. He could sit here for fifteen, twenty minutes and feel nothing, think nothing, know nothing, and it was entirely pleasurable. Even Half-Dead's dark company could not mar the first rush from a hit of crack.

He could understand how some people, Half-Dead for example, had given themselves over so

completely to the rock. Why not? Who wouldn't
want to feel like this? You had to have the strength
of a black Pullman porter during the early 1900s to
stand up to the lure of the crack call. But Dancer
thought he was strong enough—he could take a hit
every now and then and still keep his life from falling apart, he could dabble without destroying himself. Now, he too closed his eyes, watching the
changing pattern of lights on the inside of his eyelids.

Aside from the strains of soft funk that fluttered
around them, everything was quiet. For a summer
Saturday morning, things seemed incredibly lazy.
But then, with the ride into the mists of euphoria,
everything slowed down.

In his reverie, his meditation, Dancer played the
saxophone behind the Vandross ballad. Sweet. So
sweet. He was a fashion photographer, a writer, he
sought beauty.

Across from him, Half-Dead was momentarily
in communion with the essence of his name. This
was full, living death, twirling around in the haze,
complete in its loneliness, open-ended and seemingly
without punishment.

They sat there together, drifting to and fro with
the pattern of afternoon sunlight penetrating the ve-
netian blinds that were still shuttered.

Absalom was there too, as oblivious of them as
they of him. But make no mistake. Whether they knew
or not, this was Absalom's living room. He would

come home from work at three o'clock every afternoon, eat, then stretch himself out on a comfortable chair in front of the television. Occasionally he broke the routine to take Sonny and Rainy for a ride, or play ball with Sonny. But for the most part, this space was his. He lived in this room.

Neither Dancer nor Half-Dead could have known that by three in the afternoon, Absalom had worked ten to fifteen hours. For most of his life, deep in the blooming morning hours, Absalom had to break his sleep, and his nestled closeness to Gwen, get out of the bed, and go to work.

Collapsing into the chair in the early evening, Absalom would fight sleep all night, nodding, bobbing his head, until someone prevailed on him to go upstairs into the bedroom.

Rainy had developed the greatest skill in moving Absalom from the living room couch to the upstairs bedroom. It was an important skill for anyone who wanted to control what was on the television, because when Absalom was in the room and awake, he lorded over it. And because she loved to sit up and watch television as long as her mother would let her, Rainy had made it her business to master the art of getting Absalom to go to bed.

At the first sign of drooping eyelids, Rainy would say, "Daddy, why don't you go stretch out on your bed? You look so uncomfortable sitting there like that."

Absalom's eyes would pop open. "I am really tired tonight, baby girl. They had me running all over the place today."

"You should get yourself a good night's sleep, Daddy." Rainy sat back in her chair and waited. On the television was a wrestling match. If he'd hurry she would be in time to watch the movie. In a few minutes, Absalom would again be asleep. This time snoring with conviction.

"Daddy." Now Rainy could play her trump, a technique she had learned from both her mother and from Absalom himself. "Daddy." Absalom stirred. "Daddy, you better get up from there right now. You're snoring and sleeping and if you don't get up your back's gonna hurt all day tomorrow."

Absalom stared at her, trying to get his bearings. "Well, I guess I was sleeping pretty good there. Probably should get myself to bed."

And before he could sit back and fall in again, Rainy would run over to him and grab his thick hands, pull him until he rose, and head him upstairs. Victorious, she'd change the channel and sit back, until Sonny or her mother challenged her for control.

This nightly ritual continued for years in the same room where Dancer and Half-Dead now sat staring into the tunnel of empty moments. The smoky stillness was punctured by the off-key clunk of the doorbell.

"Who the fuck is that?" Dancer opened his eyes

wide and focused his vision.

"Yo, home." Half-Dead remained blind and numb. "You ain't gonna find out sitting there."

Dancer slowly rose out of his chair and walked to the door. He faced a young man of about eighteen with bamboo skin and a taut, high-energy, keen street awareness. His upper arms were a series of tight elongated muscles melded into a threatening mass. Dancer broke a smile. "What's up, Spider?"

"Sorry man, you know I wouldn't have come here if it wasn't important." In Dancer's eye, Spider was the foreground. The one-dimensional façade of row houses, with their cement-step tongues stuck out in defiance, stared at him. Because of the heat, the black streets were soft and could hold the impression of a basketball shoe.

Whither Street, which ran east to west, was a poseur, always in masquerade. It changed like the Nile from one end to the other. You could find Whither Street in white middle-class Wynnefield in West Philly and you could find Whither Street in the spare meanness of white working-class Fishtown. In between was the dense blackness of North Philadelphia that Dancer knew so well.

In the 2500 block of West Whither Street, as in most of North Philadelphia, the surface of the summer sunlight that reflected hope was deceiving. The internal hemorrhage of unemployment, the open flow of drugs, and governmental indifference all added to the gradual deterioration that was affecting the neighborhood.

As Dancer looked over Spider's shoulder he could see people going into Benson's store down at the corner. The neighborhood still had a corner store. But Benson, like other merchants, had to try everything, iron bars, bullet-proof glass, chicken wire—in an attempt to make his establishment safe from misguided, wounded, hopeless rage. The middle-class fire that had sustained Absalom and Gwen and their neighbors had given birth to melancholy. It joined the gush of sad life that lived in North Philly, adding enough apathy to make it dangerous. To the eye, Whither Street offered an alternative to abject crime and poverty. In reality, Whither Street had succumbed to it.

Dancer kept Spider standing on the stoop—none of his boys ever actually crossed the threshold. That was Rainy's rule and it was fine with him. He didn't trust most of the guys he knew in this tight, compressed North Philadelphia community. In the business of their lives, the code demanded distance, strength, and swift action. If someone was doing you wrong—messing with your lover or cheating you out of money—the response was generally quick and extreme. What used to be settled with fists could now quickly result in death.

Behind Spider, in the midday sunlight, Whither Street was now alive. A block of Spike Lee colors and people. Children played in the middle of the block, while a group of men gathered in front of a green 1980 Nova, gesturing, their heads buried under the hood. Down the block near Twenty-fifth Street, the paper man stopped his car in front of Doc's house to collect. Newspaper delivery was no longer safe for children, but too lucrative to go to older teenagers, so the paper was now delivered by an adult. On Friday nights and Saturday afternoons, with his private driver (and bodyguard), he slowly rolled down the street in a 1979 red Buick, stopping to collect at every house that took the daily paper.

Dancer saw a group of teenagers standing on the corner directly across the street from him. They were listening to rap music on a large portable tape player. It was a sleek black box, the size of a saxophone case, with a sound that was as powerful as his own expensive stereo system. But this morning they were subdued, the volume hung low. Dancer could still feel the bass line rippling across the street; it tunneled under the drooping asphalt and resurfaced under his nose. It circled his head and forced it to bob. He shook it off. It was too early to be acting like that. Still he couldn't completely ignore the call. The bass was a deadly killer wave of funk, seeking a victim.

He knew the song, a popular hip hop cut, ''Times Are Gettin' Ill.''

> *Gettin' ill with the boys*
> *somebody yelled kill that noise*

The young men nodded and gestured to Dancer, who waved back, joking, "Yo homes, why don't y'all kill *that* noise, it's too early for that kind of mess." Dancer smiled a big smile as he screamed across the street. They knew that he wasn't completely joking.

One of them yelled back, "It's never too early, homeboy."

"So, what's up?" Dancer turned his attention to Spider, who had been standing there the entire time. Dancer opened the screen, took a step outside, and tried to focus on Spider. He liked the boy. Spider was one of the few who could actually hold a reasonable conversation when he wanted to.

Even Dancer was dismayed at the plight of the younger generation. Although he exploited them, they made him sad. He couldn't understand what they were going to do with their lives. They were like a lost tribe, wandering in circles, hoping that when they got where they were going, they would know it. It angered Dancer that none of these kids ever talked about *becoming* anything. Nobody ever talked about dreams. Their lives were spent mostly with their heads down, rocked out, or jamming to the bumping rhymes of the pervasive hip hop air.

Two weeks before, Dancer had talked with a group of nine- and ten-year-old boys in front of Benson's store, at the corner. The main theme of the conversation was how they didn't think Martin Luther King was so important. One kid had turned to Dancer and in a true homeboy stance—hands in his blue sweatshirt pockets, hood up and shadowing his face—said, "Shit, man, tell me one motherfuckin' thing King did. That's old-time bullshit. You old folks believe the hype, but I ain't down for that shit."

Dancer was stunned. Okay, so it was a rocked-out world and education was a joke. But you still had to know *something*. "Why don't you pick up a book? That's what you need to do before you come out here talking about Martin Luther King," he told them.

Dancer didn't have any children and what he was seeing didn't make him want any. No one seemed to be going anywhere. Some folks talked about Jesse Jackson and the Black Muslim leader, Louis Farrakhan, but there was no one representative that everyone believed in. They breathed apathy like air.

Even though he lived among them and did business with them, Dancer tried to distinguish himself. He placed himself among the teachers, artists, entertainers, and the steady professionals who kept the race moving forward—he just went at it differently. He could not see working nine to five every day for twenty thousand dollars a year for the rest of his life. He needed time to think and time to have fun. Selling drugs had come to him as an answer, and it had proven very lucrative.

The only problem was the people he came in contact with. At one end of the drug business, there were lots of young people who had nothing going for themselves except a tour on the rock pile. And at the other end were a small group of ruthless, greedy bankers, Italians, or Panamanians, or Jamaicans.

Spider had worked for Dancer for about seven months. During the second week of employment with Dancer, Spider had asked for a loan. Dancer didn't trust him. He asked Spider, whose given name he still didn't know, to give him a good reason why he should loan him money. Spider told Dancer that his little sister (who turned out to be a complete fabrication) needed to go to an eye specialist or she would lose her sight. The explanation was long and obviously well thought out. He had impressed Dancer, and in turn had gotten what he wanted.

"Yo, man, I need my stash for the week. Now." Spider stared coldly at Dancer.

"Why? What's up?" This was completely out of the usual. No one ever got a week's product in advance. Each of the people who sold crack for Dancer met him in an approved place, every other day. That was Dancer's way of making sure that they were never tempted to take the drugs or the money and run.

"Nothing's up, Dance, I just want the whole stash." Spider held a single-dip cone of vanilla ice cream, which he now slid between his thin red lips.

Dancer saw his tongue dart out, scoop some of the ice cream from the cone, and slip quickly back into his mouth.

Dancer fought against a growing suspicion. He didn't want to be paranoid of everything. "You got the money?"

Spider shuffled his feet and looked around. "I'll give it to you next week at the Sunday spot."

"Spider, I don't know what the fuck is up, but you better get right, homeboy." Across the street, the music had changed as Public Enemy's "Yo, Bum Rush the Show," ripped the air. But the music began to fade as the boys headed down Whither Street toward Twenty-sixth.

Spider sucked in a chest full of air. "Look Dancer, things are changing man. I got to get the shit and get in the wind."

Now Dancer's mind was completely clear. Spider's eyes had exploded with terror. Something had unhinged his composure. Suddenly everything started moving with incredible speed. A long black BMW turned the corner at Stillman. Dancer looked past Spider to see who was driving, but the window was opaque. Spider quickly twisted around to see the car.

Dancer felt a pressure building around them. "What's going on, Spider?"

"I don't know, man. I don't know." Spider was almost crying. "I don't know anybody driving a car like that."

The BMW sat in the middle of the street, right in front of them. It stole the sunlight and recast it black-yellow. Dancer couldn't help but admire it. He would have gotten one if Rainy hadn't objected. She didn't like BMWs. She thought they were too common, especially among successful dealers. Sometimes she called them Black Man's Wheels.

The red Buick, loaded with old undelivered papers stacked in the back seat, blocked the narrow street. With cars parked on either side, there was barely enough room to drive a large car down the street. The paper man exited the last house on the block, got in his car, sat there a moment counting money, then slowly pulled away, across Twenty-fifth Street, and into the next block.

"Spider, I'm not giving you shit until I know more about what's going on. Now, does this have anything to do with BuckTeeth Rodney?" The words had barely left his mouth when the rear window of the car began to drop. From where Dancer stood, he could see nothing inside the car. Suddenly he felt queasy.

Spider started unconsciously bouncing up and down on the balls of his feet. "Forget it, man, forget it. I got to jet, man." He turned to the street.

Now Dancer saw something in the open window of the car. It was the flash of gold trim around a pair of sunglasses. Then he saw the gun. From the barrel it looked to be an automatic machine pistol, the newest rage, holding more status than an Uzi. He immediately slammed the door shut and dove for the floor.

He heard the burst of popping sounds, *pata pata pata pata,* from the street and the tearing of the aluminum screen door. Behind him he heard the maple wood stairs leading upstairs resound in three loud *whacks.* Dancer looked up to see Half-Dead approaching the vestibule. *"Down,"* Dancer screamed. "Get the fuck down!" Half-Dead immediately crumpled into a ball of bones and black skin.

Through the closed door, they heard the car take off down the street. Suddenly Dancer began shaking. Tremors riveted his body as he clutched a coat that had fallen from the coat rack just inside the door. He held it tightly, eyes closed. It was totally silent outside. No cars going by, no children playing, nothing. It was as still as Whither Street could be on a Saturday afternoon.

Half-Dead sprang out of his crumpled crouch. He stood over Dancer, who had pulled the coat over his head. "Who the fuck was it, man? Did you see who it was? Damn. I don't believe this shit." Half-Dead was straining in his skin. All of his senses were pushing him to action, but he didn't know what to do. He needed Dancer to direct him.

Dancer heard the words coming to him from above. He knew he had to get up, but he didn't want to. His body was still shaking. For a second, he forced his body to be still just to make sure he had not been shot. He felt no blood, no wetness. Everything seemed all right. But he wasn't sure he could actually stand up. If Half-Dead wasn't standing over him, he would have crawled into the crevices of the hardwood floors and stayed there forever. He wanted to stay in the safe feeling of his fetal crouch, it was dark and warm. But Half-Dead's eyes burned holes through the coat. Abruptly he flung the coat off.

"Dead, man," he started, as he pulled his heart back into his body. "This goddamn black Beamer pulls up and sits there a minute, them bam." Dancer felt lighter than air. "They tried to kill me, man." He was pacing now. "Why would somebody try to off me?"

"Maybe Rodney's crazier than I thought he was." Half-Dead stared into Dancer's face.

"It just don't make sense." Dancer jerked his hands into the air. There had never been any trouble, no hassles. Before him, the neighborhood had been open to freelancers. "What the fuck does this mean?" He fought to keep his nerves from fleeing into the hot North Philadelphia air, screaming.

He and Half-Dead looked at each other as they heard sirens closing distance quickly. Half-Dead cautiously walked to the front door. As he looked outside, he talked to Dancer.

"Are you okay?"

"Yeah, I'm okay, I think."

"Well you better thank your lucky stars, home-boy." Half-Dead's voice added extra weight and fell to the floor around Dancer. He turned back to face

Dancer. "Your boy Spider ain't okay at all. He's wacked out."

"What?" Dancer collapsed into the couch.

"Blew him away. You know, man, I don't think they wanted you at all. If they wanted you, they could of got you. You said they waited out there a bit. They was probably trying to wait for you to let the youngboy walk so they could get to him."

"You think?"

"Don't really matter, they got him and you're still bookin'." Half-Dead leaned against the wall, surveying the scene. There was no broken glass, but the screen had holes in it, the wooden door that Dancer had slammed had three half-inch holes in it, and the stairs held the bullets. "By the way, home, I hope you got your dope put away. They gonna want to see what was up in here."

"You're right." Dancer had sat dazed listening to Half-Dead. He heard the cars approaching outside and jumped to a new terror. He ran around the room quickly gathering up the two pipes, a set of small, empty plastic bags, and other paraphernalia and raced into the basement, where his small supply of rock cocaine was also hidden. Under the cellar stairs in the original stones used for the foundation, Dancer had created a small compartment. He put everything away.

As he rushed through the dining room, Absalom stared at him. Though his vision was blurred, he felt the panic swelling within the house. And yet, he was

powerless. A thought occurred that at such a time,
in his own house, there was no one there who loved
him. Who even knew him.

Hurrying back up the steps, Dancer walked to
the front door. Half-Dead was sitting quietly in the
living room. Obviously he wanted to be left out of
it.

Dancer opened the door on a terrible mess. Spider had gone up in pieces and his red blood ran
down the gray cement steps into the crevices separating the blocks of concrete sidewalk. There the
blood, nearing the end of its journey, soaked into the
dirt. But enough blood remained—a stain on the cement that Rainy would eventually have to scrub
away. Alongside the flowing blood, Dancer saw the
thick, slow-moving stream of melting ice cream,
white and sweet. Where the two streams met, the
river was pink. He turned his head away.

But instinctively, against his better judgment, he
turned quickly back to see Spider face down,
sprawled across his front steps. Part of his head was
missing. Dancer looked up, seeking some relief, only
to find a wall of people pressing forward.

Breaking from the crowd, a fair-skinned black
woman of about forty-five threw herself across the
street toward Spider's body. "They shot my baby.
They shot my baby. No. Please, Robert. Don't die,
baby." She cradled Robert's lifelessness in her arms,
looking up to Dancer. She had just left the corner
store when she had heard the shots. Her radar had

gone up and led her to her son's murdered body.

"Why did they shoot my Robert? Why?"

"I don't know, ma'am. I don't know. We was just standing here talking."

"They didn't have to kill him." She cried a flowing barrage of tears that ended in sentences. "My baby didn't have to die."

Dancer was stunned, drawn into a place where he felt full and empty at the same time, where he felt deeply, but found no facility to communicate it. "We were just standing here. He was eating the ice cream cone." As he looked down, he saw the flecks of cone spotting the stoop and the back of the boy's T-shirt. He looked back to the woman who was sobbing. "He was all right. Spider was all right. I liked him."

6

Absalom felt like a balloon full of water being tossed between a crowd of memories at the beach. Background music played softly in the deep folds of his consciousness. He couldn't place the song but he knew it was the Duke. He loved Ellington and it seemed only right that that sound would carry him forward, through whatever.

His hard work, the Duke's music, his belief in love—they had carried him this far. Absalom believed his main responsibility was to make life happy for Gwen, and to give his children the chance to have a better life than his. The formula was simple—you had to give everything you had, work until there was nothing else to do, and then you had to trust that the reward would be just. That your children *would* have what you didn't.

He could clearly see what some people had, how

well they lived, and he knew *he* was always struggling to make ends meet. Absalom accepted that as *his* life. But not for Sonny or Rainy. His life would only have meaning if they had a better chance.

He was moving again, this time with the whisk scratching the skins, the thumping bass, and the lilting piano thick within him. And it was Ellington's music floating in his mind that took him to the moment of struggle, when the blues defined him. A time when he thought he was losing Gwen. When she was almost gone, along with the faith that fueled his dream.

It was early evening, on the twenty-third of December, 1958, and Absalom stood in the kitchen watching Gwen cook the fish he had brought home from the market. Then, in his prime, Absalom was a large-framed brown-skinned man. His body was dense and strong. He was a truck driver, a deliverer of heavy trays of sweet-smelling baked goods. His clean-shaven, bright-skinned face beamed like a schoolboy's as he watched Gwen place the fish in the hot grease.

Absalom loved Gwen's fried fish. She dredged them in cornmeal and gently tossed them into the frying pan. The fish would sizzle and crackle until they turned a deep brown. Then she would stack them on a plate lined with paper towels.

The grease popped and splattered all over the stove, sometimes taking flight, escaping the frying pan to form perfect little darkening droplets on the white walls. Absalom, whose voice was not deep, had to talk loud to be heard above the noise of the frying fish.

Gwen was listening, but as usual she didn't seem to be paying attention to him. She was in a frenzy of preparation and cooking. The fish needed frying, the cornbread needed mixing, and the coleslaw needed stirring.

"I told Sy I wasn't going to drive no truck all over the city without being able to stop a couple of times a day to get me something to eat."

"I'm telling you," Gwen said over her shoulder.

"I got to haul all that bread around and I can't even take an hour off to eat, myself. That's ridiculous. I'm not going to stand for it."

"Well, don't do anything silly, Ab. We can't afford for you to lose your job right now."

"I know what we need, Gwen, but I'm not gonna go without eating for no white man or his small-time job."

"What do you mean? Sy's been good to you. Besides it's not small time, Ab. Who else you know drives a truck for white folks in this city? Not many. So don't go putting it down."

"I'm not. And I know he's been good to me. I'm just not gonna kiss his behind. By the way, how long is it gonna be before we sit down to dinner?" He was both excited and nervous. He wasn't sure how Gwen was going to take the news he had to tell her.

"Shouldn't be too long. Why don't you go wake up Rainy and get her ready for dinner. I told Sonny to be home by six, but he said he was gonna play football over at the athletic center with his friends so I'm not sure he's gonna make it back by then."

Absalom stopped, his tense, anxious eyes wide on her. "Don't you think a nine-year-old boy should be home by dark?" He continued focusing his eyes on her. She kept on with her cooking. "Besides, it's pretty cold out."

"He was dressed warm," Gwen said, not even looking up. He decided to drop it. He wanted her in a good mood.

The smell of fish frying permeated the house. Absalom's stomach growled as he turned to leave the kitchen. She couldn't see his face, but he was smiling when he said, "I'm starving. Well, I'll go roust that wild little girl of yours and get her ready for dinner."

"If she was mine, she wouldn't be wild like she is. Now just go and get ready for dinner."

Absalom walked out of the kitchen, through the breakfast room, and into the dining room. He turned and headed up the stairs to Rainy's room. He stopped at her doorway. She was only five years old then and, with her plaited hair tangled all over her face, she had deflated into a small tan ball of resting energy.

As he stood there, he thought he heard music. It

was a slight tinny sound that seemed to waft about her bedroom.

"Rainy. Rainy. Wake up, sweetheart. It's almost time for dinner." He gently shook her as he talked.

She slowly climbed into consciousness, violently stretching, extending her thin body. Rainy looked up at her father. "I was really sleeping," she said with emphasis.

"You sure were." Absalom could see the imprint of the blanket on her face. "Dinner's almost ready."

Her small nose flared. "Fish, huh?"

"Yup. Smells good too."

"I don't like fish, Daddy. Can't you go to Barnett's and get me a cheesesteak?"

"You do like fish, Rainy, why you want to tell a story like that? The way I remember it, the last time we had fish, you ate so much your stomach hurt." Absalom sat down on the bed next to her. He took her small, slender hand and held it.

"Rainy, what is that noise? I keep hearing music." He held himself still. "Do you hear it?"

"Of course, Daddy." She used her free hand to pull a black plastic transistor radio from under her pink flannel blanket.

"A radio. When did you get a radio?"

"Sonny gave it to me last week."

"And where'd he get an expensive piece of equipment like this?" Absalom picked up the radio, from which Fats Domino's "Blueberry Hill" thumped.

"I don't know. He knows all kinds of people."

"Well, I don't want you to get too attached to this radio. You hear? Because I got a feeling that you ain't gonna be having it too long."

Tears formed like morning dew. "Why, Daddy?"

"Just because. I got to find out where it comes from. So don't you take it outside or let nobody else play with it until I tell you. You hear me?"

"Yes."

"Now, get your ashy butt out of this bed, washed up, and dressed for dinner." He got up from the bed and walked out of the room as Rainy limped unsteadily to the bathroom.

As he reached the bottom step on his way back to the kitchen, he saw the folded end of the day's newspaper slide in the mail slot. He picked up the *Philadelphia Bulletin* without looking at the headlines. Instead he pulled out the sports section and headed for a chair at the breakfast room table. The breakfast room was what the white real estate agent had called the small room separating the kitchen and the dining room.

"Rainy was sleeping like the dead," he said to Gwen as he sat down.

"She comes in here from school every day, ripping and running, going next door, outside on the steps. She don't stop until she's plum wore out. She ought to be sleeping, much as she runs around.''

Absalom heard the words rise above the grease as he flipped through the pages until he reached the professional football statistics. He always checked the leaders in every category, searching for the black players. When he found one, he almost leapt out of his chair.

''Gwen. Gwen.''

''What?''

''Herb Adderley's leading in interceptions.''

''Who's he?''

''Colored defensive back. Colored guy. He grew up down South, I think. Yeah. Heck of a young ball player.''

''Oh.''

Absalom wanted to get on with dinner and realized that he didn't hear Rainy moving around upstairs. ''I bet Rainy went back to sleep. I don't hear a thing up there.''

Gwen stopped to catch her breath. She used her white apron to wipe her damp forehead. Even in December she could work up a sweat in the kitchen. It wasn't that she was such a good cook. She would readily admit to being only adequate. In her words, ''I gets the job done.'' But Gwen put great effort into everything she did, regardless of her expectations of the outcome.

Picturing the cute five-year-old girl collapsed in the bed, half-in, half-out, half-dressed, she smiled. ''Well, maybe she'll eat a little later tonight. It is

Friday. No rush. No sense in disturbing her.''

''But if we let her sleep now, she's gonna be up all night.''

''No she ain't, Ab. Just relax. We'll just eat by ourselves tonight. Don't look like Sonny is gonna make it on time either.''

''Well . . .'' Absalom wanted to tell everyone the news at the same time. He knew he'd have a better chance of Gwen going along with the program if he could get the kids on his side. ''I kinda wanted us all to sit down together, for once, to eat dinner,'' he spoke into the paper.

''What are you talking about, Ab? We almost always eat together. We ate together last night.''

He knew she was going to say that. ''Yeah, but that was unusual, Gwen. You know that. You always got some meeting to go to or something. More often than not, I'm sitting here with the kids and you're out somewhere.''

Gwen picked up her pace again. She wasn't in the mood for fighting. That was one of the reasons she had stayed home last night. She tried to vary her movement just enough so that he couldn't detect a specific pattern.

Gwen loved Absalom, but in the middle years of her marriage she needed, more than anything, to get out of the house, to experience a little nightlife, to dance and socialize with her friends. She smiled and demurred, but two or three times a week, around eight-thirty, Gwen was stepping out the front door, on her way out.

"Well, you and I can eat together tonight, can't we?"

"Yeah, I guess so. I wonder where that Sonny is?"

Gwen walked into the breakfast room carrying the plate of fried fish. "I told you, he's over at the Rec with his friends. He'll be home soon."

"Oh well." Absalom realized he had no control over the situation. "That fish sure does look good."

"Porgies are always good, fried up like this."

Sitting down at the table, Gwen watched Absalom as he picked the sweet white meat from the fish. "Is there something wrong, Ab?"

"Why you ask me that?"

"Because you've been acting very strange."

"How am I acting? I'm trying to eat this fish. I'm not acting no way."

"It's like you're afraid to start talking. Like if you do, you're gonna say something you don't want to say."

"I swear for God, woman. You always up in my face," he said, smiling. "I can't even eat my dinner in peace. Okay. Yes, there is something I want to say."

"Well?" Gwen ate a forkful of coleslaw. The creamy white mayonnaise left traces on her soft red lips. "I'm waiting."

"Well, you know we can't afford to buy presents this year.'' Absalom reached for another piece of fish.

"Yes, I know that. We've already settled that.''

"Well, I got to thinking. I want my children to have Christmas just like everybody else. That's why I'm working so hard.'' He continued eating. He wanted her approval.

"So? If we don't have the money, we can't do it, can we?''

"Well, I went to a finance company and got a loan.''

Gwen put down her fork and picked up the green paper napkin from the table. "You did what?''

"I got $500.''

"You borrowed $500?'' She paused, utterly angry. They would never get out of debt. She didn't want to have to use every dollar they made to pay back money they had already spent. Gwen was thinking about the future. She wanted a different kind of life. She wanted a better house. A lawn. A garden. Better clothes. They would never make it unless Absalom changed.

She said the first words that formed in her mouth. "How are you gonna pay it back? How? This is ridiculous. We don't have enough money to buy groceries so how in the name of God are we gonna make payments on a $500 loan?''

Absalom was prepared for her. He knew she'd be tense. He knew how much she hated debt. But everybody around him was deep in debt—that was how people lived. "I already thought about that, Gwen. Now just give me a chance. I'm gonna take about $200 to buy Christmas stuff. Everything. We're gonna have a big tree, lots of gifts. We're gonna have a great Christmas this year." He spread a wide smile around her as he searched her face for a response, but he couldn't wait. Before she could react, he found himself saying. "I'm just tired of working like I do and then it comes down to Christmastime and we can't even go out and buy Rainy and Sonny gifts. And I'd like to buy you a gift this year."

Gwen looked at him. He had changed. There was less of the energetic, playful boy she had once embarrassed on a long bus ride. Family had become so important to him. Absalom's sense of responsibility was like a fully loaded cart he pulled around. You could almost see the bit in his mouth.

"So, it ain't gonna be that way this year. We're gonna celebrate big-time. Anyway, I'm gonna take the rest of it and pay off some of our bills, so we'll have some more spending money."

Gwen got up from the table. "More spending money? That's a laugh. I never heard of such foolishness. You done gone out and borrowed money, put us deeper into debt, just so we can spend more money that we don't have."

"I'm trying to give my family a decent Christmas. Ain't that what a man's supposed to do?"

"Ab, don't you see? We'll have a good Christmas. Yes, that's true. But what about February, when all those bills come due? What then?''

Absalom reached into his pocket and pulled out a roll of money. He held it up close to her eyes. Then in a fluid motion he flung it onto the table. ''This here is our Christmas and we're gonna take advantage of it.''

The next day, Christmas Eve, Absalom came in the door at four-thirty in the afternoon, his arms full of packages. He had to go back to the car for two larger boxes. Gwen stood by the foyer and held the door open. She didn't say a word as he hustled everything into the basement. Both Rainy and Sonny were outside playing. Rainy was down the block with the Harper sisters and Sonny was out again, playing football.

Absalom stacked the bags and boxes neatly in the basement, then headed back into the street. Thirty minutes later he was back with the largest spruce tree the Goodman house had ever seen. ''Well, that's some tree, isn't it?'' he asked Gwen, who was sitting at the mahogany dining room table. The gleaming veneer of the table was visible through the white, loose-knit lace tablecloth.

''It's nice,'' she said.

''When the kids get in, we'll trim it.'' Absalom stepped back from the tree, which was leaning against one of the living room walls. ''Now, that's a Christmas tree.''

''Yeah, I guess it is. I should probably go on

downstairs and see if I can find last year's decorations."

"That would be nice," he said with a hint of sarcasm. "I'll get it in the stand."

"I don't feel much like Christmas this year for some reason," she said as she walked toward the cellar door.

"You won't relax, that's what the problem is. You're always worrying about something."

"Who else is gonna worry? You sure won't. You got the nerve to go out and put this family into hock. I don't like it, Ab. I'm sorry."

"Gwen, why don't you just go get the decorations. I'm going to put on some Johnny Mathis. We'll have fun." While Gwen got up from the table and headed for the basement, Absalom fought the tall tree into the red stand.

Later, after Rainy and Sonny had returned and eaten dinner, they all went into the living room to trim the tree. Absalom wanted the tree in the middle of the window that faced Whither Street. He kept going outside to see how it looked.

Rainy was very excited. Absalom had let slip at the dinner table that there were going to be lots of nice gifts for Christmas. Sonny tried to act as if he didn't care. But he was there, right alongside Rainy, Gwen, and Absalom as they trimmed the tree.

Absalom suddenly remembered yesterday's moment with Rainy. "Say Sonny, where did you get the radio you gave to Rainy?"

Sonny, standing on a chair, trying to hang a sparkling silver thin glass ornament, froze momentarily. "Radio?"

"Yes, you know what I'm talking about."

"You mean the little radio that I let Rainy have?"

"Sonny, don't fool with me now, I'm not one of your friends out there on Whither Street." Absalom was putting a hook in a straw angel.

Sonny shot a glance at Rainy, who was busy looking through the box of ornaments. He tried to wait for her to look up before he responded, but her head was buried in the box.

"I traded with some guy at school. But I decided I didn't want it. I want a new one. So I gave it to Rainy." Sonny hung the ornament and stepped down from the chair.

Absalom stood there, holding the angel. "What did you give him for it?"

"I don't know. I can't remember."

"You can't remember? Don't give me that, Sonny."

Rainy looked up and Sonny put a fist over his eye, signifying the penalty for having betrayed him.

"I think I gave him my watch."

"The watch I gave you last Christmas?"

"It was a Timex, Dad. I had it for a year already. I thought the radio for the watch was a good deal."

"You traded away a gift, Sonny? I don't believe it. Don't you understand anything about the spirit of things? You don't go around giving away things that people give you."

Gwen, ignoring the discussion, walked over and grabbed Rainy by the waist. "Come over here and tell me what you want for Christmas." Rescued, Rainy flung herself at the couch, pulling her mother on top of her. They laughed. Gwen had changed clothes and was now wearing a sleek black dress that caressed her tall, thick body. Her hair, full and flowing, was freshly done and glistened. A single strand of fake pearls rested against her small breasts. The force of the two of them crashing into the sofa brought Gwen's stockinged feet into the air with a whoosh.

"I don't understand you, Sonny. You're old enough to know better," Absalom continued, undistracted.

"I guess I didn't think."

"You never think, boy. That's most of your problem."

"Ab," Gwen cut in, "I thought this was going to be a special Christmas. Let him be tonight. It's Christmas Eve."

Absalom almost immediately broke into a broad grin. He was glad she had finally given in. "Well, don't tell me that the great Mrs. Gwen Goodman done suddenly got the Christmas spirit? I thought for sure you was gonna be Mrs. Scrooge this year."

Gwen made coffee for Absalom and her. Rainy and Sonny drank milk and they all ate the holiday cookies Absalom had brought home. As usual, Rainy needed only for Gwen to suggest she go to bed and she was on her way upstairs, but Sonny balked.

"Mom, don't be funny. I'm almost ten years old. I'm not anywhere near sleepy. It's only 9:30."

"I know what time it is, Sonny. But I want you to go to bed. So don't give me no more lip about it. You don't have to go to sleep, but I want you in your room and the lights out."

Sonny pounded his retreat up the maple stairs. As soon as he was in his room, Gwen said, "I'm going out for a while."

"Going out? It's Christmas Eve."

"I promised Vi that I would visit some friends with her."

"I don't believe it. It's Christmas Eve, Gwen. Why would you want to go out? Why can't you spend the night at home? With me for a change?"

Gwen found it hard to say anything other than, "I promised Vi. I'll be back early."

"If you go out, it don't really matter when you come back."

In fifteen minutes, a car pulled up outside and Gwen ran out to get inside it as Absalom tried to concentrate on picking up the fine strands of aluminum tinsel that had escaped the tree.

He silently put Rainy's bike together and set up Sonny's chemistry set like it looked on the box. Nat Cole's voice sugared the air and produced the fire to light up the Christmas tree. He laid out three gifts for Gwen and went upstairs to bed.

Rainy got up at the first shatter of light. She fairly slid down the stairs, hypnotized by the grand tree, its lights still popping on and off like a neon sign, presents sparkling underneath it. The sight was wondrous. Nothing ever looks as good as it does the first time you see it under a Christmas tree on Christmas morning.

She surveyed her gifts: a black Raggedy Ann doll, a doctor-nurse set, a china set, and the coveted bicycle—everything she had asked for. She took off, back up the stairs to wake Sonny up.

Early on Christmas morning, Sonny forgot his preadolescent distance and bounded out of bed. His breath was short as he discovered the chemistry set, a few books and a new pair of roller skates. He had gotten even more than he had asked for.

Gwen had come in at about two-thirty. She had stopped in the living room to gaze at the tree and the booty that was under it. She noticed the gleaming maple hardwood floor with the decorative lights streaking it in the dark. But she only stood there for a heartbeat before heading upstairs to bed.

Sometime later, in the early breaking hours of the day, before the sun, and before Rainy awoke with Christmas on her mind. Gwen and Absalom silently sought each other out. And, in their sleep, they held each other close, whispering night words that loved only their ears.

Rainy returned to the tree with Sonny. Together

they crouched in the tentative light of the early morning, playing with their new toys. Rainy tried to ride her bike on the slippery floors and fell on Sonny, who was already reading the chemistry experiment manual.

When Absalom walked down the steps at nine-thirty to make himself a cup of coffee, he found both Rainy and Sonny still so caught up in their gifts that they barely heard him. But when Rainy looked up, she exploded from the floor.

"Daddy, look what I got. Look. I got the bike. I got Raggedy Ann. I got—"

"Slow down, baby girl. Slow down," he said. "Anyway, I know what you got. Merry Christmas." Rainy dove back into the pile of wrapped gifts.

Absalom bent down to Sonny. "Merry Christmas, son. You like it?"

"Merry Christmas, Dad. Yeah, this is fantastic. It's got phosphorus and sulfur and everything. It's even got—"

Rainy interrupted, "Merry Christmas, Daddy. Here's your gift." She handed another package to Sonny. "This is dad's present from you."

Absalom took the boxes and sat down at the dining room table. He looked back at the tree, still twinkling, blinking behind his children who stood before him, waiting for him to unwrap their gifts. He smiled. For the moment he was happy. He hadn't thought once about receiving gifts. He fingered the wrapped boxes; the small square one from Sonny was obviously a jewelry box. Something deep inside him caused him to shudder, suddenly overwhelmed by a feeling of gratitude.

"I didn't know you were gonna buy me a gift," was all he could say. They smiled awkwardly at him, shuffling nervously. He had never before felt a direct sense of thankfulness from them; they had been too young to express it before. He fondled the wrapped packages, holding the moment.

"Aren't you going to open them?" Sonny said, looking down. He couldn't wait to see the expression on his father's face.

"I love you. Both of you," Absalom whispered to them. "Thank you."

Rainy's gift was a white dress shirt and Sonny's a set of cuff links with Absalom's initials engraved on them. Absalom hugged each of them. The cuff links thrilled him. His own initials. He held them up to the light and beamed. "Never had nothing with my initials on it before."

Both Rainy and Sonny asked to go out. Absalom nodded to them and they went upstairs to change. He went into the kitchen to make coffee. He sat down, cuff links and shirt in front of him on the breakfast room table. The hum of the refrigerator asserted itself. Sonny and Rainy were ready and gone quickly.

Everything was still as Gwen descended the stairs at noon. The Christmas sun nearly overran the tree lights. The living room floor was awash in golden hues. She walked into the breakfast room in a rush, startling Absalom.

"You could have said something, scaring me like that."

"I didn't mean to scare you. Just getting myself a cup of coffee."

"Gwen, what time did you get home?"

"It was kind of late. Vi had to drop off some other friends before she brought me home."

"Where'd you go?"

"Went to one of her girlfriend's house."

"Where?"

"Why, Ab?"

"Because I want to know."

"Why?" Gwen was fully awake and not liking the conversation.

"Because I want to know, that's all. I *am* your husband."

"I know that."

"Where were you?"

"Ab, now you know I don't like you trying to make me account for every little thing I do. I just don't like that. I'll tell you where I was. Not right now though."

"Gwen, last night was Christmas Eve. You never went out on Christmas Eve before." Absalom put his coffee cup down and put his eyes on her.

Gwen sat down and tightened her housecoat around her body. "I know what last night was. But I didn't feel like staying home."

"How come? What's wrong with staying home every now and then?"

"I do stay home every now and then. You just want me to be home all the time. I can't do that. I just can't do that." She poured herself a cup of coffee and waited for Absalom to respond.

"Gwen, it was Christmas Eve, for crying out loud. I don't know what's going on, but I want it to stop. I want you to be here. This is your home. Not out on some street with a bunch of wild people." Absalom's voice had started to rise, its softness gone, his anger on the surface.

"Don't get me started, Ab. Ten years, that's how long we've been doing this. I've been here. I know where my home is. But don't ask me to give up going out every now and then."

"It ain't every now and then, Gwen, it's every other blessed night. I won't put up with it."

Gwen sat back in her chair. She sat there for the longest second. "Don't you dare tell me what you'll put up with." Her voice now screamed out. "I do everything around here as it is. You're always working, always gone. And when you come home, all you can do is sit around here and watch that stupid boxing on the television. We never go anywhere, we never do nothing. I'm not gonna sit around and wait for you, I'm just not. So don't go getting up on your high horse. If you weren't so damn boring, maybe I'd stay home a little more."

Absalom was motionless. Finally, after drinking

the remainder of his coffee in silence, he said, ''Did you see what Rainy and Sonny bought me for Christmas?''

Gwen looked at him, then down at the presents on the table. She slowly got up from the table and headed upstairs to dress.

Absalom cried. In the mist of his pain. In the depth of anesthesia that brought on the dream, he cried. And Ellington must have known the same tears, because the music matched the pain. He knew Gwen had struggled to find her love. And once found, it now seemed so brief.

7

People like a blur of lights, pressed against Absalom's tears.

The song ended. He was moving, physically this time, being wheeled through the corridors. He knew the territory. The pimpled ceiling. The distant sound of voices. The fear that ran through the halls like an African griot announcing the history of pain. From his vantage, the sounds of the hospital were like poetic chants that elevated the process over the people. He felt like a part of the poem, not the poem itself. The story was about how people tried to save lives, not about the lives.

The door to Absalom's hospital room was open. Gwen, quiet and motionless, sat in the chair. Sonny and Rainy were sitting together on Absalom's cheerless hospital bed. Outside the room, in the corridors, the bustle of nurses and patients picked up. Traveling barges of complicated machinery maneuvered through, led by the noiseless march of nurses. The patients inched by the door, some attached to rolling metal contraptions that fed them medicine and food. Others, led by relatives, sought some relief from their pain through movement.

Rainy broke the silence. "I hope Dad is strong enough. I hope he can do it."

"Yeah," Sonny exhaled.

"Your father's a strong man. He's come through a lot over the last year. He's gonna make it. I know he is." Gwen's lower lip trembled.

Sonny got off the bed and put his arm around her. "Dad is very strong, Mom. We all know that. If anyone can beat this, he can." Sonny smelled her perfume. She still wore Avon's Evening in Paris.

"I just wish they would let us know something." Rainy pulled herself from the bed. She walked to the door and tried to find a nurse.

Without Absalom, Gwen's strength crumbled in silence. Sonny's hand felt like a lead weight on her shoulder. She felt her arms going numb. Everything seemed to be sinking into her center as she sat there. She took a deep breath. Then another. Gwen pumped her body back up to its proper size. Now Sonny's hand felt warm. She reached up and grabbed it, patted it.

As they sat in silence, Absalom came closer. He couldn't wait to be with his family, where he belonged. He heard them talking in his white room.

Sonny looked at his sister. "Rainy, I've been thinking about the old house. I kind of miss it. How's it holding up?"

"It's holding up just fine, Sonny. What do you mean?" Rainy tensed. She recognized the tone of his voice. It reminded her that he was her older brother and thought he had a right to evaluate everything she did.

"It's pretty old, that's all. I was just thinking about it. You know me. I'm always thinking about the future." Sonny couldn't help it. He lived among accountants and people who always talked about the bottom line. The house seemed like a disaster waiting to happen.

"So am I," Rainy shot back. "That's just what I'm thinking about. In a few years, white folks will be spending big dollars for property in our neighborhood."

"You must be joking." Sonny thought about the narrow, red brick house on Whither Street—it would never be worth more than ten thousand dollars. Whither Street was one block north of Girard, the line of demarcation between the blue-collar, white ethnic neighborhoods and the black folks. Sure, the white urban pioneers were encroaching, buying the property south of Girard, which was closer to center city, but they would never bring their gentrified touch to the heart of North Philly.

Why must it be a joke, thought Absalom? Why? Why couldn't what he had worked for, what he had

*created, become something that other people valued
and that would be held for all time by the Goodman
family? Landed people. Voting people. African
American gentry. But who was to say what could
become valuable? In this he differed with Sonny. His
son was moved by cynicism.*

"I'm not joking at all." Rainy stepped into the
saddle once again. "Dancer and I think this is a great
investment. If we can just hold on until we get our
acts together."

"Rainy, there's no way in hell a property on
West Whither Street is going to be a great investment. You're dreaming."

"Some people have no ability to dream." Rainy
walked over and put her arm around Gwen, who sat
quietly listening. "Do they, Mother dear?"

*Absalom liked Rainy's spirit. It rivaled Gwen's
when she was young. When he had offered to rent
the house to her, he had done it expressly to keep
the Goodman name in the neighborhood. In a way,
he had hated to leave North Philly.*

Sonny looked at his mother. He didn't want her
to misinterpret what he was saying. "Mom, I know
we have to keep a positive attitude, I know that. But
if something happens to Dad, we can't afford to keep
that house." Sonny had been thinking it since he
found out his father was sick. He worried about his
mother. Her pension would not be enough and he
wasn't in a position, now, where he had the money
to help her.

He was making more money than he ever had, but like many of his friends, as he tried to discover what the "good life" was, he was overextended. He lived from paycheck to paycheck, just as his father had always done. The only difference was that the amount of money he was in debt would have scared his father to death a long time ago.

Gwen forced herself to speak. "I don't know what you two are talking about. Nothing is going to happen to your father, so there's no reason to be talking about the house."

Absalom smiled. He loved Gwen. She would stay with him forever. She could supply his words when his lungs failed to support his thoughts. He could see. He could feel. She would talk for him.

Rainy was slowly steaming. "Mom's right. And anyway, you're talking about the house I live in. You can't come flying in from some ridiculous place like Minnesota and make judgments about my house."

"Rainy, I'm not making any judgments. But, you know as well as I, that unless you can afford to pay rent—"

"I pay rent," Rainy said through clenched teeth.

"I mean market price."

"It doesn't matter, you want to raise the rent, go ahead, I can pay it. I swear to God, *Mister Landlord*." Exasperation threatened her. She took a deep breath and reconsidered her approach. "Where the hell have you been? Mom and I have to deal with Dad's illness and where have you been? Minnesota?

Where the hell is that? Don't come in here talking all this trash to me. As far as I'm concerned, you walked out on us. You don't have the right to tell me anything.''

''Rainy.'' Sonny held up his hands to soften the attack. This was her main weapon against him and it always hit home. Yes, he had left. But he left to make himself into something. ''I went up there to get me a job. I work. I don't like being so far away.''

He remembered that last meeting at Data Central. He could still see everyone frozen in their places with Templeton's hand outstretched in sympathy. Rainy had no idea what he had to deal with. And he couldn't explain it to her now.

''You haven't been here, Sonny. You can act bourgeois if you want to, trying to tell me about what we should do about *my* house, but you ain't been nowhere around when Dad needed someone to take him to the doctor, or pick up his checks, or nothing.''

Gwen stared first at Rainy and then at Sonny. *Absalom flinched at the sharpness*. But Gwen said nothing.

Sonny slowly deflated. ''I'm just worried that that old house is going to fall apart and you won't be able to deal with it and it's going to fall on Mom. If we get rid of it now, she can take the money and put it in the bank. We don't have to wait for some catastrophe.''

''We're not selling the house.''

Sonny, seeking a way out of the argument, said,

"Well, it's too early really to get into this."

"You're damned right it is." Rainy was sweating now. Sonny had worn out his welcome. She cut her hazel eyes into him, piercing his skin in a number of places.

Rainy was deft at destroying her opponents. He knew that. She would do whatever she needed to do. But in this case, he felt righteous. Someone had to protect his mother. If Rainy wouldn't, and Absalom couldn't, he would.

When it came to Rainy, Sonny couldn't control himself. It was an intense and irrational reaction to his love for her. He wanted her to *be* something, not just his sister, who always talked about being a singer or an actress, but someone who was working as hard as he was. And when he looked at her, dressed even in her designer clothes, he felt that she had never materialized. Something was trapped deep inside her and had never been allowed to surface. Perhaps she was afraid to see if she could be who she wanted. It made him angry—he loved her, he really did. But ever since they were young he had nursed a feeling of disappointment with her. Disappointment that he never told her about, but held her accountable for anyway.

There were times when Sonny realized that feeling this way was paternalistic and unfair. There were times when he loved her purely, like brother and sister, but these times were few. Mostly he faced her with his stomach knotted. Rainy never knew how to take care of herself. He always had to come to her rescue.

When she was twelve he had surprised her at Major Torrence's party where the punch was laced with grain alcohol. It was 8:30 on a February Friday night and Sonny was standing outside Benson's grocery store, waiting for Rooster to get his favorite *Tastykake* lemon pie, when Frankie Sawyer walked up.

"Guess you ain't goin' to the youngboy's set?" Frankie was a chubby kid, two years younger than Sonny and two years older than Rainy.

"What youngboys?" There were any number of cliques of younger guys.

"You know Major Torrence, don't you? Well, he's having a party tonight. Right now, I guess."

Sonny didn't like Major Torrence, a boy of about thirteen who had a reputation in the neighborhood for wandering around the streets during the day when he was supposed to be in school. "Nope, I didn't know about it and I don't care."

"They got *beaucoup* wine, so I hear."

"Ask me if I care, Frankie, I don't want to go to Major's party. He's an asshole and his friends are too." Sonny could imagine the kind of people there. Slick-headed, rough-minded dudes getting drunk and raising hell. "Are you going?"

"I don't know yet. The only reason I'm telling you about it is I just thought I'd pull your coattail."

"Pull my coat about what, Frankie?" Sonny was

losing patience. Rooster had finally exited the store and joined them.

"Well, I know for a fact that Rainy is down there." Frankie swallowed and looked off into the distance. It was cold on this February night. Whither Street was quiet. Across the street from Benson's, Fred's Barbershop still had people sitting high in the chairs. Fred was steady cutting hair and talking. The two establishments lit up the corner of Twenty-fifth and Whither.

Sonny pulled his leather jacket closer to his body. "My sister Rainy?"

"Yup."

"She's at Major's?"

"Yup."

Sonny looked at Rooster. "I'm gonna go get her."

"I'm with you, man," was all that Rooster said. They both turned their back on Frankie and headed up Whither Street toward Major Torrence's house.

Rooster, the shorter of the two, had to walk extra fast to keep up with Sonny. "You sure you wanna crash this party, Sonny? I know they're youngboys but they don't have to let you in. You know me, I'm good for lifting shit from a store, but I ain't no good fighting. I'm more of a lover, you know. Don't like to take chances with my health."

"Rooster"—Sonny was a step ahead—"you're always taking chances with your health. Every time you dip into Gimbels to try to cop a radio or something, you're taking a chance with your health. Anyway, you don't have to come in. My sister is in there and they ain't gonna stop me.''

When they got to the house, Rooster held back. ''Are you sure, man? We could go down the street and call.''

Sonny looked back at him. ''You just wait right here. I'll be back.'' He rang the doorbell. He could hear the sweet sexy voice of Smokey Robinson's ''The Fork in the Road.'' Through the small window at the top of the door, he could see that Major had replaced all of the house's light bulbs with blue ones. The house buzzed with blue light.

Finally Major appeared. He was a tall, incredibly thin boy with an overbite. Sonny looked at him and almost burst into laughter. ''Let me in, Major.''

The door opened. ''Can I help you, Sonny?'' Major's voice was like a waiter's.

''Yeah, you can tell Rainy to get her butt out here.''

''I can't do that, Sonny. You can't tell her what to—'' Sonny brushed past the boy. He found himself in a blue, sweat-drenched living room. He waited for his eyes to adjust. Finally he saw Rainy at the punch bowl talking to another boy. He walked over and grabbed her arm.

When she looked up to see him, her face exploded into terror. Her soft brown skin glowed in the blue light that reflected from the punch bowl. Her hair was straightened and pulled back into a small bun on the back of her head. She was wearing a pink sweater and a red tartan plaid skirt with a big safety pin holding it together. Her skinny legs, shiny from Vaseline, were slipped into pink socks and black saddle shoes. Even back then she dressed carefully.

"Let me go, Sonny." If he told on her, there was no way of knowing what Absalom would do. Still, she had made a decision. It was hers to make, not Sonny's.

"We're leaving."

The guy she was talking to was a winesap-colored boy who wore a tan English driving cap over his curly hair. He looked at Rainy and asked, "Who the hell is this?"

"Just my stupid brother." Rainy tried to free her arm from Sonny's grip, but he wouldn't let go.

Sonny never even looked in the boy's direction. "I'm not leaving without you."

Rainy spoke through her clenched teeth, "You can't make me."

More people were suddenly around them. Major stepped between them. "I think you had better let her arm go."

No one was supposed to invade the space between brother and sister. Rainy was *his* sister. "Major, you better get yourself from in front of me. This is my sister and I'm taking her home. She's got no business here." He turned his attention to Rainy. "Now come on." He yanked her away from the table and pulled her toward the front door.

Just as they reached the vestibule, a thick dark boy stepped in front of them. He extended his hand and grabbed Sonny's shirt at the chest. Sonny looked up at him, completely oblivious to everyone else around them.

"The party ain't over yet. We was just gettin' started."

Sonny, still holding Rainy's arm, spoke with a steel voice. "If you don't get your hands off of me I'm going to give you a party all right."

The boy looked past Sonny to find Major, who was now coming up behind them. Major smiled and looked at Rainy. "Do you want to stay?"

Rainy shook her head. Major motioned the boy to let Sonny go, which he did by pulling Sonny's shirt downward in a jerk. There was an instant when Sonny's instinct was to hit the boy, smash him in the mouth and run out the door. Instead he pushed past him, dragging Rainy behind, leaving everyone standing in the smoky blue haze.

Sonny still had her arm, but Rainy no longer resisted. In a way she had been impressed by Sonny's resolve. "I can't believe you did that, Sonny. Are you crazy? You could have gotten killed in there."

"You're twelve years old, Rainy. You ain't got no business at no party with those jerks. If I ever hear of you hanging out with them again, I'm going to kick your butt myself. Then I'm gonna tell Dad." The three of them, Rooster, Sonny, and Rainy, worked their way back to the Goodman house on Whither Street.

"Sonny," Rainy's soft voice broke into the room from the open door. "Mom, the doctor's here."

In walked a young, dark-haired man, who, Gwen had first felt, could not have been old enough to have a family, to understand what she was going through, much less save Absalom. But he had surprised her. He had talked to her, cared about her. They had come to know each other very well. In the year that Absalom had been sick, Dr. Fred Mamen had learned a lot about the Goodman family, and about Gwen.

"Mrs. Goodman." The doctor, short and stocky, energetic, clad in his whiteness, bent down and hugged Gwen. "I wish we didn't have to be here today, Gwen. I really do." The young doctor carried the lives of his patients on his back like a pack mule with too far to go and not enough water.

Gwen said nothing as she pulled the doctor closer to her. "This is it, isn't it?" she said into his ear.

Absalom felt as if someone had kicked him in the stomach. It didn't matter that he was free of the binding life of physical movement. Absalom didn't want to believe that he had to stay where he was.

"I'm afraid it is, Mrs. Goodman. We took another good long look at the growth and it's spreading very rapidly. And, like I've said, it's in a place where we just can't get to. I'm very sorry.''

Gwen, still holding the doctor tightly, closed her eyes. Sonny, standing in front of the window, saw the first large tear leave her eye. Rainy, standing in the doorway, saw the second.

"Isn't there something, anything you can do?" Sonny said, touched by Gwen's open emotion. He walked over to Rainy and took her hand.

"I'm afraid not, Sonny." The doctor extended his hand. "Dr. Fred Mamen. Your mother has told me so much about you. She's very proud of you, you know. So is your father.''

"Thank you. Nothing you can do?''

"I'm telling you, Sonny, if I knew of anything that would save your father I would do it right away. I've never met a nicer man. I was saying to Rainy in the hall that I have come to really like both your father and your mother.''

Suddenly Sonny felt his arm shake violently. Rainy was trembling uncontrollably. "I don't believe it. I don't believe it,'' she said over and over, tears punctuating the falling words.

The doctor hugged Rainy quickly and stepped outside. Sonny, still holding Rainy's hand, bent down and hugged his mother, who was quietly but steadily sobbing. He straightened himself and opened his arms to Rainy, who allowed him to envelope her. She broke into loud, piercing sobs.

Holding her tightly with one arm, his other on his mother's shoulder, twisted in a macabre scene of grieving, feeling death before death had visited, Sonny finally began to feel something stir inside him. Suddenly he tasted himself as his mouth filled with a rush of inner fluids. His stomach felt as if it were rising out of his body. His father was dying. There had never been a time without him. Never a time when there wasn't a living connection.

The doctor walked back in. "Listen, I know this is really hard. But we're bringing Absalom back in. I can't tell you how long he's got . . . maybe two days, maybe a week, ten days maximum. I want you to talk with one of our counselors here and, most important, think about your father. Try to make his last days as comfortable as you can. We'll do our best here."

"Can he talk?" Rainy asked.

"Well, when he comes to, you'll be able to talk to him. I'm not sure if he's going to be able to talk back, but he'll hear you."

Finally Gwen stood. "Thank you, Doctor, for everything."

"You're welcome, Mrs. Goodman. I'll keep stopping by. I wish it could have worked out differently."

A nurse wheeled the gurney in, with Absalom's frail, shrinking body centered in it. He was unconscious. Gwen was gliding on air, elevated beyond the misery before her. She smiled a strong pure smile. She looked down on Absalom, saw the fitful, uneasy stillness of his body, the dark marks on his face and hands, the plastic tubes snaking out of his body, the white gauze encircling his head, the stains of blood, the rose petals garnishing his bandage— the swaddled heap of flesh was a study in life captured by life. His body, a pillar of black marble for so long, striking, upholding, overarching, had ingested its own power. Now inside him, in residence where he could least afford it, was another life. It held his head in its arms. It would have felt soft and warm. It would have loved him, its host, were it not for nature, the order of things. There was no room in Absalom for this cancer, its malignancy a garbled, misunderstood scream. So, angered, psychotic, the cancer spun itself into cannibalistic corkscrews that bore into Absalom, eating, sucking, transforming everything into itself. The cancer had this power and used it, seemed hell-bent on ending Absalom, his body, his thoughts, his existence, and itself. Everything within his world would soon end as cancer continued to prance through his body. It danced its exaggerated dance in his head.

"Oh, look, Rainy. He doesn't look so bad. You know, Doc, if I was you, I wouldn't plan on going away on any vacations in ten days. I know this man. He's my husband. He's likely to be around much longer than you think." The attendants transferred him to the bed.

Dr. Fred Mamen looked at Gwen. As usual, her eyes glowed with determination. He shrugged. "Gwen, if you and your husband need me, I'll be here. You can count on that.'' And he left the room.

"Sonny, you get a cup of water and a face towel,
I want to keep his lips wet,'' Gwen said, coming to
life. Sonny stood next to the bed, staring into his
father's face. His skin had lost much of its texture.
It was shiny and seemed to stretch even tighter
against his bones in some places and collected in
clumping masses far away from the bone in others.
As Sonny tried to swallow, the arch of his foot sank
to the floor. He stood flat-footed, staring. His father's
mouth was wide open, his breath struggled out. Each
of his closed eyes held a glistening plea. Before he
had come to the hospital this last time, he had cried
for many things. Now, the crying was a conditioned
reaction against the unknown.

Through the fresh white bandage wrapped
around Absalom's head, Sonny could see that most
of his father's hair was gone. Under the blanket, it
seemed as if his father's mass was gone. "Who are
you? Where's my father?'' Sonny thought.

"Did you say something?'' Rainy came up behind him.

"He doesn't look like Dad anymore.''

"I know.''

"Are you two gonna just stand there? Rainy,
why don't you get his shaving stuff out of the bathroom. He hasn't been shaved in a couple of days.
He'd like that. And Sonny, will you get me the water
and the cloth like I asked you to?''

"Yes, Mom, I'm sorry.'' Sonny shook himself.

He needed the solace of solitude. The air of the city was shut out of this room. The room existed in a place far from the bounding, free-running sunshine and gardenia-laced air of the summer. The energy of the street vendors, the noise of the kids on the streets, the clanking of the trolley still skidding down Tenth Street, right in front of the hospital. All of that and everything else was kept out while armies of technicians tried to keep people alive.

He filled a cup full of water and grabbed a towel from the bathroom. Gwen was in full swing, straightening, cleaning. In a minute she would be daubing water on his lips, the next coating them with Vaseline. A little later, shaving him as he slept.

Sonny looked at his father. When Gwen put her hand on his forehead, it seemed that his father sighed, took a big breath, and drew strength. Realizing that he hadn't actually touched his father, he walked up and kissed him on the forehead. Rainy was standing by the window, still quietly crying.

Sonny walked over to her. "I understand how you feel, Rainy. But crying now, and crying here, isn't going to make things better for him."

"I know, Sonny, I just wish I could talk to him. I've got so much to say."

"So do I, we'll have time. But for now, let's help Mom." Sonny picked up the volume of his voice for emphasis. "You know how she is. If we don't help her, she'll try to do everything herself.''

"And why should anything change?'' Gwen wiped Absalom's brow. "I've always had to do everything."

8

Absalom fought what he had become. If he couldn't go forward into consciousness then he would let go and wing into the creases of clouded sky. He willingly traveled his past. Without it, he would not even be a wisp. Now, instead of struggling with the outside, Absalom embraced the inside.

For some reason he found himself staring at his father, a rising panic in his heart. He was sixteen and he knew his father was about to beat him. As always, his father used a switch from one of his pecan trees to carry out the punishment. Absalom hated the sight of that ugly pecan tree, as if it had been created to produce wiry, stinging branches with small knots on them just big enough to eat into a brown boy's skin.

His father grabbed him by his undershirt, held him in his strong hands, and stared into the boy's face. He stood in front of Absalom, his Southern black features set in stone, long, thin, and haunting, looking through him into oblivion. He stood that way for a long time, all six feet of him, motionless, his lanky body shriveling in the North Carolina sun. Absalom knew what he was supposed to do. If there were any chance at all, this was it. An opportunity to beg for leniency. And beg he did. Yes, indeed.

"Daddy," he said, "I ain't knowed nothing 'bout them fellers lettin' the hogs out. I was just playin' with them. I ain't knowed they was gonna open the pen like that. I thought they was just playin'."

His father stared out at the cornfield that separated the front of the house from the road. Absalom looked up into his father's eyes, caught his gaze and followed it out into the field. Absalom couldn't help thinking that his father was looking at one particular kernel of corn out there. So he made a game out of it. He tried to find which kernel it was. He tried to lock onto his father's red eyes, fix on an ear of corn, see through the husk, and find that kernel.

He continued his plea. "Anyway, I helped you git all them hogs back in the pen. I ran around all over the place for to get those hogs, didn't I, Daddy? I wouldn't o' let those hogs get away, that's for sure."

The tears streamed out of his eyes. But the man just stood there, as if he were in a trance.

"Ab, now, I done tol you too many times to keep a track of, there ain't no good to come out of messin' with them Frazier boys. They come out of bad stock. Take it from me. You ain't got no business foolin' with them. You should'a known better. But you don't want to listen to nobody.''

"I'm listening, Daddy. I'm listening." Absalom started crying again. "I won't do it again. I promise, I won't do it again," he said.

"I know you won't. Go on over there and grab me a good switch. I don't want no thin little thing that's gonna just bust in two neither.'' His face was totally blank.

Absalom's father watched his son walk up to that tree and look around for something he could be beaten with. Absalom tried to find a young soft branch, one firm enough to pass his father's test, soft enough to spare his own flesh. But the same thing would happen everytime. He'd reach up to get his idea of a good licking stick, and his father would stop him still.

"Not that one. That ain't no switch. That's a twig, a young one at that. I want one with a little more age on it. Something sturdy. Naw, son, that ain't nothing there.''

So Absalom had to jump up to get a higher branch. On his first jump, he grabbed a branch and put all of his weight into the fall so that he brought the branch down with him as he hit the dirt in a ball. His father just stood there waiting, almost like a statue.

"Yeah, that's it," he said. "Now you know

what a switch is. Get on out there behind the out-house." That was the verdict, he was gonna beat this black boy's behind. Swack. Swack. Lord, let me tell you, Absalom's daddy could swing a tough switch. He'd make a child throw his hands up to God, begging him to intervene.

"Please, God, please, God. No, Daddy. I'm sorry." Absalom couldn't stop him from swinging that switch. His father became a shadow, not a real man, but a dark shadow. The pain from the stick struck fire in his backside and worked its way across his body. It extended outward and caused even his fingers to hurt. But he would not cry. He would not let his father have that satisfaction. Absalom tried to wrestle himself away from that Carolina scene. Away from his father.

Absalom wanted Gwen and his children to know how he struggled to be a man. How it hadn't been easy to leave his father's farm and his father's strong hand behind. He knew brutality. He knew it from the dirt-encrusted hand of his father. He could only guess what his father, just two generations out of slavery, had had to go through. Absalom could only imagine the anger, the rage that flowed within the man who, when angry, knew only one response.

Absalom had to learn gentleness from Gwen. Her delicate hands, her soft voice, her fountain of forgiveness. He had tried to distill it into something he could use for himself. To soften himself. It was not a small accomplishment.

In his dream he heard Gwen speaking. It soothed him. He felt her touching him. It calmed him. His scars disappeared. He drifted into her arms. Absalom let her define his reality. Gwen. A beautiful woman who had more spirit and fire than anyone he had ever met, she was a woman who could make him cry. He wanted to give her everything. But no matter how hard he tried, he always wound up giving his paycheck up to buy food and pay the mortgage. That was it.

Still, he faced her every day with a smile and the hope that she found him worthy. And when he faltered, she was there to console him. He was suddenly crying now. Deep in the thick air of the hospital, his mind was racing.

Suddenly he was staggering home drunk. It was a Friday night and he had been at the union hall. He stopped there occasionally to play checkers, drink beer, shoot the breeze. But when he got there on this particular Friday, somebody had hired a stripper.

Absalom sat down next to a truck loader, Grady Jenkins, a short, stocky guy. Grady bought Absalom a few beers. Absalom, who was not much of a drinker, was already slurring his words after the second one.

At some point a brown satin doll came switching out into the middle of the floor. She had a great big molasses smile. She wore a sky blue nightie with white trim over her full body. On her feet were gold bedroom slippers; the strap across the top of her foot was white fur. Her legs and thighs rippled.

She strutted her stuff all over the place. Absalom drank more than he had ever drunk in his life. He laughed and screamed right along with the rest of the men. And when he had the chance, he touched her. He felt her round soft ass. Not roughly as Grady did, but softly. He had thought about it all night long. She had a lot more back there than Gwen did, so it was especially appealing to him. He let himself get all turned around. Before the night was over, he was bleary-eyed drunk.

Grady brought Absalom home. He stumbled in the door. Whither Street was still alive at 11:30. He would never be able to remember who was out sitting on their steps, but he knew some people were still out.

Gwen met him at the door. "Thank God, you're all right. Get in here." Then, in a whisper, she said, "Ab, you smell like a brewery. Get in here." She led him to the couch.

"Tsk, tsk." Gwen sucked her teeth. Then she began, in a calm, loving voice. "Dead drunk. Man, what is your problem? You scared me to death. You know I love you, Ab. I love you so much. I know you got to work hard. And it's hard every day to take all the crap you have to take from them white people you work for. They just use you up like a farm animal. But you have to find your own happiness. If that means you have to leave me alone, okay. If it means drinking until you can barely walk, okay.

If it means not being here with Sonny and Rainy, okay. No matter what you need to do to make yourself as happy as you can possibly be, you do that. Because I don't want you if you gonna be unhappy. Ain't no sense in living if you got to live unhappy. Too many unhappy colored men out there already, acting like they been runned over by a tractor or something. And you know how they are. They always want to blame it on the woman. Ain't that how the blues got started? Well, I ain't gonna be your blues girl, Ab. You done made a big mistake if you expect me to make you miserable. Whatever misery you got, you can't blame on me."

She went on like that for about an hour. The lamp by the couch highlighted her fine brown features. The light mussed her hair and created a halo effect.

Absalom's eyes were running every which way, but he could see Gwen, with the light behind her, talking to him in such a soothing voice.

"So please, Ab, be good to me. When you are unhappy and you need to do other things to make you happy, please, by all means, do what you want."

Absalom couldn't help it. As she talked he started crying. He tried to stop but couldn't. The alcohol destroyed his defenses. He cried because he realized how stupid he had been. He had neglected them on a rare Friday when he had money and time. In a few minutes he was in her arms. She let him cry. He cried a long time that night. He cried for what he had overcome and what still faced him. He cried in happiness that Gwen was there.

And all she did was say, "You cry, Ab. You ought to cry every now and then. It's good for a man. I know you hurt. And hurt should find its match in tears. They cancel each other out. It's okay to cry. This world changes so slowly and even if you are successful, your legacy can only be so big. It's okay to cry."

Absalom shrank as she talked. He became smaller as he sat there, like a fifty-pound burlap sack of pecans somebody had punched a small hole in. He just kept losing himself.

Absalom's mouth was still struck open. Gwen periodically daubed the corners of his stretched, parched lips. The white paste that had materialized was wiped away. Water wet his resolve. He felt the deep stinging, rolling movement of pain stir at the base of his neck. It was not unbearable now, but he needed help to hold it back. He felt Gwen's hand. He wanted to reach up and pull her down on top of him. She treated him so carefully now, like delicate glass.

9

Hey, Dead are you still with me?'' Dancer asked, feeling Half-Dead's presence without seeing him. The dark-skinned, thin man slouched, enveloped in the shadows of the black leather sofa. The shaded windows blocked the sun and hid him within the folds of the couch.

Half-Dead opened his eyes. He hadn't been asleep, just invisible. It was his new hobby. Whenever he was alone in his small apartment on Jefferson Street, he practiced. Now, when it was important, when to be found near a murder and drugs might send him back to the real rock—prison—invisibility was an advantage.

"I'm sitting right here."

"I didn't see you."

"Yeah, I know."

Dancer was sweating, and his sweatshirt was

stained with dark circles under his arms. "Those motherfuckas are so goddamn slow. It's hot as hell outside."

"It's cool in here, with the blinds closed and quietness." Half-Dead hadn't moved, but his mouth groaned the words. What he had brought in with him, the confusion and chaos that swirled around him, was still present. But he, himself, was calm, motionless.

"I bet it is, home." Dancer couldn't help but chuckle. "I'm out there, kissing big behind to the Man and you're in here sleeping."

"I told you, Dancer, I wasn't sleeping. I just know how to disappear at the right time." Half-Dead smiled.

"That's just what you did, too. I looked around for my partner, my ace number one boon coon and what do I find? Nothing. Fucking cops are staring at me, some kid has just gotten his head blown off on my front steps and I look for my main man, my homey home homeboy and what do I find? Not a goddamn thing." Dancer walked to the window and opened the blinds, emptying a dump truck's load of sunlight into the room. "I thought, for a minute, that they were going to search the house."

"That's what I thought too, that's why I was in here making myself invisible."

"Say what?"

"You heard me." Half-Dead was still. His eyes were closed now, as he tried to keep the sunlight away. "I know how to protect myself. Even if they had come in here, they wouldn't have seen me." Half-Dead paused, stretched his long thin arms into the air, stiffened his thighs, and brought his knees up. He captured the pair of bony shins for an instant and let them go.

In the sunlight, Half-Dead's blackness radiated a Caribbean beauty, a Zimbabwean freedom dream, a healthy wonder. All the chaos of trouble and danger that swished around him in the darkness fell away in the light. Suddenly Half-Dead was a black man with a wild gleam in his eye. He had his moments.

"You probably won't believe me, but I can make myself invisible. I been working on it." Half-Dead stared at Dancer with an expression that carried no additional information.

Dancer focused on Half-Dead's eyes; they were there, in this time, dancing with each other, holding each other. One feeling for the other's essence.

"Listen, cuz," Dancer began, "I don't want to rain on your performance or nothing, but I almost got arrested out there. I tried my fucking best to keep those assholes from coming in here. Why? Not because I think they're smart enough to find my last load of rocks. Nobody could find that, but you, maybe. Not because I'm ashamed of the crib or that I got anything I should hide. Except one fucking thing. You."

Half-Dead pulled his body out of the chair and

walked over the gleaming maple floor to the window. Dancer continued. "Obviously, when you didn't come outside, I figured I was on my own in trying to explain why this kid gets shot in front of my house. And, I also figured, wrongly I guess, that you wanted me to keep the cops out of here for you. You know what I'm saying?"

"Yeah, home, I know what you're saying." Half-Dead sighed.

"So, what do I find out when I get back in here? You're just sitting here, talking some shit about being invisible. Are you crazy, motherfucka? Huh? What is your problem, man?"

"Don't have a problem, home. I told you. I've been working on making myself invisible and I think I can do it."

"Dead, you are totally crazy man. What are you talking about? You were asleep in the goddamn chair."

"I hear you keep saying that."

"Then what the fuck are you talking about?"

"Did you see me sitting here?"

"No, I but knew you were there."

"Yeah, but that ain't seeing me, is it?" Half-Dead turned and faced him with a smile. "If the pigs had come in here, they would have walked right by me." Half-Dead nodded his head rapidly up and down in exaggerated excitement. It was the most animated Dancer had ever seen him. "I can do it. I really can."

Dancer's body was still visited with tremors. He had seen the insides of another person splattered. He had survived intense questioning. Now he had to try to pierce the dense fog that separated him and Half-Dead.

Across from Dancer, Half-Dead basked in the sunlight cascading through the window. Something inside him had changed. He had always suspected he was special. Even though things never seemed to work out, even though life had given him mostly pain, he had always felt strongly about his potential. That's why he had gotten so close to Dancer. He had never met another black man like Dancer.

To Half-Dead, Dancer was successful, he was smart, he could talk his way out of certain death, he had money. Dancer was going places, and Half-Dead saw their relationship as a way out of the one-disaster-after-another life he had been living.

But now, as his confidence about his ability to become invisible grew, he began to experience a new feeling. For the first time in his life he could do something no one else could do. He didn't know how to celebrate. He had no knowledge of how to react. Now he stood facing a man who had come to be his best friend, his only friend, and he didn't know how to get past the teasing and disbelieving looks, to express his profound sense of accomplishment.

They were locked in a stare. "Okay. Okay. You disappeared." Dancer, finally dismissing Half-

Dead's behavior over the last couple of hours entirely, was anxious to get to the business at hand.
"Now, sit your black ass down and help me figure
out what the fuck is going on."

"What's up?"

"I don't know exactly. I haven't had time to put
it together. Spider comes over here looking for some
dope. A car pulls up and he freaks. But they freak
even more cause they put the smoke on him. In
broad daylight, Dead. On Whither. Now, brother,
you know that is totally out there." Dancer waved
his hand in a halting, rhythmic gesture. "I just don't
believe it. They blow this guy away in broad daylight. On Whither Street no less. Not Oxford Street
or Harlan, or any of those other scuzzy downtrodden
alleys. But Whither Street. That's a trip. Rainy is
gonna have a baby over this one. On our steps. Shit.
I don't think people on this block ever seen no shit
like that. And what for, homeboy? What for?"

"I don't know, man. Dance, do you think Spider
knew something was up?"

"He said he didn't know who they were."

"Well, like I said before, they clearly didn't
want you. They had a whole bunch of time to take
you both out if they wanted to."

Dancer agreed, but was still puzzled. "Are you
sure they didn't want me, too?"

"Check it, man, they blasted your door, to let
you know they saw you. They know who you are.
That's all. They didn't want to kill you, home. They

had plenty of time to do that.''

''Yeah. The cops seemed like they knew what was happening. That's why they didn't press about searching the house.''

''I didn't think they would, my brother. After all we're talking about black folks. Do you think they give a shit?'' Half-Dead turned back to the window. ''Hey man, there's Buzz. I bet you he knows what's up.''

''Yeah.'' Dancer ran to the door, called the teenager over and asked him in.

Buzz was a thirteen-year-old child of the streets. He lived on Ingersoll Street, two blocks north and three blocks east of Whither, in a tough neighborhood, Rock Garden. He had been out of school for a year, was into everything, and was considered a terror in the neighborhood. Both Dancer and Rainy often stopped to talk to him, sometimes to stop him from doing something he had no business doing. Buzz liked them both.

Dancer and Rainy's popularity in the neighborhood was due, in part, to the nature of their business, which rewarded them with plenty of necessary relationships. But there were also a number of people who genuinely liked them. Rainy for her stiletto eyes, her unexpected generosity, and Dancer because he was always upbeat. Dancer was always on the street, his Nikon banging against his chest, taking pictures, and mixing.

''Yo, Buzz, we was wondering what the fuck is

up around here?'' Dancer spoke as soon as the maple-skinned boy walked in.

Buzz looked up to see Half-Dead. ''I didn't know this stupid motherfucka was in here. I would'a rapped to you outside.''

''Who you talking to, youngboy?'' Dead's voice broke into small pieces of stone and rolled toward Buzz.

Buzz paused. He really didn't want to escalate his running conflict with Half-Dead. He didn't like the dude, but he knew Half-Dead's reputation and besides he was an oldhead. ''Nobody, home. Nobody. Sometimes I just like to talk to myself.''

''That's cool, as long as you the one who answers back.'' Half-Dead put his eyes right on Buzz.

''C'mon man. I didn't ask you to come in here to get into no stuff with Dead. Who offed Spider?'' Dancer waved Buzz onto the sofa.

''Aw, man. I thought you wanted to know something.'' Buzz crossed his legs. He wore white high-topped Nike shoes, with black stretch biking shorts that hugged his thighs. ''You got anything to drink?''

''What do you want, Buzz? I got some soda.''

''What about a beer.''

''You're too young, homeboy.''

''Give me a Coke, then.''

Dancer turned to Half-Dead. ''Dead, would you get me a beer, and my man Buzz here a Coke.''

''Now I'm waiting on this bug,'' Half-Dead

muttered as he walked into the kitchen.

"What's up?" Dancer plunged back in.

"Ain't that much to it, man. Spider ain't the only one. They gonna burn a bunch of dudes before it's over."

"Who, Buzz?" Dancer asked as Half-Dead walked in and handed him a can of beer. He gave Buzz a Coke. As Buzz took the can, he smiled at Half-Dead.

"Who they gonna off? A bunch of folks from what I hear." Buzz obviously had not understood the question.

"I'm not talking about who's going to get popped. Do you know who's doing the popping? That's what I want to know." Dancer didn't like the game Buzz was playing with him. But he clipped his rising anger by taking a swallow of beer.

"Oh. That's what you want to know? Well, the way I hear it, your boy Spider has been double-dipping. He's been getting some of his stuff from you and some from Rodney."

"Rodney's behind this shit." Half-Dead put his head on the top of the couch and slid down again. He closed his eyes and watched the inside of his eyelids vibrate against the August sunlight.

"So, okay, Rodney's back in business?"

Buzz looked at Dancer like he was crazy. "Back in business? Homeboy, tell me you've been away on vacation or some shit. Tell me you been sick for a couple of months, but don't tell me you didn't know

Rodney is back in the game. You definitely don't know the rules. He's all hooked up with the Moon.''

''The moon?'' Dancer felt lighter than air. What was going on? People getting shot on his doorstep, invisibility, and now the moon? ''What the fuck is the moon?''

''Let me take you to school, cuz.'' Buzz leaned forward. ''The Moon is a bunch of brothers rolling in from New York. And they're taking whatever territory they can get. You know what I'm saying? They just bust in, say, 'Hey, this here whole territory is ours, bet. Now you got to buy from us or you don't get nothing.' Are you getting the Kodak now, homeboy?''

''So, Rodney is tied into these dudes?''

''Bingo.'' Buzz sat back, turned to where Half-Dead was sitting, just to see the impact this was having on him. The sunlight split his eyesight. Half-Dead hid behind the glint.

''Okay, so, Rodney is in with the Moon. And the Moon is into taking over this part of the hood,'' Dancer said out loud.

''And these motherfuckas are totally ruthless, man. As you found out today.''

''But why did they whack Spider?''

''Like I said, they knew Spider was dealing with somebody else and when he came up short this week, they just decided to off him. But they also figured he'd lead them to you. And he did.''

Dancer was shocked at the amount of information he did not have. Even though he played the game, selling crack to people who in turn killed themselves with it, he still didn't see himself as a dealer. In his heart he was a photographer. Whether business was strong or not, Dancer still climbed into his jeep twice a week and headed for the park or the rich suburbs of the Main Line to take pictures. His photographic eye sought out beauty. He hated the disorganization and chaos in his work. Dancer's pictures were sparkling reflections of orderly existence. He liked to take pictures of lawns and hedges. Their textures, their varieties. His work, on display in the basement, was a portfolio of exciting and unusual lawnscapes. One day, he intended to exhibit in galleries downtown. One day.

And even though he spent a fair amount of time roaming the streets, stopping at the corner bars, talking to the clusters of people gathered at various spots in the neighborhood, he had never managed to keep up with the "word." That was what Dancer needed.

In the beginning, he had believed that dealing drugs would be an easy way to make money. Buy for a low price and sell for a high one. Don't even think about what it is you're selling or who wants to buy or why. What difference did that make? Life was what it was. If people didn't know that crack was a killer, that it could sink its sharp claws into their very flesh and never let go, that was their fault. The evidence was all around. Broken lives, whole worlds of black people sucked dry by drugs. Your

will had to be a bomb shelter to withstand the beck-
oning sweetness of the rock. Dancer laughed at those
who wondered why people do drugs. Why not an-
esthetize yourself? Why not escape? He thought a
better question was, why doesn't everybody use
them?

But no matter how he rationalized it, he knew
what crack was doing to the community. Increasingly it was harder and harder to do the only thing
that gave him the freedom to take pictures.

"Well, how come they didn't shoot me, too?"

Buzz broke into laughter. "I knew you was
gonna ask me that. I knew it. Get real, homeboy.
Don't you understand nothing, man? They don't really know what you're up to. They don't know how
much muscle you got or how much business you're
doing. All they know is that Rodney don't like you
and they want your turf. It's just starting, man. But
I'm going to tell you one thing for sure." Buzz put
the soda can down on the floor in front of the couch
and got up to leave.

"What's that?"

"If you want it, you gonna have to bang for it.
Forget Rodney. Yeah, Buck Teeth is gonna be in
charge, but the guys you have to worry about are the
dudes who came in from New York to help him get
established."

"Yeah. Thanks, Buzz."

"No problem, cuz. Glad I could help."

Buzz was gone and Dancer fell into the chair,

exhausted and riveted by a creeping insecurity and fear.

"That's one slimy little motherfucka," Half-Dead said softly.

"Yeah, well, at least I get some goddamned news from him. How come you didn't know all that?"

"Who said I didn't?"

"If you did, homeboy, you know you should have told me."

"How do I know what you know and what you don't. Shit. I can't remember to tell you all the shit I hear on the street. You have to ask me questions."

"I don't believe you." Dancer looked at Half-Dead.

"Tell you what, Dance. I think it's time I started giving you some lessons."

"Lessons?"

"Yeah, I got a feeling you're gonna need to know how to make yourself disappear. Like me, you know." Half-Dead sat up.

"No lessons, okay. Not now. Listen, it sounds like we're in trouble."

Half-Dead interrupted. "My guess is that you shouldn't sweat it. They probably won't fuck with you as long as you don't make trouble for them."

"Yeah, but suppose it don't go that way? Suppose they want everything?"

"Well, then, we're gonna have to decide how ugly we're gonna act."

"Yeah."

Half-Dead turned his head to face Dancer. "And you know, brotherman, we can act pretty ugly if we wants to, now can't we?" He held his palm out for the ceremonious slap, the dap. Dancer enthusiastically responded. The resounding clap echoed throughout the room, waking all energies, good and bad.

Dancer felt instantly better. "Yo, home, super ugly." They both broke into laughter.

They sat in the falling afternoon sun for an hour before Half-Dead spoke again. "Spider was a good little brother. He could have had it going on."

"I know, man. I know. I don't think I've ever seen somebody shot like that, laying there, everything spilling out. I could barely breathe."

"Well, I seen a few. I've left a couple motherfuckas laying there myself. And I know one thing, Dance, it's better to see someone else go down than to go down yourself. You can tell right away by looking at a dead man that they ain't gonna do nothing in this world no more. That is the end. Where their spirit or soul or whatever goes and all that, well, I don't know. But you can damn well believe his body is finished."

"Man, let me tell you. That was a wild scene. His mother was out there. It was a mess."

"If they blew him away, they must have figured he threatened them. So, to them, they'd rather see him die than them."

"I know that, Dead, but I'm not talking about bullshit gang theory. I'm talking about the young-boy's life. Something deeper, man. What I'm saying is all this gang-banging shit is getting totally out the pocket. I mean, he was a young man. He shouldn't have been mixed up in no shit like he was. You know what I'm saying? His whole life is gone. Everything. He never knew shit."

"Well," Half-Dead got up to leave. "I know some shit. I know that they ain't gonna blow me away like that, without a fight. Now, do you know what *I'm* saying?"

"Yeah, Dead." Dancer was very tired and it was still early. "But I need to know exactly what I'm up against. I don't want to let this sweet situation go up in smoke for some okeydoke bullshit. My instinct says it's time to go to war, but I got to know how treacherous these motherfuckas really are. I need to talk to Rainy." He walked Half-Dead to the door. The police crime laboratory people were still taking pictures and drawing on the ground. Spider was now a chalk outline on Whither Street.

10

Gwen stood back as two nurses attended to Absalom. Each time she was forced to get up from the bed, to let his hand go, to move away from his thin breath, it took longer to feel his presence again. The nurses talked to her as they worked. She in turn told Absalom what they were doing.

"They're fixing your IV, sweetheart. Don't worry."

"They going to give you something for that pain now. You're okay, aren't you?"

Soon the movement of the faceless attendants ended and Gwen returned to the bed. Sonny and Rainy had watched the episode in silence. Absalom expelled a long stuttering sigh. Rolling backward, in free fall of spirit, head back, turning, forming elegant spaceless spirals, Absalom forgot his pain. He forgot present moments. He could only remember the wonder of discovery. The joy of being new. Of finding love and knowing it. Again, the blackness of his open mouth hid the voice.

He saw Gwen hustling up to the bus station, carrying her two suitcases, trying her best to get to the ticket window and then to the bus before the driver slammed the heavy metal door shut. It was an old red and silver Trailways bus, the only one that stopped in Newton Grove, North Carolina.

Absalom found himself crammed in the back seat. Sweat poured out of his body and ran down the inside of his khaki army uniform. He sat there buttoned up tight, the picture of an American GI.

The army's system of justice scared Absalom. At induction, they had told him, "When you put that uniform on, there is no between, you are all army." That meant you didn't open the collar wider, you didn't roll up your sleeves, you wore the uniform the way you were supposed to, no matter how hot it was. You never knew who was watching. Being black only made it worse. He had decided from the beginning to be a model GI.

And there was no relief on this fire-hot day. Even with all the windows open, the bus sweltered. He was on his way to Fort Dix in New Jersey and she was going north to Philadelphia for the first time. Looking out the window at the baggage handler loading the last of the luggage, Absalom saw Gwen as she emerged from the ticket office and rushed up to the bus.

The first two-thirds of the bus weren't very crowded, but the last three rows of seats were packed full of black people. He looked around; there were no more seats left in the colored-only section. He could tell by the way she kept shifting the weight on her feet that Gwen was nervous. She stood at the front of the bus staring at the bus driver, who was as thin as piano wire and barely existed inside his uniform. Absalom could hear his voice ring off the curved roof.

"Sorry, miss. Don't seem to be no more seats."

"There's a seat." Gwen raised her finger and pointed to a seat in the last row reserved for whites. When she pointed to the seat, she was ignoring, actually looking over, at least six other unoccupied seats in the whites-only section. Absalom figured she pointed to the one she did because it was the closest to the colored section. She had hoped the driver might not make a big deal about the last open seat, in the last row, of the whites-only section. Of course, she figured wrong.

"Now you know you can't sit there."

"But I got a ticket."

"Yes, I can see that, but there ain't no seats, are there? Now what you want me to do about that, missy? Huh? If you want, you can go on in the back and sit on the floor, or you can stand up. Pretty as you are, somebody's likely to give you a seat. But whatever you gonna do, I want you to do it. We're late enough as it is."

Absalom could see the driver's gray hat, with its shiny vinyl black bill bobbing in the shadowy cockpit of the bus. Gwen just stood there looking toward the back.

"Well?" the driver said as he closed the door. The bus gasped and jerked forward as he released the emergency brake.

Gwen turned and began walking toward the back. Absalom looked around and realized that all the black people around him were sitting straight up in their seats, straining with anticipation. Everyone, including Absalom, felt her boldness. She was fresh from the North Carolina earth, bound for the glory of the big city. And she carried that hope like an umbrella.

Gwen strolled down the aisle and right up to the last row. She looked up and down the bench seat. For the first time Absalom realized that all of the other passengers on the bench were women, except him. Then he felt the weight of her eyes hit him upside the head.

She wore a tan blouse with black trim around the collar and on the breast pocket. In the pocket, a starched white linen handkerchief stood straight up. A wide-brimmed tan straw hat with a thick black band around the crown completed the picture. He could feel her beauty squeezing itself into the back of that bus, trying to hook an arm around him.

She broke a smile and winked at him. He could feel the stares of everyone in the back of the bus.

She stood there, white bobby socks in white and brown saddle shoes with a dark brown Sears & Roebuck skirt that started narrow at her tiny waist and flared to a width wider than the aisle she stood in.

"Soldier?" she said sweetly. Gwen had decided when she walked off her father's farm that she would never again shy away from a challenge. Never hold her thoughts back again.

"Yes, ma'am." Absalom's throat was dry.

"How much space can you make between those strong legs of yours?" Gwen knew she had everyone's attention. She could see only eyes peering over the back of the bus seats.

Absalom looked down at his thighs; the crease of his khakis cut the sun. He didn't understand what she meant.

"That's right." She stared directly at his crotch. "If you open those thick brown thighs of yours, how much space can you make?"

"I guess there's enough room here." Absalom spread his legs as wide as he could. She left the suitcases in the aisle and slid over to where he sat.

"I'm not usually so familiar, but I really need to get to Philly," she said as she sat down.

"You *need* to get there, or you want to?"

"Well, sometimes, when I want something, it's the same thing. How you gonna tell the difference sometimes between needing and wanting?" She tried to get comfortable, but her dress was so full, it exploded around them.

"One way to tell is just not to get it. If you live through not getting want you want, well, then maybe you didn't really need it." As he talked to her, she was busy tucking material here and there, trying to fit somehow between his legs, and building her confidence. She felt mischievous, playful.

"What's your name, soldier boy?" she asked softly.

"Absalom."

"Absalom?"

"That's right. My name is Absalom Goodman. I'm from Fayetteville, on my way to Fort Dix."

"Well, hello, Mr. Absalom Goodman, my name is Gwen Tillman." His hip had already started to ache as he strained, trying to give her as much space as possible.

"Absalom Goodman, what kind of a name is that? Sounds like some kind of African name or something."

"What?"

"I said, is that some kind of African name? Who in the world would name a boy Absalom?"

"What's wrong with it?" He kept smiling even as his face tired.

"Nothing's wrong with it, exactly. Just never heard nobody called Absalom, that's all." Gwen still felt the back of the bus caught up in their conversation. She felt herself playing to them.

Absalom smelled her freshly pressed hair as it flapped into his face. Every time she talked, she sort of leaned back and tilted her head up. Her skin was smooth and creamy. He imagined his fingers melting into her flesh.

"What do you mean? There ain't nothing wrong with my name. My father got it from a minister." Absalom didn't know how to quell the disturbance that was brewing in his lap.

Then her voice raised another notch. "Now," her voice pierced through everything, the voices of other passengers, the whine of the tires against the hot tar, "y'all know what I'm asking him, don't y'all? I'm just asking how in the name of Sojourner Truth, a colored man get a name like Absalom. Is you Arabian?" She smiled and looked back at him. A couple of people started chuckling.

"No, I am American. I got a uniform on, don't I? I might look African and my name might sound African, but my daddy grows more tobacco than any colored man in North Carolina. We are Americans."

She turned her head back to him. "I was just playing with you, Mr. Absalom Goodman, American. I was just playing."

The bus moved slowly. It stopped at every little town between Newton Grove and Wilmington, Delaware, on its way to Philadelphia.

During the ride, Absalom fell in love. The softness of her buttocks, which rested between his thighs, her sharp eye, and her pouting, teasing laugh taunted him all the way to Jersey.

"You ever have a girl sit between your legs like

this before, Absalom Goodman?''

"No ma'am,'' he answered without thinking.

"I don't usually act this way you know. I could stand for a while.''

"Oh no, Miss Tillman, don't you even think about it.'' He didn't want her to move. The danger of her being there caused his skin to peel back. He was giddy for the first time in his life. "If anything, I guess I should get up and let you have the seat. But don't you move a muscle.''

"Well, Ab, can I call you Ab?'' He nodded. "It's gonna be real hard to go all the way to Philly without moving a muscle.'' Gwen smiled and brushed her hair against his face.

"I was afraid you might say that.'' Absalom bit his lip. He was worried that she would feel him stirring. He wasn't sure what he would do if she called attention to his rising excitement. He thought that such shows of affection and desire should be presented gently. He didn't want to seem crude. Even though she had been the one who had eased herself into *his* lap, she made it seem right. He didn't want anything to spoil the perfectness of the feeling. Suddenly he didn't want the rattling, hot, noisy, fried-chicken-smelling bus to get to Philly.

Suddenly he didn't want anything but for Gwen Tillman to sit between his legs, chew her gum, and talk about the cars they passed and the size of the farms that became a blur of colors and animals and sunlight and sweat. He feigned disinterest and made small talk. From time to time, he would accidentally let his hand rest on her waist. It made his palms sweat. He wiped them on his uniform. Damn the army anyway.

As he sat there, bouncing with the bus, listening to her pop chewing gum in his face, watching her read a copy of *Tan* magazine and answering her occasional questions about his life and childhood, he cared less and less about the uniform, the army, and Korea.

In the course of one bus ride, Gwen helped him realize that he had joined the army because it was the only way out, the only way off the farm. But it hadn't taken him long to figure out that the army wasn't the greatest place for a black man. From the moment he felt the denseness of Gwen's hips, he knew that whatever he was going to do, she would be a part of it. And she had been, as she was now, right beside him.

His mouth was dry as if it had been open for a long time. Absalom cleaved distance between him and the thing that nibbled his brain. He again drew breath and plunged further into the emptiness, away from consciousness, away from the dragging weight of despair. The numbing thing that now coursed through his body and closed the door to a future of pain. For now he was free of it. But that freedom felt shallow. The pain that had held him in bondage was replaced by gray mist, a feeling of swimming, perhaps drowning. He couldn't do anything. He was just free of pain.

Through his closed eyes the gelid, flickering light taunted him. Absalom stretched his arms out wide, caught an airstream, and glided into the light.

11

Absalom now understood how much of a luxury it was to expect the future, no matter how terrible it might be. The existence of a future gave a person the chance to be completely comfortable with the present. He was being denied that. Absalom was filled with sadness—it had replaced the air in his lungs, permeated the thoughts in his mind, become his blood.

When he was a young man, just back from Korea, his future was always in front of him like a series of ornate doors. Now, there was only one door and it stood at the end of a long dark corridor.

And around him Absalom felt the gathering energy of his family. They were like a choir of singing papier-mâché masks placed on the walls of the corridor. Were they trying to conjure a healing or usher him toward the light of the open door of death?

• • •

Rainy sat quietly in one of the two hard blue plastic chairs. Gwen was in the multicolored cushioned chair. The pattern in the fabric was a series of connecting circles, moons of blue, gold, and red, which grew in size as they changed color. The same pattern was painted on the hallway walls throughout the hospital.

Rainy turned to face the bed. Gwen was once again stroking Absalom's forehead. His eyes had been closed so long Rainy couldn't remember seeing them open. Absalom's dark chocolate eyes were seemingly sealed. Gwen sat there, talking to him.

Through it all, Absalom lay nearly motionless. Occasionally his eyelids would flutter, feign opening, and then relent to soft darkness. At other times an arm might twitch, or he might cough, but, as Gwen whispered in his ear he barely moved. His skin was ashen in spots. When Gwen detected those areas, she would retrieve the skin lotion from the table next to the bed. The thick, milky liquid rushed into his cracking, thin, paling skin and instantly transformed that spot into a glowing proof that life existed inside. Absalom sometimes sighed.

"How are you doing, sweetheart? You're tired of this place, aren't you? I sure would be. You been here way too long. But I just want you to realize that you have to keep thinking about that war. We're fighting this thing together. Ain't no reason to think you're going through this by yourself, cause you're not. I'm here, Rainy's here, and so is Sonny. The Goodman family is all here.''

Absalom's two children stood in the doorway of his hospital room and watched their mother talk to him as if he were sitting up facing her.

Sonny grabbed his sister's arm and asked, ''How about a cup of coffee?''

Rainy broke a smile and turned to her mother. ''Do you want anything, Mom?''

''No, you two go on. When you're done, maybe I'll get a bite to eat.''

The phone, which had been silent all day, rang. Almost instantly, Gwen had the receiver to her ear. ''It's Dancer, Rainy.'' She handed the telephone to Rainy.

Rainy brought the phone to her ear. ''Yeah?'' Dancer's voice was barely audible. Rainy knew something was wrong. He was asking questions, he wasn't saying anything. ''I'm fine. Well, it's not good. He's holding on. She's fine too. Mom, Dancer says he hopes you're doing okay.''

''Tell him I'm doing just fine. Well as can be expected.''

''What?'' Rainy gasped as she heard about Spider. She instinctively turned inward, huddling the telephone close like an infant, trying to disappear from view. ''Where? On our steps?''

Sonny watched her. She was trembling. Gwen, oblivious, was now making her way to the bathroom to wet a washcloth for Absalom's dry, flaking lips.

The conversation ended and Rainy gently replaced the white receiver. Sonny was still standing in the same spot he had been when the telephone rang. ''What's up?''

''Nothing . . . nothing really. At least I don't think. . . . ''

''Rainy, what happened?'' Sonny persisted.

''Some neighborhood kid got killed on the block today.''

''What block?''

''Our block. Whither Street.'' Rainy almost stumbled into the chair of the colored moons. When she sat back she felt herself fall inside one of the larger circles.

It was a tunnel. The chair had no back. She was tumbling through the tunnel. Like Alice. Her feet flailed in the empty space. She resolved to let everything go. To fall in grace. To fall singing. She would float silently, effortless, down to whatever bottom there was. Far enough so that Spider's face wasn't hovering in front of her. She fell free-form, buffeted by an occasional fluttering breeze. Was that her father's voice streaming beside her? Was that his pajama gown fluttering in the wind? Is that where he was?

Absalom felt the fear that Spider's death brought to Rainy. If he could have, he would have wrapped a large arm around her and whisked her away. He would have renewed his pledge of fatherhood to protect her.

• • •

When he had finally consented to buy the house in Mount Airy, Absalom had said to Gwen, "Now we got to figure out what to do with the house."

"I know." Gwen was so happy about her new house, a ranch style house on a block where the houses were not connected, that she almost didn't care about Whither Street. At least they had reached the stage where they could leave North Philly. Take another piece of the dream. But she knew that if they couldn't satisfy Absalom's concern for the old house, he would never enjoy the new one. "We could see if Rainy wanted to move back here and live in it."

"Rainy?" Absalom hadn't thought about Rainy. If Gwen hadn't spoken so quickly he would have suggested calling Sonny in Minnesota and asking if he was interested in moving back to Philadelphia.

"Well, who else you gonna ask? I know you weren't thinking about Sonny?"

Absalom was always startled by Gwen's ability to anticipate him.

"You know good and well that Sonny ain't never coming back to North Philly to stay. Anyway, Rainy's living in an apartment in West Philly. I bet she'd love to move back home."

"I guess you're right." He had wanted to give the house to Sonny but, as he thought about it, Absalom knew that Gwen was right. The house had become the first and most important asset he had. It had come to him mainly because he was a veteran, a survivor of war. It was his status as a veteran that allowed him to keep the Whither Street house even as he bought the new one. By tradition, Sonny, being both the oldest and a man, should get it. But Gwen was right, Sonny would never come back.

As it turned out, Rainy jumped at the opportunity to lower her monthly bills, have more room, and greater freedom. This had been her neighborhood, too. With more money available she would be able to buy voice lessons.

"Now, you be careful down here, Rainy." Absalom had held her hand as he was about to leave for the new house. "You take care of it."

"I will, Daddy." Rainy felt him wanting to walk up the stairs one more time, maybe even to sleep in his bed one last time. "You and Mom come over any time you want. Don't worry."

Absalom looked at her, thinking that Rainy, at least, had made a decision to stay in the neighborhood. That was important. The community needed youth. It needed a new start. "By the way, I left the Bible upstairs for you. I think you should have it. It belongs in this house."

Rainy was surprised he was prepared to leave the Bible behind. "Dad, don't you think you should take it with you?"

Absalom just smiled at her. He had very little to give to either of his children. The house was one thing and the Bible was the other. It just seemed right that the two not be split up. Besides, Sonny was even less likely to care about the Bible.

That night Rainy replaced the plastic bag that had enclosed the book for many years and put it in the night table beside her bed.

And then, in a gentle rush of movement, Rainy was pulled up and back to the rough reality of the small white room.

"Who was it?" Gwen had heard and now wanted to know details. "What kid?"

"His name was Spider." Rainy walked to the window. For a moment, she regretted having talked so openly on the telephone.

"Who killed him?" Gwen stared at her.

"I don't think anybody knows."

"Where on Whither Street?"

Rainy needed a tissue. The tip of her nose had started to sweat. The makeup she was wearing underscored the tiny dewdrops. "Dancer said they shot him while he was standing on our steps."

Gwen flared, "Our steps? Our steps? What was he doing standing on our steps?"

"I don't know, Mom."

"I swear. What is that neighborhood coming to? People killing each other just for standing on somebody's steps. Just for being there."

"I don't know why they killed him." Finally Rainy took two steps and pulled a white paper tissue from the box.

Gwen turned away from Rainy, did not look at

Sonny but instead faced Absalom. "What difference does it make? When you find out, you're still not gonna know anything, because people who kill people only *think* they got a good reason. But it ain't never really a reason. It's just something somebody made up. It's nothing but craziness, that's all. I'm sure enough glad your father got us the hell out of there. I couldn't live with all that killing going on. Course, it's always been bad, but now, these new drugs they got is making our folks act completely foolish. Killing somebody on my doorstep. I declare."

"It's amazing." Sonny was watching Rainy. She was obviously still very shaken by the news. "Did you know the boy?"

Rainy put her back to Sonny and looked out at the wall of windows that faced her. "Yes. I knew him. He was about thirteen or fourteen."

"Maybe I haven't been down there in a long time, but I see the neighborhood hasn't changed much." Sonny paused. "Or maybe it has. I can't remember anybody ever being shot on Whither Street before."

Gwen looked down at Absalom but her voice was loud. She meant for everyone to hear it. Everyone. "People get shot everywhere. How can it change? Ain't nothing changed in the world. People still got to fight for their own dignity. That ain't never changed. Just cause it's harder for the colored don't mean it can't be done. People just get beat down. I don't know what they expect. Nothing is gonna change until we get *ourselves* together."

Rainy looked over to Sonny, who seemed genuinely caught up in his mother's speech. Even though it was simplistic, Sonny agreed with her.

Rainy felt the energy slide out of her body. It was as if a plug had been removed. She walked up to Sonny. "Do you still want to buy me that cup of coffee?"

"Will you be okay, Mom?" Sonny asked his mother, who was back to Absalom, softly brushing the remaining gray patches of hair.

"Oh yes, yes. You two go. I don't mind. It will give me time to think. Talk to Absalom a little. I'm fine."

Sonny smiled. He loved her. She was pure, perfect, not real, an image to the end. Even as her husband held tight to a thin life, she flashed strength. He and Rainy might need a break, but not Gwen Goodman. It would take exhaustion to pry her from Absalom's room. He turned to Rainy. "Sure, let's go. But I want to make a quick telephone call first. I'll be right back." Without looking at Absalom, Sonny walked out of the room.

The decision to have coffee with Rainy had broken the spell of the hospital room. He understood suddenly how easy it was to manufacture a new life inside them. In hospital rooms you argue, laugh, and cry, all in the spirit of tending the sick. If you are a visitor, you have the power of health, and still the world shrinks to the size of the room.

He passed Angela on his way to the phone. She looked up and smiled at him. Sonny wondered how hard it must be to smile at people who were going through such apprehension and pain. He knew that she knew how sick his father was. She knew he was not going to walk out of the hospital, and yet her smile was real. That was probably what had brought her to nursing. A compassion for those in pain and their loved ones. A desire to soothe.

He punched his credit card number into the telephone. He heard it ring.

"Hello?" It was Allison.

"Hey, woman. How's it going?"

"Sonny?" He felt instant tension.

"Yes, Allison, it's Sonny. Expecting somebody else?"

"Where are you?"

"Where am I supposed to be?" He had called to ask about work. He figured she'd know whether there had been any problems. But now he was deep in the hollow space between them, and it was lonely there. There *was* something wrong.

"What the hell are you talking about? You're supposed to be in Philadelphia with your father." He could hear exasperation in her voice.

"Yeah, I'm here." He had never felt this feeling with her. As if she weren't happy to hear from him, as if she were glad he had to leave, and was momentarily afraid that he hadn't actually left.

But Allison quickly recovered. "Well, Sonny, how is he?"

"He's very sick. I don't think he's going to make it."

"Oh . . . I'm very sorry, Sonny. I wish I had met him. I know how much you love your father."

"Yeah . . . it's tough. This is very tough."

Allison was now all softness, nearly liquid, as she flowed through the telephone lines, through the air, into him. "How are you?"

"I'll live," Sonny said and immediately realized the ugliness of language. A situation can change any word to something ugly. He breathed deeply. "I just called to see how you were. I wanted you to know."

"I'm glad you called."

"Are you really?" Sonny wasn't up to a revelation, but he couldn't stop himself from asking the question.

"That's a stupid question, Sonny. I love you, you know that."

He closed his eyes. There were tears there and he fought them. Suddenly he needed her to love him and that frightened him more than anything. His father was dying.

"Sonny . . . are you okay?" Allison felt him struggling.

"Yeah." Sonny pushed the sound out of his mouth. "I'll be all right. I'm just tired. Look, sweetheart, I've got to go, Rainy's waiting for me." He tugged at his wilting suit jacket, pumped his energy up, "Hey, Allison, before I go, tell me how the project's going."

"Well...I...ah...Sonny, why don't you go and call me back. I heard some things, but I can tell you later."

"Shit. Shit. What the fuck happened? Come on Allison, I have to know."

"Well, our part went fine. The press got everything on time and the press conference went smoothly..."

Sonny sighed. "Well, what the hell is wrong then?" He didn't care if some other department fucked up.

"Well, some community groups held a press conference right after ours and claimed we were introducing a computerized mind control system into the inner city. Can you believe it? They called our computer-based education system a Eurocentric brainwashing tool. When I heard that, it completely freaked me out. Can you believe that?"

Sonny was deflated. "No," he said flatly. "No, I can't believe it. Damn. What do they want, a chisel and stone? Damn. This is the twentieth century, technology is a fact of life."

"I know that, but you know it's more complicated than that. They were complaining about the content of the program, not the computer itself. I know how important this is to you, I just thought you should know."

"How did Templeton take it?"

"I don't know."

"Damn."

"Listen Sonny, I do know one thing. Your father's sick and all of this shit will take care of itself. It will be here when you get back."

"Yeah . . . thanks Allison. I love you. Well, I should go. I'll call you tomorrow. Take care of yourself."

"You too, boyfriend."

Sonny hung up the telephone. When he reached the door, Rainy was waiting for him. He didn't remember walking down the hall. He didn't remember passing the nurses' station. Hadn't seen Angela.

Just behind Rainy, his father lay motionless, his mother leaning over him. To hell with work.

As they walked to the elevator, Sonny couldn't help but feel Rainy's strong presence. The men they passed slammed adhesive glances at Rainy. There was something about her. She was obviously attractive. Something more than her tight slender body, her well-shaped legs. Maybe it was her smile. Something.

At the lobby level, the elevator opened and forced them into the stream of moving people. They had been silent the entire time. "The coffee shop is right over here," Rainy said, pointing and leading the way.

She liked being with men, even Sonny. They

tried to act as if they knew it all, but in every man Rainy had ever known there was a sense of bewilderment. It was as if they didn't know why they were living. No matter what his profession, Rainy believed that at the base of every man was a deep emptiness. A lack of purpose. To her, men spent most of their time trying to figure out what their reason was for existing. Why did they exist? Rainy knew men who were so confused with this question that they never did anything that made sense. They cheated on their women. Would do anything to get ahead, would fight, indeed kill, for no reason.

They picked up sandwiches and coffee and sat down, still in silence. A sterile electronic version of ''The Girl from Ipanema'' whipped the air around.

Rainy looked into Sonny's eyes. She knew, no matter how his posture protested, that he was empty, that he had not found his reason for living. Volvos, Armani suits and custom shirts didn't do it. There was something missing. Still, she admired him. He had gone to college, moved away. He had changed the terrain of his exploration. She envied him, envied his ability to leave, to disconnect. She had been unable to do that.

''Are you okay?'' Sonny returned her stare, a soft smile sweeping his face free.

''I guess. Everything seems to be happening at once. Dad's sick and now it seems like things are getting complicated at home.'' She took a bite of her egg-salad sandwich.

"With Dancer?"

"I guess."

"So, did you have something to do with that kid getting killed?" Sonny was thinking fast. He knew something was wrong.

"No. Ah . . . no." She paused, staring at him. "That's just one more thing. Spider was an okay kid. He used to stop by and talk to Dancer and me. I don't know anything about that." Rainy realized she had slipped. Unexpected pain had a way of changing what you wanted to say. She hadn't wanted to get into all this. "It's just that things could be better, that's all." She felt Spider's death inside her. She knew she was connected to him.

"I'll drink to that." Sonny looked around the cafeteria. There weren't many people there. The evening visitors hadn't started arriving yet, so there were only a few people, dressed in hospital whites and blues, smoking cigarettes and drinking coffee. "Do you think Dad's gonna make it?"

"I don't think so, Sonny. I wish he would. I really do. But I don't think so. It's like he's already gone."

"I know. I didn't expect that. In the movies, when people die, they lie there in their hospital beds for a long time, making last speeches and stuff. They call their children to their bedsides. We're not going to get any of that."

Absalom wished he could convince them other-wise. He had no use for a deathbed himself. But he slept against his will. He was trapped in his own body. He tried to find a voice but nothing stirred.

Rainy sipped her coffee. "I don't know, though. Mom seems to be in direct communication. Maybe it's us. Maybe we should stop trying to act like this is just another part of our lives. Maybe we should really slow down and be like Mom, single-minded about this."

"Yeah, maybe. But I just feel that we've got to plan for what's ahead."

"Like selling our house?" Rainy held the cup in the air like a torch.

"Rainy, I'm talking about an old broken-down house in the ghetto of North Philly. It could destroy us." Sonny paused; he wanted to convince her. "You see, if you can't take care of broken hot water heaters, leaky roofs, and stuff like that, it will eventually become Mom's problem."

"First of all, Sonny, it's my house. Mine. And secondly, I've got everything under control." Rainy breathed deeply. "Listen, what's wrong with you? Why are you on my case so heavy right now? I don't know, Sonny, but for some reason I feel like there's something the matter with you. What is it?"

Sonny's face stiffened. "Dad's dying. Isn't that enough?"

"But I don't think that's it. What's all this stuff about the house? How's your life in Minneapolis?" Rainy could tell that she had touched a nerve. Sonny immediately hunched his shoulders.

Sonny wanted to open up. Could he put into words what he was thinking? "I'm sorry if I've been on you too much. Things are kind of a mess in my life, too. I just feel so frustrated."

"Frustrated about what?" Rainy sipped her coffee.

"Everything, Rain. Everything. I mean, here I am riding you about your life and I'm not doing such a good job myself."

"You still have your job, don't you?"

"Yeah. I guess so. But when I see Dad up there I start to wonder what the hell I'm doing. I'm working my butt off up there and for what? Besides, I think my girlfriend is going to dump me. All of a sudden nothing feels right."

"I know what you mean, Sonny. I really do."

"Rainy, I thought I was really happy with my job and my life and everything and then Dad gets sick and now I don't know what to think. He worked like a dog his entire life, and for what? What did Bonansky give him? And now he's dying and it's like nothing happened. The world just closes up around people when they leave. Especially black men. This is our father. If he dies, who will know it? Who will care?"

Rainy fought the tears again. "We'll know. We'll care. I guess I'm dealing with the same shit." She wanted to find Dancer and convince him that they had to change their lives. Sonny was right. The only way they could make Absalom's life more meaningful was to do something positive with *their* lives.

"Listen, Sonny, I'm going to have to go home soon. I think Dad's okay until tomorrow, don't you?" She hoped Sonny understood. She wanted to keep talking, but something inside her was pulling her home. There was another crisis brewing. She felt it.

"I guess so, Rainy. Mom and I are going to have to go home for a while eventually, too. If you need to split earlier, go ahead. We'll call you if anything changes." Sonny was almost in a daze of melancholy. Allison. Absalom. Templeton. Sonny.

"Thanks, Son. You know I love you, don't you, brotherboy?"

"Yeah, Rainy. I know. I love you, too."

She paused. "So maybe we won't fight anymore?"

Sonny cracked his face again, smiling at her. "I suppose I can survive a couple of days without fighting with you."

"Good, because I think we're wearing Mom out."

"Rainy, that's something I don't think could actually happen."

Absalom watched Rainy leave the cafeteria and make her way toward Whither Street. As he turned back to Sonny he could see the stress play itself out on his face. He could not penetrate the space that

Sonny held. He hoped they would have a chance to talk. Absalom didn't like the floating tension between his children. As the father, it was his place to help them get along. He had not always treated them equally, perhaps he hadn't given enough to either of them, but he had tried to teach them to respect each other. Absalom looked over Sonny's shoulder as his son stared into his cup. The cream was separating from the coffee, forming swirling beige rivers. Rainy's energy was still present.

Sonny felt abandoned. The image of his father's skeletonlike face hovered in front of his eyes. Underneath the image, a radio from within the cafeteria kitchen broadcast a Phillies game.

The sound of the announcer and the faint roar of the crowd flowing from a radio somewhere behind the cafeteria's steam table brought a reluctant smile to Sonny's face. He remembered the times he and his father went to Connie Mack Stadium to see the Phillies. It was one of his favorite things that he and Absalom did together.

Suddenly he felt his father's presence. He turned around quickly.

"I can feel you, Dad. I can."

Absalom was startled. He had never contemplated what he would do if anyone turned to face him in this space. Sonny, though, looked right through him. Absalom knew his son was searching for him, needed him. But there was nothing he could do. He felt happy enough that Sonny had actually felt his being there. At least he would know that life had greater possibility than most people ever imagined. Sonny's momentary vision was a gift.

12

Even as his spirit-willed self traveled from place to place, seeing his children, remembering his life, Absalom lay in the gentle care of his wife. In some way she gave him the power to keep moving. Without movement he would have surely disintegrated from the pain. And without Gwen's soft hands, movement would not be possible. She coaxed him on. Built his courage.

Gwen had breathed a smoother, sweeter breath since Sonny and Rainy had left the room. She didn't care where they were, she was just happy to see them go away for a while. Being with either of them alone was good, strengthening. But together, right now, they were like two bees caught in the same pink honeysuckle blossom.

Absalom seemed to be resting comfortably. Gwen carefully wiped his face and hands. She heard him sigh a deep, longing, painful sigh at least three times. She had a feeling that he knew she was there. She felt him holding her. She felt his love for her fight through the thick shroud of threatening death.

Gwen let her head fall backward; her fine gray-brown-black hair reached her shoulders. She smiled, let a sly snicker escape.

"I don't believe you're doing this, Ab. I just don't believe it. We was just getting started, you and me. Just getting started." She brought her head upright, bent down and kissed him on his brown-red, cracking lips. She let her tongue search along the lips. She wanted him to feel the sweetness of her. She would not let him go easily. He would have to leave her, feeling the heat of her presence.

"I just don't know what I'm going to do without you." She took his hand. "It seems like the whole thing happened so fast." She paused, thinking about wasted hours. "I missed you a lot, Ab. You know? When you were working all the time. Up early in the morning. Home late in the afternoon. Asleep all the time. We missed a lot of what we could have seen together. It seems like we never went anywhere, did anything special." She paused to catch her breath. "I missed you."

Absalom moved. Her heart stopped beating. She felt it the moment it stopped. Her whole body was silent. No whoosh of rushing blood near her temples. No pulsating thumps in her wrists. Her body was still.

"Ab?" she whispered into the air. She didn't look at him this time. Every time she felt his body move she expected him to sit up and talk to her. Every time.

But he didn't say anything. She knew he wasn't going to speak. Still, she heard something. It came from someplace deep inside him. The sound was so faint, she wasn't sure she actually heard it. He was saying something. She felt the blood pumping again.

"Ab? Can you hear me?" She looked at him closely this time. His eyelids fluttered briefly. "Ab?" She spoke to him and this time it wasn't said off into the stale hospital air. It wasn't spoken to the dying figure of a man in the bed beside her. It was said to Absalom. Directly.

She grabbed his light hand, opened it, and placed her small round palm against his. "I know you can hear me. I know you're there. Don't leave me, sweetheart. I don't know how, but you've got to hang on." She paused. She realized what she was doing. His movements were slight. There were no identifiable, recognizable signs of communication. But she felt it anyway. She could not stop talking to him. They had shared so much. Done so many things together. She couldn't talk to him now as if he were not a man.

"We didn't really have our proper goodbyes, you know." She brought his hand up to her lips. "You can't just walk out on me without giving me a big fat sloppy Ab special. You know that. I won't have it. So don't get no ideas that you can just lie here and I'll forget that you're my husband, or that you've got some husbandly duties to perform.''

She smiled at him. ''That's right. I ain't letting you off the hook.'' She paused again. ''I need you, Ab. I always have. But right now I need you more than ever.'' She listened to herself talk. It was a bizarre sensation. She talked. She listened. She talked back.

Depleted, Gwen got up from the bed and went to the window. She could see outside. She could look down on the courtyard and the McDonald's below. Then, when she turned to face Absalom, she saw herself sitting there, holding his hand. She wanted to run back and take herself into her arms. To hug herself tightly. She needed arms around her. She was already missing strong arms.

But she did not run to herself. She stood there, staring. She saw the increasing gray sweep of her thinning hair. She saw her caramel skin slowly losing its grip on her face and arms. She almost felt sorry for herself until she realized that, next to Absalom, she was the symbol of health, like the Lady of Liberty was of justice. Age was different than death. Age had its benefit, namely life. She found it difficult to grieve for herself in the midst of a larger tragedy.

Gwen looked at Absalom again. She really wanted him to come back home and be just the way he had always been. She wanted him to recover, to recuperate, to win. She didn't want him to suffer. She wanted him to get up out of the hospital bed and walk out that door with her. "I want you back, Ab." She spoke loud enough to get through the pain and darkness that had cloaked him.

"Look at this woman, will ya, Austin?" The shrieking, grinding voice pierced the energy of the moment. At the door was Selma Mae, Gwen's sister, a chunky, dark-skinned woman a few years younger than Gwen. Behind her was a tall, scalpel-thin, dark-skinned man in a shiny silver-gray suit. He wore a black fedora with a brim that broke almost down to his nose. He was Selma Mae's new boyfriend, Austin.

When Selma Mae's voice barreled into the room, it caught Gwen out of herself and in mid-thought. Gwen scrambled to put herself together.

Absalom moved a finger as Gwen recovered her thoughts. Surprised to feel visitors around him, Absalom threatened to take flight.

"Selma Mae. What are y'all doing here?" Gwen instinctively walked back to the bed and sat down. Her sister met her there. They hugged quickly. Gwen smelled the alcohol in the air around them. She wasn't sure if it was her younger sister or the man who stood behind her. "I ain't told nobody about Ab being sick." She had only told her children. It was all a part of the war. Deny defeat, don't let it exist. Besides, she didn't want to be bothered with visiting relatives and a bunch of people who would stand around trying to figure out what to say when there was nothing left. When death comes, when it is finally imminent, talk becomes irritating.

"I know you didn't, but chile, everybody knows. You can't keep something like this a secret. I don't know why you even tried. I s'pect that in a day or so, the whole Goodman and Tillman family will be here in Philadelphia."

"I wasn't trying to keep it a secret. I just hadn't had time to call everybody."

Selma Mae walked around Absalom's bed as if she were conducting an inspection. She gently tugged the corners of the bed at Absalom's feet to check the tuck. "Well, how're you doing, girl? And how's my brother-in-law?"

"We're both hanging on." Gwen looked away.

"This here," Selma Mae walked to the door, reached out and grabbed the bag of bones behind her and pulled him through the doorway. "This here is Austin Parker."

"Hi, Austin."

"My deepest sympathies, madam." Austin pulled his hat off to reveal a nearly bald head. He was clearly older than Selma Mae.

Gwen didn't know what to say. She hadn't prepared for visitors. She sat very still, turning her head slightly to find just the narrow band of empty space.

"We was down in New Orleans, early this week, at Aunt Freddie's funeral, when we heard about Abbie being sick," Selma Mae said, taking off her white gloves. She wore a pink and blue floral print dress that fit her solid, slightly cubed body snugly. She was still walking around the room. She checked the glasses, the water pitcher. She read the labels on the plastic containers that dripped fluids into Absalom's body. She ducked into the bathroom.

"Naw, Selma Mae. That ain't right." Austin's voice sounded like walnuts in a nutcracker. "Early this week we was in Savannah, Georgia, at Clem Diggs's. You know that."

"Was that this week?" Selma Mae reappeared from the bathroom and looked at Austin. "I could of swore that was last Friday or Saturday."

"Nope. Last Friday we were in Tampa at my Uncle Fremont's niece's wedding."

"Oh yes, that *was* such a wonderful ceremony, wasn't it?" She took a quick look and closed the bathroom door. She walked back to the bed and began to circle it again.

"Simply wonderful, Selma Mae, simply wonderful."

"God can be so beautiful sometimes, can't he Austin."

"Beautiful, Selma Mae? God is beauty. And what about Scott Whittaker's funeral two weeks ago. Talk about beauty. There was at least five hundred people at his services. Never seen so many people at a black man's funeral."

"In Norfolk, Virginia, no less." Finally Selma

Mae had completed her review and sat down in the chair with the circles.

Gwen sat and watched them. They hadn't come for her or for Absalom. It was just like Selma Mae. Something had happened to her sister along the way. She had always been quiet, a loner. Selma Mae had been married twice, both times to men who cared more about her than they did themselves.

But five years ago, her second husband died in a car accident. Two weeks later, his brother-in-law had a heart attack. Within a month, three more cousins of theirs passed away. In a very short period of time, five people who had been close to Selma Mae had died.

Now, with no husband to stay home with, no reason to be anywhere in particular, Selma Mae chose to visit sick and dying relatives as a vocation. She prided herself on her ability to manage the process of living in the face of death and despair. Her life was now a conveyor belt of movement from one funeral to another, one hospital to another, with an occasional wedding or baptism thrown in for renewal.

"Now those was some well-to-do black folks in Norfolk. You never seen so many diamonds and furs in your life." Austin walked to the window and perched his narrow behind on the sill.

"Can you believe it? In Norfolk, Virginia? I just never thought about there being that many uppity Negroes in Norfolk." Selma Mae looked down at her shiny black patent leather shoes.

Gwen was determined not to speak anymore. From time to time she smiled or tightened her grip on Absalom's hand. But she was not about to get involved.

"Hell, Selma Mae, there's uppity black folks everywhere. In some towns you can't even tell who they are, unless you go to church or to somebody's funeral."

"Gwen." Selma Mae stared at Gwen, who seemed to be rocking on the bed to some internal song. "You know how some people can be. Come Sunday, or when somebody's done died, they come out looking like a million dollars. I don't believe in that. Simple black dress will do. I don't believe in putting on airs. That ain't the Lord's way."

"Amen to that." Austin brushed his thin fingers over his bald head.

"Look at him, Austin. How are you doing, Abbie honey?" Gwen barely heard her. "Look at him, Austin. He's trying his best to be strong, but he looks so weak. Two years ago he was so handsome and strong. Abbie is my favorite relative."

"God has a plan," Austin said quietly.

Selma Mae turned quickly to Austin with a big smile. "He does Austin, he truly does. I know that. My sweet sister knows that too, don't you?"

Absalom wanted to walk into Selma Mae's body and pinch her from the inside. First of all, he hated being called Abbie. Somehow he knew his father had never contemplated how Selma Mae would destroy his name. And secondly, how did she know how strong he was? What could she tell from just looking at him? She had to know that what he was couldn't be measured from just looking at him. He was more than an outline of a man on a hospital bed, he was more than Selma Mae could see. He was everywhere. He could be with anyone. His power increased as they seemed to pass him on.

Gwen closed her eyes. She could feel Absalom's heart beating through the palms of her hands.

"Selma Mae?" Austin was digging through his pants pockets. "Where'd you put my cigarettes?"

"We left them in the car, Austin. You can't smoke in here anyway."

"Why not? I smoked in that hospital in Tuscaloosa."

"That was in Tuscaloosa." Selma looked at Gwen and said, "We was in Tuscaloosa when Uncle Fred's brother Jeffrey was dying from cancer, too. He looked terrible."

"Damn. I want a cigarette."

"You can wait. You already smoke too much," Selma shot over her shoulder at Austin. But to Gwen, her voice softened. "You just got to have faith, sis. You know?"

Gwen looked at her. Again, Austin broke the connection. "Is he gonna go home?"

This time, Selma Mae turned completely around in his direction. "If you don't shut up, man, I'm gonna put *you* in the hospital. You act like you ain't seen nobody sick. You make things worse asking stupid questions like that. The Lord is the only one who knows. The Lord is in control now.''

Gwen nodded. She was in complete agreement. The Lord, Jesus, Yahweh, Krishna, somebody, Allah, whoever it was, it wasn't her. She felt powerless.

Again Absalom bristled. He fought against Selma Mae's voice. There was no reason to give up so much control. The Lord had the man to work with. The man was more than an image. The man, Absalom, was a partner and had his own power. That is what everyone forgets when they give control to God. God must have a partner.

''Where are we staying, Selma Mae?'' Austin was rubbing his day's beard growth. It had seemed to creep over his face during the time they had been in the hospital. Suddenly he looked even older.

Selma Mae walked over and stood next to Gwen. ''Gwen, how's he doing? I mean, is he gonna get better? He don't look that bad to me.''

''He's very sick, Selma. He really is. The doctors don't think he's gonna make it.'' Gwen spoke with no emotion.

Austin looked out the window. When he saw the golden arches below, his stomach growled. ''Selma Mae, we're gonna have to figure out where we're gonna stay. I'm getting hungry and I need a shave. This beard is starting to itch the devil out of me.''

''Hush, now. I'm talking to my sister. Why

don't you go take a walk or something." Selma waved at him.

"Naw, that's okay. I'll just wait for you right here."

Selma Mae turned her attention back to Gwen. "I guess what I mean is, ah . . . is he gonna live a few days, a week, or what?"

This time it was Gwen who sighed. "The doctor said it might be a few days. That's all I know."

"I'm sorry, Gwen. I really am." Selma Mae paused, as if trying to find the right words to say. "I just need to get up to New York to see Verta. She's really sick too, you know. I was thinking that we'd keep on going up to New York and stop by here on the way back to Goldsboro, where Thelma's husband is having heart surgery. We'd be back in about two days. I just didn't want anything to happen to Abbie before I could get back."

Gwen looked at her. She knew that Selma Mae's heart was in the right place, but still her presence, her attitude, were beginning to work on Gwen's nerves.

"Selma Mae, I appreciate your concern. I'm really glad you came. But why don't you go on to New York. I'll be here when you get back, and so will Ab. I promise you."

"That's my sister." Selma Mae bent down and hugged Gwen tightly. Gwen never let go of Absalom's hand. For a second she felt almost as if Selma Mae was squeezing life from her body into Absalom's. For a second, she didn't want Selma Mae to let her go. But that feeling passed, leaving her gasping for air. Selma Mae relented.

"Come on, Austin. We've got to get on the road if we're gonna get to New York before midnight." Selma was already gathering her things and heading for the door.

"New York? I thought we was staying in Philly."

"Just get your things and let's get going. Oh, say goodbye to Gwen and Abbie."

Austin paused only a second. "Ah . . . good evening, madam. It was a pleasure to meet you. I truly wish it had been under better circumstances. I look forward to seeing you on a happier day. And to you, sir, I wish you God's love and good luck."

"Thank you," was all that Gwen said.

Austin squeezed by Selma Mae, who was standing at the door. She stood there staring at Absalom. "I know how it is, sis. I truly do. Don't give up. I'll be back in a couple of days. Take care of yourself. Remember, I love you both."

As soon as Selma Mae and Austin were gone, the air settled. Gwen, still holding Absalom's hand, now placed it at his side. She walked to the bathroom and filled a basin with cool water. She found the thin damp white face towel she had used earlier and sat them on the table next to Absalom's bed.

"Well, what do you think, Abbie?" Gwen chuckled, knowing that Absalom might reach up and playfully smack her. "Has she completely flipped her wig or what? I think you're right. She's gone stone crazy. I know you always said my family was nuts, now I got a sister that's proving it. But I promised her. And you know I don't break my promises."

Absalom, lost in himself, continued his search. He reached out. His arms fell off. His legs broke into pieces. He cried out to her and laughed at his life. She was a dancing figure he'd swim the sky for. Even in this smothering smoke. Who else could make him smile at a time like this? He was with her but felt she could not tell it. She didn't feel him like he did her. He wasn't reaching her and he needed to. He sought the comfort that she'd always be there for him. Giving him strength, holding him up. It was an uneasy comfort.

It was uneasy because Gwen had always kept him off balance. There were times when Absalom thought she might actually leave him. And then there were those nights when he was shocked by her nerve to go out without him. When she wouldn't even tell him where she was headed, or what was on her mind. After dinner, Gwen would often just get dressed and ease out the door, leaving Absalom nodding in the living room.

Most of the time, he was too tired to care where she was going. But sometimes, his eyes would open and he'd wonder: Was there someone else? At the center of his heart, Absalom didn't think so, but he was never completely sure.

Gwen would be like a flash of light in the early evening, making dinner, cleaning up. And come night, instead of fading out, her light would burn brighter and she'd start fidgeting. He knew she had to get out.

Gwen put her lips close to Absalom's ear and held tightly to his hand. "I know you always wanted me to be home with you. But I couldn't then. I needed to know I could be free. That I could decide what I needed. I had to get that out of my system. And I did. I told you you didn't have nothing to worry about. I had to learn how to be happy with you. And now . . ."

Gwen saw the nurse at the door. She stopped her whisper and let Absalom's hand go. She knew the routine. She would take a short walk while the nurse turned and cleaned him. He needed the rest anyway. She kissed his forehead and walked out.

"I'll be right back, Ab," was all she said.

13

Absalom knew in his heart that Rainy's life was becoming more complicated, and it scared him. He also knew that she was under the consistent stare of family judgment in a way that Sonny was not. Sonny had gone away.

But when Rainy agreed to live in the house on Whither Street, she had been sucked back into the vortex of North Philadelphia. She had to face the reality that she was once again in the house she had grown up in and had a legacy to live up to. Everyone knew how hard Absalom had worked for his family. Everyone knew how much love and attention Gwen had given her two children. When Rainy accepted the key to the front door, she became the last symbol of the Goodmans in the neighborhood.

Rainy had been lonely for a long time. There had been only two serious boyfriends before Dancer, and a handful of lovers. But no one had managed to make her feel fully loved. No one had made her forget that she had something to protect, and the mere fact that she was a woman made her a target. For Rainy to experience the full measure of love, she needed to believe that the man was not interested in taking something from her. Didn't need *her* to make himself whole. Still, to know love, she figured, you had to put everything on the table to be taken. You had to invite a potential thief into your house for the weekend. If, when you returned, you still had something, love was possible.

She had not met a man who could put aside her cautious, untrusting nature. Rainy watched her girl-friends, one after the other, enter relationships that slowly degenerated into quiet, steely, bitter disappointments. And yet, there was something about Dancer that made her take a chance. In spite of all she thought, she had offered herself to Dancer on a gamble. It was a calculated risk, all based on the fact that Dancer had a dream. He wanted to be a photographer.

Absalom was sure that Rainy had made the wrong decision. He watched her nervous eyes scan the streets as she drove home from the hospital. He spirited into the car. When she walked into the envelope of Dancer's world, she dragged the Goodman history behind her like a lead train, heavy and majestic. It worked against her.

The world turned quicker and quicker in its ro-

tation as Rainy drove home. Her head rejected the
fast-paced disco music on the radio and took off into
the rolling white noise of her thoughts. Her silk
blouse, damp with the perspiration of dread and heat,
clung to her racing body.

Although she wanted to get home to see Dancer,
to see her house, to be reassured that everything was
all right, she knew deep inside that it wasn't. She
knew he wasn't. Rainy was frightened by what was
probably waiting for her. Her future was now as ten-
uous as the air in the hospital.

The hospital. The word itself had come to be the
manifestation of dread. And once felt, dread was an
unshakable companion, present until fulfilled.

Death held life in low regard. She was already
mourning her father. She groped in the dampened
light for a way to connect to him. In the past weeks,
she couldn't get close enough to him. As close as
they had been, suddenly she felt a growing distance.
The memories were clear. His life stood out like
flowers in a desert. Still, she felt an unfulfilled longing to say something she was incapable of saying. It
was like a ghost stomping around in the basement
of her body. A presence. Guilt.

Rainy couldn't help but feel it. As she drove she
began to regret the time she had let slip away. The
times she could have pressed, moved closer to him.
He could, probably would, die before she had a
chance to recover. Tears started to well up in her
eyes.

"I love you, Daddy," she spoke aloud into the North Philadelphia air. Her eyes squinted and blinked in rapid succession.

"I love you too, sugar." Absalom wanted her to focus on her own life. The missed opportunities between them could be made up in an instant. Anything could happen in an instant. They could be alienated for years, live their separate lives and then, in an instant, when a father looked into the eyes of his daughter, everything could be forgiven. Two lives could become one.

Rainy turned onto Whither Street. Two blocks away from the house. She knew the truth: it was Absalom's. His and Gwen's. She had seen the young years of the street, after the last Polish resident had fled, when the children of working black men and women exploded with color and energy on the sidewalks. The summer nights of "Mother May I?", of relay racing down the middle of the shadowing, simmering street. She remembered the whistling, popping, scraping sound of Double Dutch. Spin the Bottle, Five Minutes in the Dark. She remembered the love that bounced out of one house, from one family, into the house of another. It had been a childhood. Many black children did not have that experience anymore. She could not remember domestic violence, rape, robbery, crime of any sort on the 2500 block of Whither.

The adults were always out, sweeping the sidewalk or washing it down with long snaking green hoses that screwed into spigots in the basement. Instead of nurturing lawns, the water hoses, which were pulled through the basement window, were used to move trash off the bricks and cement. It was used at high pressure to bore between the cement blocks of the sidewalk, shooting dirt, toothpicks, and gum wrappers into the brick gutter of the street.

Absalom felt the heat of North Philly. He knew they approached Whither Street.

On the surrounding streets—Seybert, Ingersoll, Taney, Stillman, Master, Jefferson, Oxford, on every side of Whither—gangs and crime had existed forever, it seemed. But Whither still held tight. People sat on their steps at night and watched the city moon show off. The block club, the Cub Scouts, the Jaycees, the PTA, all found their leaders among the parents of Whither Street.

But nothing disgusted Absalom more than the spray-painted scribbles that shouted from the walls. It was the clearest clue that time had not left Whither Street alone. Even on Whither Street the graffiti filled almost every vacant wall.

Absalom remembered how the graffiti had come like a scourge through the community when Rainy was a little girl. He and the other men of the neighborhood had kept track of its changes. In the 1960s, it was the simple, clear markings of territory like 2-8 Ox for the Twenty-eighth and Oxford Street gang. Then, in the seventies, because of rich downtown whites, graffiti artists disconnected from the gangs that had spawned them. Their work went uptown, downtown, freelance. Their work became art. Absalom remembered seeing some of the teenagers from the neighborhood interviewed on a news show about graffiti and how it was art. Of course, a couple of years later, those same kids would be back on the corner, aimless. The white people would be on to other fads. Absalom shook his head.

But now, he could see a new graffiti. The markings were clearly gang identifiers again. No pretention of art. Each was distinctive, with its arrows and letters and circles. Each was intricate. But instead of art, it was evolving into crests. The gang members coveted their symbols and they didn't care whether you understood it or not. All of the corner houses and buildings with long, blank walls offered themselves for announcements.

As the car approached Whither Street, there was a new symbol. It was spray painted in deep magenta and stood out like a neon sign. It was a rough, hurried circle with a line running through the center. It rested on another line that was drawn horizontally under the circle. Under the line were the words, THE MOON SHINES ALL DAY. One side of the circle was filled in with the same magenta color. The other side was empty and took on the beige background of the house it was painted on. On the beige side, along the outer circumfrence, were little squiggles signifying rays. On the other side were lightning bolts like the SS used as insignia during World War II.

Absalom closed his eyes to it.

Rainy, who rode by this corner every day, had not noticed it before. It scared her, too. It made her think about Spider. Until this day she couldn't remember someone dying like that. Rainy knew about drive-by shootings; how drug gangs used them to scare residents and competitors. Now someone had died on Whither Street. At her doorstep. In Absalom's lap. Was this what she had let happen to her?

Rainy pulled into a parking slot on the tightly packed street. She noticed a squad car parked on the red brick pavement in front of her house. She stared at it as if it were refuse someone had forgotten to pick up. A delicately featured, light-skinned cop was leaning against the car, talking with Doc.

Doc was a man who lived up the street. He was now about seventy-five, a short, stocky, almond-colored man who had lived on the block since Rainy was a little girl. He had been called Doc since she could remember. He claimed an extensive knowledge about everything. In fact, the Doctor, as he sometimes referred to himself, had a way of pontificating about abstract ideas and little-known facts, so that one would always leave a conversation with him feeling either impressed or made fun of.

Some years ago, when Rainy was sitting on the steps, Doc had walked up and sat with her. She seized the opportunity to ask him a question she had been dying to ask since she was a little girl.

"Doc?"

"Yes, child?"

"What are you a doctor of?"

"Well now, I'm a doctor of many things. A Doctor of Knowledge. University of Life. College of Hard Knocks. But for your sake, I'm going to simplify it. I specialize in the comings and goings of *things*. The moon. The stars. Our bodies. Everything. The whole kit and caboodle. Not just a few things, but the whole magilla."

At the time, Rainy had just stared at him. She had no idea what to say in response. Now he stood next to the policeman in front of her house.

"Spider's dead, huh?" she asked as she walked up to the two men.

"Splattered from here to kingdom come," the Doctor replied.

"On my doorstep?"

"Practically right in your living room, sweetheart. It's a crying shame."

The policeman's interest in her tweaked. "You live here?"

"Yes."

"Are you related to that Dancer dude?" The cop's attitude was all business, but his eyes were saying something totally different to Rainy. She wanted to straighten him out right away, but decided against it.

"We live together. Why?"

"I'm just askin', that's all. Doin' my job.

Ah . . . what's your name?''

"Rainy Goodman. Now, what's the deal here? What are you looking for? Do you know who killed the boy or what?''

"We're working on it.'' The cop shot his first smile in her direction.

She drilled two holes over his eyes and looked through them. She saw Dancer at the screen door. The door was splintered by the bullets. Rainy walked by the cop without making any more contact. As she hit the first of the four stone steps of her stoop, she turned and said, "You just keep working on it. You need to be doing *something* with all your free time.''

Rainy looked at Dancer standing behind the screen door. In the early evening shadow, the features of his face were broken by the fine mesh of the screen. She could sense the weight of his existence. He was nervous. His long right arm hung straight down at his side, and he held the door open for Rainy.

"Hi, babe,'' she said. She touched the bullet holes. "They made a mess out of this door, didn't they?'' She didn't expect an answer.

Dancer looked at her and for a moment he wanted to fling the door open wildly and gather her into his arms. He felt drained. He was tired. He was scared.

Rainy felt him calling to her. She felt the ripples of pleas and sobs buffet her body, but she was certain he would take them back if she showed the slightest bit of concern for him. That was the way Dancer was. If he felt she wasn't paying attention, he could show intense sensitivity. But when he knew she was watching him closely, he always played it tough. He treated her the same way he treated Half-Dead.

"You finally decided to come home," was all he said as he held the door open for her. She pushed past him and into the living room. As she went by him, she turned her head in his direction and gave him an exaggerated kiss on the cheek. She was relieved to see that Half-Dead wasn't there. She wanted a few minutes to relax and to talk to Dancer. There was quite a bit to go over.

"What do you mean, finally?" Rainy didn't like the tone of his voice.

"You've been gone all goddamn day." Dancer turned from the door and followed her into the living room.

"I've been at the hospital with my father. Who is not doing very well, you asshole. So don't go starting that bullshit."

Absalom realized suddenly that he was not God. Even though he could be in this room, at this precise moment, he couldn't do anything to change things. He couldn't scream. He couldn't grab his family and leave. It was a frightened helplessness. It took him back to his North Carolina childhood.

His mother stood inside the front screen door,

hand on her hip, watching the chickens in the yard. She had a name for each one. Harriet, Booker, George. There was an Alice, a Cleopatra, and a Lucille. There were maybe twenty-five chickens out in the front yard.

Chickens gave the farm music. The rooster called the first line and the other chickens took the rest of the day to give the response. And as night came, they would all gather together in the coop and continue their soft cooing melody.

Over time the rhythm of the chickens would be so natural, so much a part of the day's sound, that it was easy to forget them. They just went through their day, walking through the yard, clucking and clacking, picking up the seeds and corn kernels thrown out on the ground. Sometimes young Absalom would come barreling out of the house and trip over one of them. Send her screaming, squawking, two feet into the air.

Every afternoon his mother would break her routine, go to the front door and watch them. She had known them all since they were chicks. She had seen them grow up. All that those chickens had was in the front yard or in the coop. All they had was the food she gave them. Every day, in return, they gave her eggs.

His mother, a heavyset woman the color of wet sand, would stand there, one hand on her hip, the other on her cheek, pinching it between two fingers, wrapped up in the movement of the animals. Absalom would be in the dirt driveway or the small patch of green grass between the house and the driveway. He'd stop whatever he was doing and watch her.

He used to wonder what she thought as she stood there seemingly lost in the scratching, jerking movements of the chickens. Was she planning a meal? Trying to determine which was the fattest? The oldest? Or maybe which one had laid the least amount of eggs in the past week? He couldn't read her mind, but inevitably before many days passed one of the chickens would die. It was something about his mother that he couldn't reconcile. She loved them and cared for them just to kill them.

Absalom knew. She knew. Even the chickens knew. When they felt her stare they huddled in tighter groups and became more quiet. They didn't stop eating, they just stopped making so much noise. They were probably wondering which one it was going to be.

On a Thursday or Friday, Absalom's mother's stance at the door was more than a reverie. After a while, she would open the door and slowly walk outside. One of the chickens would stick her head up and look around. She was probably trying to guess what day it was. If that chicken saw a plate full of fried chicken in his mother's eyes, well, she'd start slowly, nervously walking toward the cornfield. She wouldn't squawk or nothing. She'd just quietly start walking, almost strolling away. Soon, the other chickens would be easing themselves toward the field, too. Chickens can be real cool. They can make a big fuss, but they can also get out of the way.

His mother wouldn't pay no mind at all. She'd just head in one direction. Toward one specific chicken. This time she was going for Alice. Alice was one of the few chickens straggling behind, acting like there was nothing going on. Alice was just standing there in a mindless fog as his mother bent down.

She moved slowly as she walked up to the chicken, and even as she bent down. But once Alice was within reach, her thick hands shot out and caught the chicken by the neck. Absalom's body flinched. He knew Alice. He fed her in the mornings just like all the others. George and Harriet were already in the cornfield with the rest of the chickens by the time Alice started screaming. She screeched one long sound that made his toes itch.

His mother then swung her arms in a circular motion. Alice looked like a wild carnival ride, swinging at the end of his mother's arm. Feathers flying, the white yellow bird, now dizzy and mixed up, gave up and just let herself be flung around.

She killed her. She killed them all, one after the other. Every week. The same thing. She'd walk out there and grab one and wring its skinny, bony chicken neck until its head separated from its body.

Alice couldn't squawk then. His mother still held the chicken's head in her hands. The body of the animal, though, was now running around in circles in the yard. Blood spurted everywhere. Her little legs just pumping, running, running. Alice was trying to outrun death. She was trying to get away. Fighting reality.

His mother threw the head away and walked over to the kettle of boiling water she had by the side of the house. By now, Alice had run out of steam. His mother would go over and get her. She'd grab the chicken's still twitching legs and carry her upside down to the kettle. Without a word she'd dip the dead bird in the scalding hot water. Once, twice, again. Each time she let the dead chicken stay in the water longer. At some point, she would start pulling the limp feathers off the bird.

Within twelve hours, their North Carolina house would be full of the thick aromatic smoke of fried chicken. Absalom ate that chicken. It was good. Nobody could fry a chicken like his mother. Nobody. It wasn't Alice anymore. Just a chicken. When you live on a farm, everybody teaches you to respect and care for animals and then they kill them for food.

And yet, watching his mother slaughter those chickens one by one had always made him feel powerless. Absalom realized how little control he had over life.

If there was something he could have done to stop what was happening around him now, he would have.

• • •

"They killed Spider."

"You already told me that." Rainy's anger was an ice pick in an iceman's crusty hand.

"I'm sorry, Rainy."

"I picked up your pictures from Fotomat." She dropped into the sofa, loosening up. Then, as she sank into leather, she noticed for the first time that Dancer had a gun in his hand. She had missed it when she came in.

Dancer saw her expression change. "Before you say anything, Rainy, I just want you to know that I hate violence, I really do. I don't want to hurt nobody and I don't want to get hurt. But shit's happening all around us." Dancer was sweating profusely. He had changed clothes and now wore a sky blue BanLon cotton knit shirt and tan khaki full-cut pants. He had his black Air Jordan high-tops on. Rainy thought he looked cute. But he was pacing like an animal, talking loudly and not looking at her.

"Dancer . . ."

"Shit's happening, Rainy. I don't even know how much. Shit, I just found out what the whole goddamn neighborhood has known for days: Buck Teeth Rodney is fronting for some New York gang. The Moon. They want our trade, babe. They want our measly little small-time traffic."

"How do you know they want it, Dancer?"

"How do I know? How do I know?" Dancer repeated the question five or six times as he paced in front of her. Every now and then, he'd walk to the window and look out. "How do I know? Because they killed Spider right on our goddamn steps, that's how I know. That was a message. That was for me."

Rainy sat back in the soft black sofa. She crossed her legs. The heat from outside had stained the air in the house. All of the events of the day contributed to the heaviness she felt. For a second she thought about her father, lying in the hospital bed, waiting. But his image quickly disappeared as she focused on Dancer pacing in front of her. She pulled the envelope of photographs from her large black purse.

"Here," Rainy said, handing him the red and green envelope. Dancer flung it to the other side of the couch.

"I'm not talking about pictures, Rainy. This is serious."

"I know how serious it is. I was just thinking, that's all." She closed her eyes for a moment. She wasn't really thinking. She had thought the whole situation out on her way home. "Well, Dancer, you know we really don't have much of a choice."

Dancer stopped his pacing. "What do you mean? We damn well do have some choices." He held the gun up. "This is a goddamn choice."

Rainy looked at him and felt something tighten in her stomach. She didn't like the way he was going about this. But then, it shouldn't surprise her; Dancer was prone to getting things twisted, going in a di-

rection he knew she wouldn't agree with. He often
pulled the wrong lever.

"Dancer, that little piece of shit in your hand
ain't gonna do nothing to nobody. You need to put
it away. The only thing it does is make you *think*
you're invincible."

"I'm scared, Rainy. I'm really scared. I
mean—" Dancer's dark brown eyes flared as he
remembered standing in the door talking to Spider.
He remembered watching the car drive up, stop
right in front of the house and wait. They waited
right there until they wanted to, and then, bam,
they did him in. "They came that close to blowing
my brains out. I could have been splattered all
over the front door."

"I know," Rainy said solemnly. She had
thought about the shooting and realized how close
Dancer had come to death. She had considered the
danger they were in, and she had made her mind up.
"Look, Dancer, we've got to get out of this mess.
It was fine for a while. We made a little money."

*Absalom covered his face with his rough hands
and like a flower in reverse, retreated to blossom.*

Dancer started pacing again. "A little money.
What the fuck is a little money?" He was sweating
streams inside his shirt.

"Dancer, relax . . ."

"Relax? You weren't here when they filled that
door with lead. I'd like to see you relax after you've

been shot at. Anyway, I'm ready for them if they come back.''

''With that?'' Rainy said, pointing to the gun.

''If I have to.''

''Well, babe, I think we had better think this out. I don't want no more shooting around here. I don't want to get killed and I don't want you to get killed.'' Rainy heard the faint sound of music coming from the stereo. Strains of a barely audible Anita Baker scented the air. That was what she wanted. To be Anita Baker blowing her voice through people.

''So, what do you suggest we do?''

Rainy swallowed her dream. She knew what she had to say but had wanted to let him think it had just occurred to her. It couldn't appear premeditated. But now, now was the right time. If it was to be said, it had to be said now.

''Well, suppose we just hand it over to them. Give it up. We don't have to do this. It's too dangerous. And, besides, maybe it's just not right anymore.'' Rainy reached over and picked up the envelope of pictures. ''You could get into your photography full time. Maybe I could find a group and start singing. We could do it. I know we could.''

''Singing, Rainy?'' Dancer tried to wave off her suggestion lightly. But inside, he trembled. He walked to the window. Panic ran through his body like a frightened child locked in a house of horrors. He fingered the gun, felt its chill in the palm of his hand. ''What the fuck are you gonna do to make money? Do you think you can sing and money will just roll in the goddamned door? Or are you going to wait tables or be a goddamned receptionist while we wait for the big break? And me? You got any ideas for me? Don't give me that shit about photography. I've been taking pictures for five years. Big fucking deal. How many black photographers do you know? Ain't no serious photographers around here. I don't want to be like Crazy Leonard walkin' around the Foxtrap with a goddamned Polaroid camera around my neck begging drunk motherfuckas to let me take their picture."

"Dancer, you know there are black photographers around here. Michael Satterwhite is a photographer, a good one too. You need to stop thinking like that."

"I'm not Michael, Rainy," Dancer shot back at her. He couldn't explain why some people seemed to be able to do everything they wanted to do. He just knew how he felt.

"What difference does that make?" Rainy could see how hard it was for him to imagine life outside the hustle, the game. That's what it was. They had been playing a game. They invested their money in cocaine and sold it for a profit. Until now the only obstacle had been the law. In a game with the law they could win. But against the wild, unmetered violence of people hungrier than even Dancer, they would lose. And if they lost, where would that put them? Instead of working out an escape route, she and Dancer had put it off. They weren't prepared for the future.

"If you're talking to me, it makes a lot of difference. I'm not going from pulling in a hundred grand a year selling a little dope to scratching out fifteen, twenty thousand dollars driving a smelly cab or working in somebody's restaurant. Naw, baby, those days are totally over."

"Dancer, we can't win this one. I don't want to fight no gang from New York."

"No? Well, Rainy, I'm not in the mood to just move out of the way and let somebody come in here and take over."

"Dancer, will you wake up? We started doing this because we didn't have any money and we were both out of work."

"Nothing's changed, Rainy, except that people realize we have a good thing going here and they want a piece of it."

Rainy looked at the pictures stacked in her hand. The photograph on top was a picture of the house. Dancer had taken it in black and white. It bled into the edges of the paper. The shades of gray outlined a building that had managed to hold itself up proudly over the years.

The picture could have been taken twenty years before. Rainy stared at it. Dancer had captured the etchings of time on its façade. She could see herself at four years old, crawling on the red brick pavement in front of the door. The front wall of the house spoke out to Whither Street. The house, the very one she sat inside now, the one with a door full of bullet holes still showing fresh wood, was sandwiched between two houses just like it. All down the street on this block, each house was identical. They did not have porches or garages, only a set of white marble or dark stone steps leading to a narrow, lonely doorway.

Each house became its own statement. But this was Absalom's house. She saw his large frame walk to the door to fetch her for dinner. This was Gwen's house. She saw Gwen walking up Whither Street after getting off the trolley on Girard Avenue. Dancer was a good photographer, he had captured it all. He had just walked too far into the grayness. He no longer understood what the images were. How closely they were connected to what was. This was her history staring at her. This was what had taken Absalom to the end of his physical life.

Rainy remembered the late fifties, when the commercials on the black radio station encouraged all of the residents to change from wood to aluminum doors with storm windows. Eventually, nearly each house did.

"Listen, Dancer," Rainy interrupted her reflection, convinced that her way was right. "We've got to cut bait. Right now. I can't be a part of all the killing and shooting and crap we've got to go through for a little bit of money."

Dancer grew increasingly anxious. "Rainy, you

don't seem to understand. This is the most money I've ever had. We've got a bank account. We've both got new cars. Look at this.'' He grabbed his running suit top that was draped on the banister. ''Feel this, this is a Fila suit. And this,'' he shoved his Rolex watch in her face, ''how would I ever buy a Rolex? How?''

''You're an artist, Dancer.'' Rainy turned away from the flash of the watch. That wasn't the point. They both were capable of so much more.

''That's bullshit, Rainy. I wanted to be an artist.'' He reached down and grabbed the bunch of photographs. ''You think this is doing something? This ain't shit. What good is it? This ain't changing a motherfucking thing.'' All the time he talked, Dancer cut a narrow path in the maple wood floors. He wore through the bottom and ended up in the basement, where his stash of crack cocaine was.

''This.'' Dancer reached into his pants pocket and extracted a roll of bills. It lifted him back to the main floor. ''This is what means something in this fucked-up place. This is what I want.''

''We're getting out, Dancer. That's it. I'm not dealing with it anymore. And neither are you, if you expect to live here.''

''Yeah, baby. That's it. Step all over me.'' Dancer knelt down, put his face right in hers. Rainy was very much aware of the gun in his right hand. ''You can't tell me what the fuck to do. Do you understand?''

Rainy knew this was a test. In the beginning she was giddy with success. They had money. It was precise and clean. They kept it out of the house. The only drawback had been dealing with Half-Dead, but even that hadn't been so bad. Now, though, the acid had eaten through the protective coating. Now it stung.

"Dancer, you better get the hell out of my face talking crazy like that. I'm out of it. And, if you want *me*, you're getting out of it too.''

Dancer stared into her eyes. He felt her resolution. He moved closer and pressed his lips to hers. Her body slowly, involuntarily began to relax. Rainy, feeling an instantaneous need for escape, circled him with her arms.

"I love you, Dancer,'' she whispered in his ear.

"I love you too, Rainy. I'm scared. I want to be a man. I want to get up and scream to everybody around me that I'm a man. I want to do what I want to do. I don't like being told what to do. I don't like being pushed around.''

"I'm not pushing you around.''

Dancer held her tightly. "I'm not talking about you. I don't really know who it is. I'm just trapped. Photography seems so stupid to me right now. I love it, but who the hell is going to give me money for it? I need to get paid.''

"If you'll apply yourself, be patient, maybe it'll come through."

Dancer violently broke free, slid the cocking mechanism of the gun back. Rainy heard the loud metal click as a bullet filled the chamber. "Maybe. Maybe. Fuck maybe." Dancer walked to the window. "Rainy, I didn't have shit where I grew up. We didn't even have a goddamned bathroom. I wore clothes from my brothers and cousins. I never had shit."

"Dancer, you can't win this one. They'll kill you." Rainy felt weary. Her father struggled, Dancer struggled, her mother, Sonny, everyone she knew struggled to hold on to themselves. The song seemed endless.

He walked back to her, released the gun from its ready position and laid it on top of the pictures scattered on the other end of the couch.

"Come on. Let's go upstairs." He stood over her, arms extended.

"And do what?" Rainy couldn't believe how he could shift to sex from any alleyway. All thoroughfares of his mind led to fucking. She sighed. What kind of a life was it that when you were scared or angry or depressed you wanted someone else to rescue you, take you away, get lost in? She looked at him. She wasn't really in the mood and she wasn't sure what had been resolved. Then again, why not end the day the way it had begun? She wanted to fly, to be catapulted into another existence, out of

this, away in the empty space of serenity. Sometimes
Dancer knew how to take her there. Perhaps this was
one of those times.

"Take care of yourself, baby girl," Absalom
whispered to Rainy as she passed him on her way
up the stairs.

14

When Sonny found his way back to his mother, she was sitting in the same spot on the bed where he and Rainy had left her. In the time that had passed, he had had coffee with Rainy, felt Absalom's presence and it seemed to him, as he stood watching her, that she had not moved an inch. Her hand was still locked onto Absalom's skin and the same soft humming sound was coming from her body.

"Where have you been?" she asked. The distance in her voice startled him. She didn't turn to look at him, and except for the question showed no sign that she had seen him fill up the doorway.

"Rainy and I had a long talk."

"Good." Gwen said, still not moving. "We had some visitors. Your Aunt Selma Mae and a friend stopped by."

Sonny looked around. "Where are they now?"

''Oh, they left. Selma said she'd come back on Tuesday, I think.'' Gwen stared at the bed as she talked.

''How's Dad?'' Sonny didn't like Selma Mae and all of her different boyfriends. He didn't like the fact that she turned up like a crow to a road kill whenever someone was sick.

He walked over to the bed. There was no way to keep going in and out of this room, being so close to the bed, close to him, and not want to touch him. To kiss him. But as he drew close, there were horrors camped around the bed. A harsh plastic tube slipped into Absalom's nostril, reached down into his stomach and stirred his pain. His dark mouth was perpetually open. His eyes waxed shut. Still, Sonny ventured closer, seeing in detail the relaxation of the skin near the bone. The ribbons of color the skin became. Some were dark like an elephant's, some light, almost white. The sinking eye sockets. The swelling on the left side of his head, at the top of the ear. The place where cancer lived.

He put his hands on Absalom's brow. Still, the more precious his skin became, the softer it felt. Even the dry parts. Gently he brushed the back of his hand across Absalom's forehead. Sonny felt the dampness from the daubing his mother periodically gave Absalom. He felt the smooth glasslike touch of vaseline. He felt his blood exit the back of his hand and pour into his father.

''About the same. He's still fighting with everything he's got." Gwen looked over to Sonny. She was glad to see him touching his father. Live with him, Sonny. Live with him.

"He really is a fighter, isn't he?" Sonny met her stare.

"Your father, Sonny." Gwen shook her head slowly from one side to the other. "Your father is some kind of fighting man. We both came up here from down South without a pot to pee in. And together we made out all right. We fought the riffraff in the neighborhood and we stood up to the white man." With great effort Gwen rose from the bed and walked to the window where her purse sat on the still. She took out her compact and powdered her face.

Sonny watched in silence. He knew her movements was simply a pause, not an end. "Now I look at you and Rainy and I feel like somebody stole something from me. I love you, Sonny. Rainy too." She talked as she powdered her face. "But it seems like the bigger and more grown you two got, the more I couldn't figure out what we was fighting so hard for. You shouldn't be offended by it. I'm just remembering how hard everything was for us when ya'll was coming up. We never had no money. Everything we did was for you. Absalom would go without, just to buy you a new toy."

"I know that." Sonny felt a sudden, odd feeling. He could feel the sharpness as his mother held him in her eyes. "But I don't understand what you're saying, Mom.'' Sonny felt the pain in her words. Yet Gwen, peeking at the circular reflection in the small mirror of her powder case, did not show it.

"It's not that difficult to understand, Sonny. I'm just saying that now, on the other side of the coin, after we've fought and sacrificed and I look at you big and strong, and him lying there like that, well, I can't help wondering if we didn't give you too much. Seems like you got more of us than we did.''

Sonny felt the rising anger in her voice. The tension, its barbs spreading like tentacles. "You're not blaming me? You can't be blaming me.'' His eyes flamed and stung. His breath caught its sleeve on a doornail.

Gwen caught herself. She listened to the words she had spoken ricochet off the walls of her inner mind. She looked up at Sonny and saw the strain that bound his face together. She wanted to reassure him, to make it clear. She wanted to say, "No, Sonny, I'm not blaming you. We loved every minute of it. We did.'' Instead she looked him directly in the eye. "Well, son, right now I'm pretty angry. I know I shouldn't be angry with you, but I can't help it.''

"What have I done?'' Sonny's voice broke into a higher pitch.

"Your father is laying there . . .'' Gwen froze. She stared at Absalom, a stream of clear drool sliding out of the corner of his mouth.

"Dying.'' Sonny completed her sentence.

"Maybe. But very, very sick at least. And you and Rainy can act like you got life on a string. You can go off talking about the future like it's guaranteed to you. Like you're entitled to it for just being here. You talk about him being strong, being a fighter, but I sometimes wonder if you really understand where he had to come from to put you where you are."

"I understand, Mom. I do. I know how hard it was. It hasn't changed that much."

"It doesn't go on forever, Sonny. That's all I'm thinking." Gwen let go with a thunderous sigh. "Sooner or later something happens."

"I think you and Dad did a pretty good job."

"I do too, Sonny, I do. But that was my point really. We were so busy trying to make it right for you and Rainy that we missed a part of our own lives. All of a sudden, I feel like Absalom's life wasn't that important. Like neither he nor I did that much."

Sonny walked over to her. He turned and looked back at his father. "I don't know, Mom. I think you're wrong. Both of you worked hard." Sonny felt his stomach tremble. Its emptiness was prey to the nervous acid that suddenly cascaded inside. "I love him, too. I miss him already. It's not like we were together all the time, but—" A part of Sonny slipped gently into the bed next to his father. He nestled him. He was nurtured by him. The other part scurried up to Gwen, begging forgiveness. "I think he should be pretty proud. For the first time I feel proud of him. He lived a good life. That's a lot to do.'' Suddenly he couldn't stop it, he fell into his mother, who dropped her compact. The mirror exploded, but Gwen held onto Sonny for her life. She felt his strong arms hold her. He dissipated into the thing he was before he could breathe. He became her again for an instant. Tears poured out of him.

Gwen wavered but held Sonny up. Finally she had to take a step back for leverage. When Sonny felt her losing her balance it was like a smack of frigid Minnesota winter air. He took control of himself. He grew in size and held her tighter. His tears became paid debt. This time he raised her an inch off the floor, kissing her butter rum cheek.

In his grip Gwen found herself with a large smile on her face. There was a rush of happiness. ''He did live a good life.'' Sonny's grip made it difficult, but she said it anyway. Finally he let her down and lowered his arms. ''He loves you, too. We'll make it, Sonny. We will.'' The neon from the courtyard below put a soft red glow over her face. The atrium roof above the center of the hospital, which hours before had allowed a bright, showering sun to reign, now clouded over with darkness.

''Mom, why don't we go home tonight? I'll fix us a nice dinner and we can come back first thing in the morning.'' Her red face took the years off. Suddenly she appeared young and enthusiastic as she stared at him.

"I thought I'd stay the night. But if you want to you can go on and then come on back here in the morning."

"I'm not leaving you here tonight, Mom. I think we should go home. We can't do anything right now." He put his arm around her shoulder like she was an old buddy.

"I'm not leaving, Sonny," Gwen said strongly, walking back toward Absalom. "He needs me. Now's not the time to be going."

Sonny needed to get some fresh air. The atmosphere thickened as the day disappeared. The growing emptiness around them screamed for them to leave. Maybe Absalom needed privacy. Gwen distance. He wasn't sure, but he knew he had to keep after her to take a break.

"Listen, Mom. This is hard enough on you as it is. Couldn't you go home and get a good night's sleep? Dad will be okay until tomorrow."

"How do you know that? How do you know he's going to live through the night?" She sat down beside her husband.

"I just know it, Mom, and so do you. The doctor didn't say he was going to die tonight." Sonny took a deep breath. "I just thought you might like to get out of here for a while."

Gwen again took Absalom's hand. Throughout the afternoon and evening he had been sleeping fitfully, never fully achieving consciousness, lost in a series of dreams. Now he was lying peaceful and motionless.

"He's resting good now. He wasn't doing too well earlier, but he's doing a lot better now." Gwen raised his hand to her chest. "I just don't think I should leave."

"Mom, suppose we go for a ride. Maybe stop by the old house and see Rainy, get something to eat and if, after all that, you want to come back here, I'll bring you back. How's that? We can always call from Rainy's to see how he's doing."

Gwen was quiet for a moment. "I guess I can go for a little while. Maybe a ride over to Rainy's will do me good. But I'll probably want to come back here later."

Absalom barely breathed. "Sonny and I are going to get some air for a little while. Okay? So, I don't want you to worry, sweetheart. We'll be back soon. Okay?" Gwen turned her head to Sonny, who stood staring. "What do you think? Will he be okay?"

Sonny found his words hard to say. They were little weights that had to be thrown off in order to move forward. So he threw them off. "Mom, I really think he's going to be fine tonight. You need a break. Just a little while. I'll go tell the nurse where we're going. And if there's any change, she can call us."

"Thank you, Sonny, that will make me feel much better." She watched Sonny leave. "He's right, you know, we didn't do that bad. We could've done worse, you and me. Everything I read or see on television keeps telling us how terrible black men are as fathers and husbands. Nobody ever takes the time to celebrate men like you.'' She paused. ''But we did *do* something special.''

Gwen bent down and kissed Absalom on the lips, lingering there as the bold redness of her own burnished his skin and left its mark. She held her lips there as the rush of history passed over her head. She felt the whooshing rush of the wind. She heard the startling bebop of the passing sounds. She saw the swirling colors of time twisting in front of her face. She was a little girl, a mother, a lover, a friend. She was eight and sixty-six.

A young mother, proud and resolute. Trapped. A mother, not a lawyer, not a mayor, holding two small strong black children. Kissing babies and fixing dinner instead of kissing babies. Gwen realized all of Absalom's regrets. Their years had passed like sculls skimming the surface of the Schuylkill River, decorating history like the lights outlining the boathouses.

''My mother wanted me to go to college. Wanted me to be somebody, Absalom, just like we wanted for them. Seems like everything grows in such little steps. Things take so long to catch hold.''

Gwen picked up her purse from the foot of the bed. She then brought her chocolate lips close to his ears. ''Now, you know how I am, Absalom. I don't like to make a big fuss. I can talk you into tears and

I can cry you into laughing. I don't usually make demands but this time I'm putting my foot down proper. If you die before I get back here, I'll never speak to your proud black butt again. You hear me?''

Sonny peeked in the door. ''Mom, everything's okay, the nurse said that she'll—''

''Give me a minute, Sonny, I'll be right out.''

Sonny flinched. Moments of intense feeling come suddenly, unannounced. Moments when everything outside that experience are relegated to the peripheral and obscure dances, flights of peach blossom and purple petunia, not clearly significant to breathing, crying, loving.

He closed the door. Everything inside the room faded into a flurry of still images. No music played, no singing was heard. Everything turned away from him.

He found himself heading for the telephone; he wanted to speak to Allison again. The phone rang three-times before Allison picked it up.

''Damn. I'm glad you picked up the phone. I was beginning to think you weren't home.''

''Sonny?'' She sounded as if she had just awakened from a deep sleep and couldn't put anything into focus.

''Did I wake you or something?''

''No. No. I was just . . . ah . . . I was just getting dressed. Why would I be sleeping this early on a Saturday evening? Actually I was . . . ah . . . I have somewhere to go. How's everything there? Did something happen?'' Allison was surprised that he had called her back so soon.

She was trying to evaluate their relationship. He had been so preoccupied with his rise up the corporate ladder that he had not seen their life together dissipating. It was late now, maybe too late. If he hadn't had to leave she would have been willing to try, one more time, to reinvigorate the connection between them. But something had changed inside her when Sonny was called away. She knew it was critical. That his father was sick. But she couldn't shake the feeling that he put everything ahead of their relationship.

''No, nothing has changed. I just wanted to talk to you again.''

''How's your mother?'' Allison sensed a chance to escape confrontation. ''Tell her I said hello. Tell her that I asked about her and that I would one day like to meet her.''

''I will. And she's holding up pretty good. She's a strong woman. That's basically what I'm doing, trying to spend as much time with her as I can. So, ah,'' Sonny couldn't stop himself, ''where are you going?''

Allison held her words. There are moments when the utterance of a group of words can change life itself. Can put new things into motion, end others. There are moments when words have power well beyond their context.

"I'm having dinner with a friend, Sonny. It's no big thing." She needed to talk to him. To talk about what she'd been thinking. Maybe there was still time to work things out. But she didn't want this conversation to go any further. She could go to dinner with whomever she wanted.

"Who?" Sonny couldn't help but be suspicious. That was the type of week it had been. He stared at the distorted image of himself reflected in the silver telephone in front of him. Suddenly he was on the telephone again and someone on the other end was stammering. It wasn't a good sign.

"What?"

"Who are you going out with?" His body stiffened.

"Just a friend, Sonny. Don't worry about it. Just take care of yourself and when you get home we can talk."

"Listen, Allison. I miss you. I can't wait to be back there. There's a lot I have to say. It's like in just the last two days I've learned so much. I mean I'm looking at my father and he's dying right in front of my eyes. And yet I feel him more strongly than ever. It's like he's more real. Anyway, the point is that I want to make it up to you. I want to show you that we can be successful *and* happy."

"Sonny, let's just wait until you get back. We'll deal with everything then. Okay?"

"All right. Ah . . . I know it's Saturday, but did you hear anymore from the office?" No matter how hard he tried he couldn't not think about work.

"Not a thing." He could tell she was ready to hang up. "For God's sake Sonny, you don't have to worry about Templeton or me or anyone else right now. Just take care of your mother and yourself." Allison was a little agitated. She was already late for dinner.

"I guess you're right. But it's hard for me to let it go. My whole life is up there."

"No Sonny. Right now your life is right where you are, with your family."

After a long, ambiguous silence, Sonny sounded her a kiss and hung up the telephone. He sat in the booth for another minute or two, then gathered himself and walked back into the Oncology ward. He was mindlessly moving toward Absalom's room when he nearly walked into Angela, the nurse he had met coming in.

"How is he?" she asked.

"What? Oh. About the same," Sonny numbly answered. His father's image flashed in his mind. "I never seem to say what I'm actually feeling."

"Let me give you some advice." The nurse's dark features highlighted her smile. "When you love somebody and they are as sick as your father is, don't wait for some special time to say what you've got to say. Take advantage of every moment you have." Sonny nodded dumbly as she walked off with a tray of medicine. Her words slowly faded into his skin.

He found himself at the door to his father's room. "I'll see you later, sweetheart," Gwen said as she rose to leave. Sonny straightened himself.

"Mom, I haven't spent any time with Dad by myself." Sonny's voice sounded almost childlike to Gwen. She was surprised by the desperation in it.

"You spent so much time talking about the house and everything else except your father. I just thought you had nothing to say."

"But that's not true. I need to talk to him."

"Now you remind me of me. Your daddy used to always ask me, when I said I needed to do something, he'd ask, 'Do you need to or your want to?' "

"Does it make a difference?"

"Not to me, Sonny, not to me. But to your dad, it made a difference."

"Well, do you think I can spend a few minutes with him now?"

Gwen took him by the arm and led him toward the elevator. "Listen, Son, I just laid down the law to your father. He'll be here when we get back. I think he's got enough on his mind right now. He knows you love him. He knows all about that, so you don't have to worry. I'm not saying I don't want you to spend some time with him. I'm not saying that. But why don't you do it tomorrow. Let's give him the night off."

"Okay. But I don't want to wait too long."

"I understand." The elevator came and they stepped on.

"I mean," Sonny was walking with her but he was not certain he was ready to leave, "suppose he passed away tonight?"

"Weren't you just telling me that he would be okay and that the nurse would call us?"

Suddenly Sonny was eight years old and on an outing with his father. They were visiting one of his father's friends. The man had a son with whom Sonny was supposed to play. They each were given a quarter to spend at the store. While Sonny debated over what to buy, the boy bought some candy and left. He was playing a trick on Sonny, just for fun. But when Sonny left the store he was completely disoriented. They had left the house just before dusk and night fell quickly. It seemed to Sonny that it had gotten dark *while* he was in the store. Nothing was familiar. He started crying. He wanted his father. He began to run. There were people all around him. The buildings grew. He was lost in the streets of North Philly, searching for someone he knew. Someone to hold on to, someone who would help him find his father, who would then take him home. Someone who could bring a sense of being found to the sense of being lost. But no one came along and he ran and ran until he found himself on Girard Avenue and heading for Whither Street.

It suddenly occurred to Sonny that losing a parent, being permanently separated, was the beginning of the end of childhood. He wanted to let his father know that he would be strong, that he would do what he could to honor Absalom.

But his mother was right, he could wait until tomorrow. After all, he had insisted on her leaving. He didn't really want to make her wait for him now. His body relaxed.

"Do you think we should call Rainy to tell her we're stopping by?" Regaining strength, Sonny put his arm around his mother.

"Naw, she won't mind. She's always telling me 'Just stop on by. You don't have to call me or nothing. Just come on by. It used to be your house too you know.' I just say, yes, Rainy, I know it used to be my house. So don't worry." Gwen cut off her thought as other people got on the elevator.

As they walked into the lobby, she said, "How long has it been since you've been down to Whither Street?"

Sonny smiled. He knew she would eventually get to it. It was a part of his mythology. "When Sonny Goodman left the ghetto of North Philadelphia, he vowed never to return." That was the way it was written by the scribes of the neighborhood. Sonny had never said it, but then he had never returned for more than a day or two either. Even though Rainy still lived there, he rarely visited her. When Sonny came to Philadelphia, he usually stayed with Gwen and Absalom in the new house.

But now, going to the old house seemed important. It was where he had been brought up. It was his home as much as anyone's. To touch a part of his history, something he shared with his father now, would help him understand. He wanted to go home. He wanted to see Whither Street again.

"It's been a while," he answered, secure in his vagueness.

"At least ten, twelve years, I reckon."

"Really?" Sonny was honestly surprised.

"You know that good as I do, boy. Don't try to play dumb with me."

15

Absalom jumped to alertness. Something was seriously wrong. Why would they leave him now? He needed them there, just sitting around him, talking. He breathed them in, the sounds they made and the smell they created, and felt his heart lurch stronger. And yet, he felt the pull to North Philadelphia just as they did. Something was going on at the Whither Street house and they were all supposed to be there.

He felt the gathering storm. Maybe it was going on everywhere. Maybe it was a fight for the survival of an entire people. Maybe the storm was all-encompassing and overwhelming. But for Absalom and his family it was now. It was time for them all to be there. And so he was compelled to fall in behind Sonny and Gwen as they traveled back to Whither Street.

Gwen left the heaviness of the hospital behind her. "It's still hot as a boiling kettle out here. Whew. Too hot for me. Sometimes you really appreciate air conditioning. I mean to tell you, I can't wait to get to Ab's car. It must be eighty degrees and it's..." Gwen paused to check her watch. "Well, I had no idea it was 9:30. Nine-thirty, Sonny. We've been in that hospital all day."

Sonny felt the heat, too. It swished and swayed all about them. "I parked over there," he said, pointing to the dark shadowy parking lot. In the little cinder block shack off to the side of the doorway, lit by a dull bulb, Sonny could see the old man still sitting. The street was full of people. The trolley passed. A boom box blared indistinguishable bass lines. The smell of onions softly sautéing crept along. The smell of beer and urine steamed off the cement and brick crevices. The city in early evening. The echo of closing shop doors, the sliding security gates, the ebb of mercantilism. The dawn of debauchery.

Sonny grabbed his mother's arm, holding it as they crossed the street. The old man now stood at the door of his shack. "You the fella with the Caddy, right?"

"You got it." Sonny reconnected with his earlier vision. The strong sense that he knew him from somewhere in his past. He turned to his mother. "Mom, I could swear that I know that man."

"Course you do," Gwen said matter-of-factly. "That's Mr. Betters. He lived around the corner from us on Whither Street. He lived on Seybert Street. He had that peach tree in his backyard."

Sonny's face lit up. "You mean, that's the dude who we used to rob those peaches from?"

"Wasn't too many people in North Philly with peach trees, Sonny. I s'pect it was his."

Headlights flashed in their faces as the car pulled up. Sonny's mind fluttered with delight. He remembered vaulting over the dark-wooded, tall, pointed picket fence that Peachy thought would keep them out. That was what they called him. Peachy. Sonny had never known his real name.

Sonny was the one they'd usually nominate to go over the fence and grab a shirt full of peaches. He had gotten Peachy's movements down to a science. He never got caught. But Peachy would always come barreling out of his back door, wielding a baseball bat or a small shovel. Peachy loved his fruit tree and would probably have hurt Sonny had he caught him. Fortunately for Sonny, Peachy was slow and awkward. Everybody knew that Peachy had a metal plate in his head from World War II. To Sonny and his friends, this, more than anything, made Peachy a target. Nobody took him seriously. If he got angry, people acted as if it were the war injury.

"I kept my eye on your car, son, just like I

told you I would. It truly is one humdinger of a car.''

Sonny was speechless. He knew his mother would not acknowledge the man. They had probably not seen each other in years and were never more than infrequent, passing acquaintances at best. But he, he had trespassed. He had gone over the fence, countless times. He had gone over so many times that he had stolen enough peaches to make soda money selling them to his friends during the summer months.

Sonny reached into his pocket, feeling for his money. He pulled a small clump of bills out. He pulled off two twenty-dollar bills and put them in the man's hands.

The man looked Sonny in the eye. ''How's your father?'' Sonny could hear the bills crumpling in the man's hand.

''He's doing okay. Hanging in there.''

''Yeah. I know it's tough, young man. I know. You take care of your mother. Hear? Don't forget the living. You know what I'm telling you? And here.'' His hand grabbed Sonny's with incredible strength and shoved the forty dollars back into it.

''You hold on to all this cash. Why you givin' me all this, anyway? Your bill is only ten dollars.''

''I know, but I just wanted you to have it.''

''I don't know why. I don't like people givin' me things when I don't know why. I ain't no welfare case, goddammit. You take your money, you probably need it more than I do.''

Sonny felt the dank dull feeling of soggy bills in his hand, wilting from the transfer. He didn't care anymore whether the man took the money or not. Suddenly it seemed ridiculous. He got in the car.

"I was about to burn up, Sonny. Did you forget I was in here? Turn this car on and get that air conditioner on." Sonny did what she told him.

The summer hues of the evening rested upon the shoulders of the urban landscape like a surrealist abstraction. The twisting colors of the August sunset, the billowing heat, cascaded around them. Safely ensconced, Sonny drove the Cadillac through center city, heading north on Broad Street. The shadow of the evening was stronger, more significant it seemed, in the valley of the concrete. Dwarfed by the buildings, Sonny felt as if he were in an animated film of the 1930s. Geometric shapes, shadows, and moving objects all asking for validation.

"Sometimes I really miss this city."

"I bet you do. It sure is different from where you're living now." Gwen thought about her two visits to the Twin Cities. Compared to Philadelphia, Minneapolis seemed so sparkling new and unbelievably white. White faces flashed everywhere. There were black people there, of course, but they always seemed to be with white people. Nothing struck her as especially black. Not like

52nd and Market, or Germantown Avenue in Philly. She remembered thinking that it must be hard to be black in Minnesota, so few reflections of yourself as you walked the streets.

"Yes. It's very different." His thoughts were running up and down the cement sidewalk. Sonny watched the years pass in fast seconds. He remembered the first time he came downtown by himself to buy shoes at Florsheim's. His first suit at Boyd's. He remembered the gravy-smothered turkey sandwich he ate at Woolworth's every year when his mother took Rainy and him shopping for Easter clothes. He blinked, the night lights creasing across his attentive eyes, and he realized that he had driven around city hall, which stood at the center of downtown like a crusty phallus. "The city of brotherly love. That's a laugh." He remembered a tradition of brutal white police officers and a taut racial atmosphere. The car then faced North Philly.

Instinctively, regardless of the changes in the landscape, buildings new and buildings gone, he headed in the direction of the house he had grown up in. It was odd, without asking directions, he wended his way through the strutting streets like a snake. Nothing could confuse him. Now quiet, Gwen stared out the window of the moving car, watching the people and the things they did without comment.

She looked through the shadows at Sonny, absorbed in driving and silent reminiscences. "Have you ever told me why you moved? I mean, I guess you probably did, but whenever I remember you live in Minnesota, I can't quite figure out how you got there." Gwen's mind continued even after she stopped talking and before a smiling Sonny could respond, she added, "I swear, you give birth to babies and you raise them up and you take care of them and all of a sudden they're living somewhere you never heard of."

Sonny found himself laughing. It wasn't the usual "what's a black man doing in Minnesota" question. This was his mother asking. "I don't know why I'm there, Mom. I really don't, except I have a good job."

"Are you going to marry this Allison girl?"

"I don't know. I need to get back to Minnesota. I know that."

Gwen watched two little black girls sitting on the steps playing jacks. "I just don't understand it, Sonny. Why would a smart, good-looking black man like you go way out there in the middle of nowhere?"

"Mom, I think it would be very hard for me to live in Philly and have the type of life I have in Minnesota." Even though he said it and truly believed what he said, Sonny knew it wouldn't make sense to his mother.

"Just what kind of life is that, Sonny?"

He sensed the slightly indignant tone of her

voice. "It doesn't have anything to do with money or things or anything like that. It's just, I'm not looking over my shoulder all the time up there. It's not so intense. Everybody's not out to do you in like they are here. There are ugly people everywhere, Minneapolis too, but I feel safer there. Things are calmer."

"But there ain't no black people up there."

"There's some."

"You know what I mean."

"Yes, I know what you mean, Mom, and I don't like that part. It is definitely white. And, yes, sometimes it wears me out. At the end of the day, I'm tired just from dealing with it."

"That's what I would think. I don't mind white people. I just don't ever want to be away from lots of black people. That's what would bother me about Minnesota. Not how many white people there are, but how many black people there ain't."

Sonny chuckled. "When you're black and you're separated from the folks too long, you start to miss them. That's why I like coming home. But Mom, let me tell you something. After I've been here for a week or so, I'm ready to go. I don't think I can deal with the city again."

Gwen sucked her teeth. "I just don't understand how you can grow up around all these black people and go live somewhere where they ain't none."

"Come on, Mom. You've been to Minneapolis." Sonny turned onto Whither Street. "You know good and well that there are black people there."

"I know, Sonny, I'm just messing with you. I know why you're living up there."

Sonny was curious. "Why?"

"Because you can be a part of this family but not have to deal with any of the problems," Gwen said flatly.

He was stunned.

Gwen turned and looked at him in the darkness of the summer night. There were stars in the sky. They wavered like they were captured on a field of billowing blue. Sonny had pulled into a parking space, shifted into park and turned the car off. The constant traffic on Whither Street brought a continuous white-blue stream of reflecting headlights into the car.

"Sonny, I'm your mother, remember? I know you pretty well. You could live up there in Minnesota or anywhere for that matter and never come back to Philadelphia if your father and I didn't live here. Now, I know that's true. You never come to the family reunions and get-togethers. So you don't have to make up any fancy excuse for living there."

"I swear, Mom, sometimes you get everything all twisted up. I went up there to work for a company. Not to get away from the family."

"I know, sweetheart. Don't worry. I understand."

"Well, are we gonna go in or what?" Sonny figured it was time to change the subject. He didn't really expect her to understand or to really talk about it.

"I just wish you'd get yourself a family."

"Like Rainy?" Sonny said as he jumped out of the car.

"That's not a nice thing to say, Sonny, especially since you haven't met her boyfriend. Now, I don't want you to be negative about this." Gwen gathered her pocketbook and straightened her dress.

Sonny slowly walked around the front of the car to open the door for his mother. He didn't look up, but felt the intense heat generated by the long day on the sun-baked bricks and cement. He felt the sweat of black men seeking respite after a long week. He felt the growing excitement for the coming Saturday night, the event, the explosion, the expression.

He remembered the summer voices of children that had filled the street during his childhood. He saw his father sitting on the steps of 2515 Whither. He saw the Hardisons sitting on their steps next door, waving, trying to be first to say hello. On the other side of the Goodman house were the Strongs, and their two daughters, Carmen and Willa. Sonny had always had a crush on Willa. Now Willa lived in Germany with an army husband. Carmen, fat and with four children, lived with her widowed mother. Doc was there pontificating on the likelihood of Sonny spending the night in North Philly. There were football buddies and cute would-be girlfriends, smiling at him. His family spilled out of the house and flowed into the Whither River. They all called his name. "Sonny? Is that Sonny? That's Sonny y'all."

Suddenly the image blurred and nearly no one was recognizable. They weren't even there. Only remnants of people guarding their own doors. Still holding on. Now he couldn't see anyone. He didn't want to know anyone. He wanted to go into the house—he wanted that experience—and he wanted to meet Dancer. But that was it. He wasn't like Rainy. He didn't need a daily fix of pain and frustration, of flapping pennants on the staff of capitalism. He worried that their despair would envelope him like a letter from an unhappy ex-lover.

Gwen came out of the car slowly. Sonny helped her. They were parked about five doors away. And so, in a family's dance of pride, Gwen slipped her arm into her son's. A smile immediately appeared on her face. Whoever was about on this Saturday night, whoever sat on their steps and watched the cars pass and talked about the day's events, whoever was standing in a window, or getting dressed for a ritualistic Saturday night out, would see her walking tall with her son.

Her son. A boy from the same block on the same street as their sons and daughters and sisters and brothers. A boy from the same place they were from but who had managed to get out. One of the few. Now Sonny, whether he knew it or not, or cared, had become one of the neighborhood's few positive role models. A part of the proof that being an African American in an American city was not a sentence to a wretched existence. She was proud of that and she wore him like a coat as she walked toward the house they had fled seven years earlier.

At that time, Whither Street had become a symbol to Gwen of the uncontrolled decay that was sweeping the community. She had fought valiantly, as had Absalom and many of their neighbors for many years, to keep the streets relatively safe for their children. But after Sonny and Rainy were older, the fight seemed endless and hopeless. After a while it was as if they were living in a community under siege. Gwen had felt the rising fear, the increased sense of heaviness in the community.

Yet it wasn't the physical change in the neighborhood that had chased her. The houses still appeared neat and brightly painted. It was the rise in the numbers of young pregnant girls, the increased flow of drugs, the children who did not finish high school, the families that broke up, the burglaries that plagued every house on the block, until the only thing left to do was to move. To her, moving was the only way of expressing outrage at the neighborhood's demise. Yes, they had worked hard, but in the end they had to flee.

The street was far from quiet. Sonny couldn't believe how many people seemed to be just standing around. There were groups of teenagers at each corner. People he didn't even know. The Hardisons weren't sitting out. Neither were the Strongs. The image had been his memory. Blared beats of myriad whispers in words and music shook the night air. Sonny heard the giggles of girls, the bravado of boys. He smelled vinegared collard greens, a smell he never smelled in Minnesota.

Instead of the Hardisons, there were two older men sitting on the steps. Standing over them were two younger men. They were involved in an animated discussion about basketball.

"I'd take Jabbar and kick all y'all's asses. Just give me Jabbar."

"You're full of shit man. Jabbar? Give me a break. Jabbar was a fucking sissy. I'll tell you what. If we put Wilt up against Jabbar, he'd go back to usin' his Christian name."

In between the banter and the insults the men laughed until they coughed and then laughed again. Fortunately, it seemed that no one recognized Sonny. But as Sonny and Gwen turned to walk up the steps, a hand shot out of the air behind them and grabbed Sonny around the neck. It was a man's hand, but it was thin, dry, and bony, with long yellowed fingernails.

Sonny froze in his tracks. He couldn't speak, he couldn't turn around. He just stood there. The men halted in their banter and turned.

"I been waiting for you, Sonny."

Sonny heard the words and sank lower on the gray stone steps of the house. He looked over at his mother, who now had a small smile on her round face.

"Doc, you better let that boy go. He might turn around and knock you into next week."

"I was just wonderin' when you was gonna get off your high horse and come visit some of us down here." Doc spun Sonny around and embraced him roughly.

"Hi, Mr. Doc." Sonny's words rode the stream of air Doc forced from Sonny's body.

"How are you doin', boy? You lookin' mighty fine. Check out these threads. Guess you pretty proud of this boy, huh Gwen?"

"You know I am, Doc. He's grown up just fine."

"Yeah, I can see that. Not like what we got around here nowadays. It's like the Wild West out here anymore. People getting shot up for nothin'. I just don't understand it. Actually, son," Doc finally stopped to take a breath, "I can understand full well why you wouldn't come down here. If I had somewhere else to go, I'd get out of here too.''

''It's not that I won't come around here. I just live so far away,'' Sonny lied. The truth was, no matter where he lived, he would never again feel comfortable on these streets.

''I understand. Well, you just keep learnin' all you can. That's all we can do in this type of situation.''

Gwen depressed the doorbell button. They both heard the thud of the bell. ''Ab was supposed to come down here and fix that. It's been broken since we moved out.''

Rainy appeared at the door in a green silk Japanese robe. A wild surprise stretched across her face. It underscored the bizarreness of her eyes. Both Sonny and Gwen stared at her. Her eye shadow and mascara had run—her sharp, polished, African face reflected a myriad of colors floating on her skin.

Gwen wondered instantly if Rainy had been crying. ''What's wrong with you?'' she asked bluntly.

''Nothing's wrong. I just didn't expect any company.''

Sonny took a step forward. ''I just thought it would be good for Mom to leave the hospital. I was going to call you.'' Sonny looked past her into the darkened house. ''But your mother didn't think we had to.''

"Oh?" Rainy's smudged face broke into a reluctant smile.

"You told me whenever I wanted to visit, all I had to do is come on over."

"I did, huh?" Rainy brought both of her hands to her hips and let them rest there. "Well, come on in then. Dancer and I were upstairs. Be comfortable, I'll be right back." She walked past them and ran up the stairs.

As he walked through the door, Sonny was struck by the unchanged air in the room. He could be a child in this room. He remembered his collection of green plastic army men—at one time, he had amassed nearly a hundred, all posed in a variety of combat positions.

Once, in an effort to thwart the enemy, Sonny had stuffed the plastic army men into the underside of a couch that used to sit just inside the front door. Sonny didn't know that Gwen and Absalom had been planning for weeks to buy a new couch.

He walked in the house one day after school to find a new ensemble. They had changed the living room, gone from Early American to the modern style of the fifties. The couch was gone; his army had been decimated by a surprise attack.

Now he stood there in the living room and he could feel his history percolating all around. The furniture was different. The paint was new. But the details of the house were exactly the same. The same cracks in the plaster walls, the same gap of black space between the baseboards and the wall. Sonny sat down.

"Wow, every time I come in here, I am overwhelmed. I grew up here."

Gwen looked at him askance. "Really? I didn't know that."

"I just feel so far away from all this now. When we lived here, this house seemed so big." Sonny's voice trailed off. The smallness of the living room was gradually agitating him. Chilled air blew from an air conditioner in the window that looked out on the backyard. The air rushed directly into his face, causing him to squint. "Now, I can't believe how tiny it really is."

Gwen nodded her head. "Sometimes I feel the same way."

Sonny sat back in the leather chair and watched Rainy and Dancer appear near the top of the stairs, standing close together. Their leg shadows painted a mural along the stairway. Sonny thought they were probably kissing.

Rainy wore a peach-colored sundress that cascaded around her, contrasting with the deep summer brownness of her skin. Right behind her was the shiny narrow foot of a tall man.

As they emerged into view, descending the stairs, they composed a curious picture. Rainy, handsome, worldly, and delicate, rode upon Dancer's arm, underlining the man's rough edges.

"This is my brother, Sonny. All the way from

Minneapolis,'' Rainy said in a steady, confident voice. She expected Sonny to be negative. Rainy expected him to try to put Dancer down, but she was determined not to let it happen.

Dancer needed Rainy's help less than she assumed. He walked right by Sonny to Gwen and wrapped his long dark arms around her. He was wearing a white short-sleeved polo shirt and the darkness of his arms, even in the dim lights of the shadowed house, startled Sonny. Dancer was the darkest man Rainy had ever been connected to. She used to joke that she would never go out with a man who was darker than she was.

"How are you, Mrs. Goodman? How's your husband?"

"We're both doing okay, as well as can be expected." Gwen sank into a corner of the chair.

"I know this is a very difficult time, but I'm glad to hear that right now, things are okay." Sonny felt the insincerity across the room. Here was Eddie Haskell's soul mate—the sign of the Rooster.

"And you," Dancer turned on his heels to face Sonny. "you must be Sonny." He extended his hand.

Sonny instantly felt the tension congeal and rise up from the floor, moving along the legs of tables and chairs and people and take shape between them. He quickly decided to make no pretense, to play no games. He didn't intend to be nice. In fact, it was suddenly clear to him that the very first thing that had to happen, was that Dancer had to leave. The Goodman house on Whither Street was not where Dancer belonged.

Sonny nodded, posting his message in a silent stare. You'll find no gullible sucker here. Instead of grabbing the weakening out-stretched hand from Dancer, he pushed himself out of the chair and turned to Rainy. "Maybe this isn't a good time. It is getting late."

"You're here now, Sonny." Rainy watched Dancer tactfully retrieve his hand. "You might as well have a seat. I'll make you something to eat."

Gwen decided to let the whole thing between Sonny and Dancer pass her by. She really didn't care. "I don't think I could move if I wanted to."

Dancer sat down beside her. "You must be exhausted. I just can't believe how strong you are, Mrs. Goodman. This is an incredible weight to bear."

Sonny sat listening, stunned at Dancer's blatant attempt to seduce his mother. He could hear Rainy rattling pots in the kitchen. He looked at Dancer and his mother. Dancer seemed almost flirtatious.

"When people are seriously sick it's so hard on those who love them. They have to be strong for the sick but, at the same time, they need support and love, too."

Gwen looked at Dancer carefully. Then she looked past him and found Sonny's eyes piercing the thick cold air. Between them a stormy ocean rolled and pitched in the August moonlight. They had been mother and son in this house. She had wiped, cleaned, and spanked his butt in this house. She felt her feet planted firmly on dry land. She would stay through the tidal onslaught.

Meanwhile she was weighing Dancer's manner carefully. She knew what Sonny was thinking, but she also heard what Dancer was saying. It made her feel better. It seemed to give her permission to relax. She knew she shouldn't trust his sincerity, but, at the same time, it seemed a moot question. Who cared if it was sincere or not? She needed to hear what he was saying. No one else had said it to her.

"Sometimes I feel like all I have to do is just be strong and believe in God and he'll get better. Sometimes I feel like it's just that simple."

"I know what you mean, Mrs. Goodman. But that can take a lot out of you." Sonny's head spun around in confusion. How could this be happening to him? Dancer's intense focus on his mother's feelings was working. He marveled at the man's deviousness.

But something else was happening at the same time. Sonny felt another force, some new shape growing around them. He felt a pull but couldn't discern its origin. So he sat there and listened.

"Son, I've sat there with my husband for two

weeks. Every day, all day. I'm so tired..." Gwen's voice trailed off.

"You can rest here, Mrs. Goodman. You just put your head back and relax for a while." Dancer looked at Sonny. "Rainy's probably about ready with something to eat; do you want to go into the dining room? I'll bring your mother's food out to her."

Sonny tore through the muck between them. "Listen, man, I can bring my mother her food. I don't need you to do anything for me."

Dancer stood up and stared down at Sonny. "What's with you, homeboy? What's the problem?"

"You, *homeboy.* You're the problem." Sonny looked past everything out into the street.

"Hey, I just met you. Don't come round here starting no shit." He shot a glance at Gwen, whose head was back on the chair with her eyes closed. She was motionless. "I mean, ah, mess."

Sonny leaned close to him and spoke in a low voice. "Maybe you just met me, but A, you're living in my house and B, you're sleeping with my sister and C, you're running bull to my mother. So don't talk about mess. I don't know what's going on around here, but—" Sonny stopped cold. He stood frozen in the middle of the living room floor, his suit feeling like a crumpled rag that hid parts of his body.

Gwen opened her eyes and looked at him.

Dancer, waiting for the rest of the onslaught, ready to deliver his response, lingered in anger two feet away. Rainy had heard the entire exchange and had moved into the living room to intervene. Everyone stared at Sonny, who was staring at the table between the chair and the sofa. His mouth was open and his eyes reflected a growing terror.

Now he understood the last feeling of ill will. "That's a gun. Rainy, Mom, why is there a gun on the table here?" Sonny pointed stiffly to the pistol.

Dancer turned and saw the silver gun, innocently lying there like a piece of gleaming sculpture. His heart fell like a darting fox caught in an iron claw-trap.

"Now I know you don't have a gun in this house, I just know that's not a gun. Rainy? Dancer, is that your gun?" Gwen could see the pistol clearly now.

"Ah . . . that's my friend's gun. I'm sorry, Mrs. Goodman. I forget it was here. He, ah, he was by here right after he bought it and was showing it to me and, ah, well, I guess we just forgot it was lying over there." Dancer hoped his story would lay sufficient cover.

It might have, except that Sonny was already in pursuit. This was the crowning proof.

"Naw, man . . ." Sonny took a step forward into Dancer's face. He put himself into Dancer's shadow, which claimed itself from the lamplight arising from the coffee table behind him. "It's not

like that. You brought a gun into this house."
Sonny stopped for effect. He felt his pulse jump-
ing, blood squirming swiftly through him.

"Do you know whose house this is? Do you?"

Dancer was caught a bit unprepared. The di-
rectness of the attack was unexpected. Rainy had
led him to believe that Sonny, while an intelligent
person, was not exactly a fighter. In fact, he had
always imagined Sonny as a punk, an aberration of
the inner city.

Dancer had been born in Mississippi and had
come to Philadelphia with nothing. To him, the
city was a marvelous place with opportunities for
everything. It was a place he could find the energy
he needed to be happy. The speed, the rolling wonder, the never-ending story that was the inner surface of the inner city.

To Dancer there were only two types of black
people—those who had hope and those who didn't.
Anybody who had was a punk. That's how he had
imagined Sonny. Now, standing there, his face a
man's hand away from him, Dancer reconsidered
his approach.

"I know whose house it is," Dancer said finally.

"Whose is it, Sonny?" Rainy had watched the
scene from the breakfast room. A solid teal blue
wallpaper was the background for her slim figure,
which hid within the sundress.

"It isn't yours, Rainy. And it damn sure isn't

his." Sonny jerked his thumb at Dancer as he turned to face Rainy. She walked toward him.

"I don't know how many times I have to say it, Sonny. Don't make me have to keep telling you. This is my house. Mine. I've been living here for five years. Dad wanted me to have it."

"How do you know? I never heard him say anything about giving you this house. But more important, I know he never would let you have somebody like him living with you."

"Wait a minute, home. I think I should warn you that I ain't likin' the way you talk about me." Dancer was smiling, but his words marched out of his mouth, fully armed and combat ready. They positioned themselves around Sonny, communicating their intention, and slowly faded into the air. Almost imperceptibly, Dancer backed up as he continued. "Cause, look here, my brother, I don't go in for a whole lot of name-callin' and all that bullshit. You don't even know me. I don't know what you got against me. But I know one goddamned thing." Dancer raised the level of his voice so it became a spear charging into Sonny's space. Dancer turned around and picked the gun up. "You had better put your butt on chill, cause you gettin' on my last nerve. I've had to deal with a lot of shit around here today. One of my partners gets dusted and now you come in here actin' like you're my father." Dancer wrapped the gun with his hand.

"You're right, Dancer." Sonny looked at his mother, who now stared at him bewildered. Rainy stood just to his left trying to decide what to say. "I don't know what's going on around here. But somebody got shot right outside. And this is my sister. And Rainy, I don't care what you say, this is my house and my mother's house and most important, this is my father's house. So don't tell me what I can and can't say." Sonny sat down next to his mother and put an arm around her. He looked up at Dancer, who stood fixed, fondling the gun.

"You gonna shoot me with that?"

"I told you once already, Sonny, to get off my case." Dancer stared at him, his anger rising up like little crackling camp fires dotting a prairie. Thousands of trembling thoughts rattled inside his head. "I could kill you if I wanted to. You talk too much. Especially about things you don't know a fucking thing about."

Sonny didn't feel scared. He saw the gun. He felt the breeze that rushed through the barrel and grazed his temples as it passed his face. He could not back down in his own house.

"Why are you acting like this?" Rainy's plea pierced the cool air.

"Rainy, what is going on around here? Why did that kid get shot on our doorstep?" Sonny couldn't let the tension drop.

"How should I know? I was with you, remem-

ber? I swear Sonny, you're acting like a real id-
iot.''

"I'm not the one holding a gun.'' The simple
observation stunned everyone, including Dancer,
because his eyes shifted quickly from Sonny to the
gun. Gwen, who had been transfixed by the sight
of the gun, broke her stare momentarily. Sonny
heard her softly whisper, "Sweet Jesus.''

Rainy looked at him. "Will you please put that
thing away? This is stupid. You don't even know
each other.''

The aching doorbell interrupted her. Dancer
put the gun on the dining room table and walked
to the door. There was a gathering of noises in the
vestibule. Sonny could feel the air change again.
Gwen had let her head fall back to the couch. How
could this endless misery give her any time off?
She resigned herself to it. She felt it was not done
with her.

Half-Dead and Dancer walked into the room.
"Mrs. Goodman, this is a friend of mine—''

"I know who he is.'' Gwen had turned long
enough to look at him and had now closed her
eyes. "Don't I, Raymond?''

"Raymond?'' Rainy broke the tension with a
smile. "Your name is Raymond?''

Half-Dead stared at her. "Uh, hi, Mrs. Goodman. How you doin', Sonny?'' Sonny nodded.

Rainy was surprised. "I didn't know you all
knew each other.''

Gwen started talking. Her eyes remained closed. "Rainy, don't you have a brain? I raised you in this neighborhood. I know everybody. I know all the people you know, plus their parents. I knew the white people who lived here before we did. I know Raymond and I knew his momma and his daddy and he knows it."

"Uh, excuse me." Half-Dead wanted to break up the discussion. His long scrawny body trembled. "Can I talk to you for a minute in the kitchen?" He turned and slowly walked toward the back of the house. Dancer was right behind him. Rainy instead walked toward her mother.

"I didn't know y'all was havin' company," Half-Dead said as they reached the marigold-colored kitchen.

"Neither did I." Dancer was thankful for the interruption. He wasn't sure what Sonny was up to or how long it would have taken them to come to blows.

"Yeah, well, if I had of known, I would have slipped in on the sly." Half-Dead was stern-faced, his narrow features and dark skin moving into a crease that seemed to extend the length of his face. "It's getting tight out there."

"What do you mean?"

Half-Dead leaned close to Dancer and whispered into his ear, "Well, I could have just made myself invisible and walked right by Mrs. Goodman and Sonny."

"What? What the fuck are you talking about?" Dancer was already agitated. He felt the tension that Half-Dead had brought in with him.

"Don't you remember? I told you earlier about how I'm learning how to make myself inv—"

"Motherfucka, listen." Dancer grabbed Half-Dead's dark blue T-shirt and pulled the man into him. "I don't give a rat's ass about your being invisible. You hear what I'm saying, homeboy? You get it? But I do care about what's going on." He spoke the words softly but they were edged with the sharpness of his growing desperation. He felt something coming down around him. The air had less space to it. Everything was dense and his breathing struggled against the environment. The quiet strength of fear's fingernails dug into his ankles. He could feel something clutching at his legs, struggling to hold him down.

"Chill out, Dancer. What's up with you? I've never seen you so freaked, man." Half-Dead stepped back and stared at Dancer. "You're scared, ain't you? I didn't think you'd be scared of those punk-ass motherfuckas."

"Hey, man." Dancer put his hands up in the air. "They killed Spider right on my front steps. Now I'm not saying I want to close shop or anything, but I ain't gonna lie to you, homeboy, I'm not feeling too good about what's going down."

Half-Dead looked at a tired Dancer and smiled. "That's why I came on over. You think I'm gonna leave you here to deal with everything by yourself. Naw, homey, we're in this together.''

Dancer knew that Half-Dead was trying to say something but couldn't understand what it was. ''Dead, man, please, what the hell are you talking about?''

''I been doing some investigating tonight.'' Half-Dead paused. Dancer just stared at him. ''Yeah, I went underground, you know. I—''

''Dead, man, I'm gonna kill you myself if you don't tell me what the fuck is happening.''

''Well, that's the reason I came right on over here. I left my shit outside in the car though. So I should probably go get it before it gets too late.'' Half-Dead started to leave the kitchen. Dancer reached out his long arm, grabbed Half-Dead and slammed him against the wall.

''Tell me.''

''They're coming for you, Dancer. They want us out of business and they're playing hardball. The deal is, they want everybody to know that the Moon is not afraid to waste people to get control.''

''They want to kill me?''

''Hey, Dance, don't worry, man. I brought my shit with me. I got the nine in the car. I think I should go get it now.'' Again Half-Dead turned to walk out of the room. But Dancer, nearly in a trance, held firm to his shirt.

''Can't I talk to them?'' Dancer's heart thumped.

"We're gonna have to show these bozos that we can take care of ourselves before they talk to us."

Dancer felt his thighs trembling. His stomach was a Ferris wheel. He was trying to maintain his composure, but he was failing. Half-Dead seemed so stupid all of a sudden. Every piece of information had to be extracted like a tooth from his melon head.

"When are they coming, and what are they going to do?"

"I think they're coming tonight and I don't know for sure, but I bet you they're going to bust a cap on you."

"I don't understand, Dead. I don't understand. Nobody has like, leaned on me or anything. I get no warning?"

"I told you, home, from what I heard it don't make no difference. That's not the way they operate. It's not even a personal thing. Seems like there might have been something personal going on with Spider, but not with you. They just want the turf. So, they're coming to get it."

"Rainy wants to give it up," Dancer said flatly, letting go of Half-Dead's shirt.

"It's an idea, I guess. I just don't like giving everything to motherfuckas I don't even know, just because they try to act bad."

"They killed Spider."

"Yeah, but Spider was stealing from them and

playing two ends against the middle. He deserved to get killed. Shit, you might have killed him for what he did.''

''Yeah. Well, suppose I just give it up?'' Dancer felt the threat hover in the air surrounding the house.

''I don't know if you can. They might be trying to prove something.''

''You think we should fight?''

''I told you man. They ain't doing a whole lot of talking. Now can I go back out to my car and get my gun?'' Half-Dead's patience had finally worn out.

''That's Rainy's mother out there. We've got to get them out of here.'' Dancer felt the energy of panic escalating. At that moment, Rainy walked into the kitchen. Half-Dead turned and walked past her.

''What the hell is going on? You look scared to death.'' She saw the façade fall away, revealing the caged animal. Freedom taken away. From predator to prey. ''What's wrong, Dancer?''

''According to Half-Dead, the Moon is going to try to waste me.'' Dancer said it plainly and without emotion. He was so frightened, he was numbed.

''What did you do? I thought you weren't going to do anything until we talked about it.'' Now she too felt the floating panic that was like a living organism, which multiplied and extended itself.

"I don't understand it, Rainy. I haven't done a goddamned thing. I didn't even know they was in the hood." The wildness spread over his face.

"We've got to let them know we're out of business." Then she thought about Sonny and her mother sitting in the living room. Sonny breathing heavy, angry, and fondling the gun that Dancer had left there. Gwen trying to escape the moment, knowing things were deteriorating all around her. Still, she valiantly sought peace in the momentary lull.

Rainy let out a sigh and leaned against the sunflower-papered wall. The avalanche of life seemed ever flowing, showing no signs of shallowness. In her youth, she would have run home to her father. She would have grabbed his large, rough, hands, hands that curled in semifists on their own and dragged him to where the trouble was. He would fix it all.

In the living room, Sonny looked at the steel gray gun in his hands. It was heavier than he would have imagined. He was not familiar with guns. Their power frightened him. Nothing should be able to penetrate the notion of life and expose the meaninglessness so absolutely. No created thing should have the power to end life. He picked the gun up and pointed it at the window. The truth was, though, that everything people created had the same power; you could eat yourself to death. But it was the starkness of the purpose of a gun. There was no other reason for its existence except to kill. We no longer marveled at the sight of smoke or the burst of an explosion. No, it was death that we applauded. The gun was the essential tool. The only tool for which there was no other purpose.

Sonny was afraid, too. He couldn't explain the intensity with which he wanted Dancer to leave. He felt the house had been taken away from him, from his mother and father, even from Rainy. Somehow it had been usurped. He wanted it back.

When he was a little boy, he would have gone down into the cellar, found his father tinkering with the furnace or the water heater or fixing something, and he would have said, "Dad, somebody's taking our house. Something's going on around here and I don't know what it is. But I'm afraid."

He closed his eyes. He could see his father walking slowly up the cellar stairs. The weak wood moaned under his weight. The stairs emerged in the breakfast room, where the refrigerator was. His father would hit the top of the steps and grab the refrigerator door at the same time. He might act like he wasn't listening, but he was.

"Dad, I'm afraid."

Absalom understood the plea in Sonny's voice. The voice held the pain of history. Every American black man had felt the same pain. He poured himself a tall glass of milk. "Do you know what it is? Do you know why you're afraid, Sonny?"

"Things are getting worse, not better. We're giving up ground. Going backwards." Sonny breathed hard. "I thought that our lives were supposed to get better, that we were supposed to have more. Isn't that what you told me? 'Go to school, work hard and you'll be able to do things I could never do.' That's what you told me. But instead, it feels like we're losing. Nobody cares anymore. We're not moving right now."

Absalom sat down at the breakfast room table and gulped a large swallow of milk. The liquid put a white stain on his robust tan face. He smiled broadly.

"Losing what, Sonny?"

"Dad, I don't know. You always said that even though it was hard to make it in this white man's world, it was possible."

"Yeah, I said that. I remember. So what?"

"It's not feeling very possible right now. Besides, it ain't always white people you got to be looking out for, is it?" Sonny was trying to work it out as he went. "I mean some kid was killed on our front steps. By black people. It wasn't a white man who blew him away. I can't get over that. I've just been sitting here, holding Mom's hand and thinking about the fact that somebody lost his life on our stoop."

"What is it, Sonny? You can't get over knowing that black people kill black people? Cause if that's it, you've got a long hard row to hoe."

Sonny fondled the gun. "No, that's not it. I know that black people kill each other. White people kill white people, too. That's not what I mean."

Absalom got up, opened the refrigerator, and pulled the half-gallon milk container out. He sat back down and refilled his glass. "So what is it?"

"Is this all there is? This constant struggle to fight off the effects of hatred. Isn't there a sweeter thing in this life?"

"Sonny, the sweetness is in your ability to be yourself. To not let what other people do affect you so much. Yes, I know I told you things were gonna get better, and I thought they were. But I'm just a hardworking colored man. Just like you now. And I had to believe in progress just to keep going. Heck, we thought if we believed hard enough it would come true. But we didn't figure that our children would get so successful that they would think the struggle was over. Everybody left and didn't look back. Left all the hurting people back here."

"But Dad, I thought that's what we were supposed to do."

"I know you did, Son, but look around you. Your success don't mean that much. Everybody in this house is black and in trouble. And all around us there are people in pain. And they're angry. It's a bomb, Sonny." Absalom paused and wiped his mouth with the back of his hand. "You like Minneapolis?"

"Yes."

"Your life is not like this anymore, is it?"

"No."

"So, Sonny, you see, you don't really have to deal with it. You'll go on back there. The people who live here have to make a decision. They have to decide what they won't tolerate. When I lived here, that's what we did. We just said we won't let you do that on this street."

Sonny looked at his father. "Dad, I love you. I'm very, very proud of you. I can't imagine having a better father."

"It's good to hear that, Sonny. I love you too. I just wish I could have done more." Absalom seemed distant; he was smiling but he sounded sad.

"Dad, what are we going to do about the house?"

"I can't do anything now, Son."

Half-Dead walked back in the door, the nine-millimeter pistol tucked in his pants. He walked past Sonny and Gwen. He walked past Absalom and into the kitchen.

"Listen y'all, maybe we should split for a while. I mean, why would we stay here and wait for them to come?" Half-Dead was animated, obviously excited.

Dancer just stared at him, but Rainy agreed.

"Good idea. We've got to get the hell out of here
and we've got to get my mother and brother out of
here."

She headed into the living room; but as she
passed through the breakfast room, the dining
room, and into the living room she realized they
had waited too long. A tall, thin, brown-skinned
man filled the front doorway. He wore a black
leather suit that was made like a track warm-up
outfit. He smiled at her. Rainy noticed the gold
caps on his teeth.

"You shouldn't leave your door open in a
neighborhood like this. You never know who will
come in."

Rainy's heart exploded, blood stained the inside of her body. Silently she cursed Half-Dead.

The man stood in front of her. "Is this where
I can find Dancer?"

"Who are you?" Rainy felt her knees breaking. The center of her body was dropping.

"Can I see Dancer, please?" The man stood
completely still.

"Can I help you?" It was Gwen. She twisted
in her chair, looking up at the intruder.

"Who are you?" The man suddenly became
jumpy. "Who are all these people? I just want to
see Dancer. Somebody had better get him out here,
now." He raised his voice at the end of his sentence.

Rainy stared him in the eye and asked, "Who are you?"

Sonny felt the increased tension. "Is this our house or what? How hard do you fight for something?"

Absalom smiled, "Until you lose your breath."

"I said, who are you?" Rainy stood in the man's way.

"But I'm afraid." Sonny put his arms around his father's muscular neck.

"I know, Sonny. And I can't say anything to help you. I'm worried about you. I'm just glad you came to see me. I missed you." Absalom's eyes sang to Sonny.

"If Dancer's here, you had best be telling homeboy to get his ass out here. You want to know who I am?" His eyes gouged holes in her head. "You tell that faggot punk-ass motherfucka that BuckTeeth Rodney is looking for him."

Rainy knew that Dancer was hiding in the kitchen. She hoped he'd stay there. There was a heavy feeling about BuckTeeth Rodney. She felt his power, as if he could will violence into happening. "Listen, we're out of it. We quit. We're out of business."

"Yeah?" Rodney flashed his golden teeth. He had lost the physical reason for his nickname, but he kept it anyway. Everyone knew BuckTeeth Rodney. "Since when? Could it be since Spider bit the dust? Could you be scared?''

Gwen got up from the couch. Sonny tried to grab her, but she eluded his outstretched arm and walked up to BuckTeeth Rodney. ''Boy,'' she said as she neared him, ''do you know that this is my house? And I don't appreciate strangers bursting in and telling us what we have to do.''

''Listen lady, if I was you I'd keep quiet. And if this is your house you've got problems because Dancer has seriously put the whole show in jeopardy. My advice to you is to get out of here while you can.''

''What are you going to do?'' Rainy cut in. Sonny stared at the floor.

''Listen, you can tell him we're not gonna kill him. We just want the shit shut down. Right now. As I'm speaking to you, this is now our territory.''

Sonny whirled around to Rainy as he listened to BuckTeeth Rodney's last sentence. ''Do you mean to tell me that this is all about drugs? You sell drugs here? Rainy, you? And that asshole?''

''Don't worry, cuz, we got that line tightened up, ain't that right sister?'' he said, staring at Rainy. ''You know what I'm saying. This is our turf. And I don't want no shit from Dancer or any motherfuckin' body. Got that?''

''I don't believe it.'' Sonny was deflated. The gun in his hands felt like a lead ball at the end of a chain. ''In our house.''

Absalom hugged him again. ''You asked about

losing. Yes, I guess we are losing some things. Still, Sonny, the fight. It's worth it.''

At that moment, Half-Dead materialized in the archway that separated the breakfast room from the dining room. It was as if he had been hiding behind the wall all the time and suddenly showed himself. His gun was pointed at BuckTeeth Rodney.

"Get the fuck out of here," Half-Dead spit at the taller man.

BuckTeeth Rodney smiled. "You don't want to threaten me."

"Get out." Half-Dead's voice was the only noise. Rainy was frozen, nearly in the line of fire. Sonny was slowly getting up out of the couch. He still had a gun in his hand.

"Okay, man. Chill. Just chill out. I'm going." BuckTeeth Rodney turned slowly to leave. Gwen heard air leaving her mouth. Rainy started to back up. When Rodney got to the front door, he turned his head back slowly and threw off a large grin. It slapped everyone gently. Half-Dead's eyes were fixed on him. And as Half-Dead feared, just as BuckTeeth Rodney was about to take his first step outside the house, he wheeled around and in a quick burst two shots from his pistol sliced back through the small house and hit Half-Dead. They stood him straight up for a second or two. Sonny didn't see the gun explode, but he did turn to see Half-Dead's chest rip open.

Rainy screamed and dove for the floor, grabbing her mother as she went down. Sonny turned to face Rodney. The gun in Sonny's hand became a neon light. Sonny stared at Rodney. He had never watched someone get shot before. He had lost his ability to hit the floor in cover. He had lost it somewhere in the space between inner-city life and a healthy existence.

BuckTeeth Rodney didn't hesitate. He saw the gun and wasn't about to take a chance. He pulled the trigger again. Once, twice. Sonny saw the bullets leave the barrel of the pistol. He could see them spinning slowly, bearing down on his head. He looked at his mother, who was curled on the floor between the sofa and the coffee table, eyes closed, hands over her head. He wanted her to know that she was safe. But he wasn't sure. Rainy was terrified and sang it out in stricken fear. He could see the bullets, imperfect weights propelled directly at him.

"I'm going to die, Dad. It's happening to me. I thought, I thought that I was a visitor. But I'm not, am I? I'm not visiting at all. The company, Allison, everything was just a vacation. I'm really dying here. And it seems so futile. Everything I've done. Everything I wanted to do. It feels so empty. I don't want the fight to be futile. What do you do with futility? Dad?"

Absalom looked at a horrified Sonny. He pulled the boy to him and said, "I love you."

Sonny felt his full lips on his cheek.

The bullets hit him sharply, tearing into his right temple and lower left side. Part of his face broke away and rolled across the floor. Blood exploded from his body. BuckTooth Rodney stood there thinking. He could kill everyone. For a moment, standing there, that's what he wanted to do. But instead, he turned and ran out the door.

16

Gwen's chest rose and fell in the motion of breathing, but it had, much earlier, emptied of flowing emotion. Now she couldn't feel her heart or hear the blood rushing. Still, she made time to do it. It didn't make sense to stop breathing now; Absalom needed her, even Rainy needed her. The only Goodman free from the thickness was her son. And she could never feel whole again, because he had always been an important part of her and he was now gone forever. But she was there fighting for everything that remained. Her family. Her house. Her community. Her life. Her husband. A struggle that was only intensifying.

They met around Absalom's bed like a choir at rehearsal, waiting for someone to assert their will, to become the translating vessel which would allow their voices to soar. Someone who would help to

create the sacred singing that worked its way under
the skin until you were a stream of blue-green water
swishing through the air like a gospel song. Gwen
was too lost in her own reverie to be the capable
choir leader. She was there, visible and present, but
she was unable to lead the singing.

Rainy sat quietly in the corner of the dark hospital room. The Monday shadows sat like black-
robed worshipers in the room. Her thoughts had
congealed together into a muddy clump that made
talking impossible. Sonny's face was impressed so
clearly in her mind. His surprise, his discovery. She
had watched as Sonny dropped to the floor, life running from him like rats from a sinking ship. And
from that moment she had been unable to speak.
Only tears and soft sounds left her body. Sonny's
death was now in her breath.

Sitting on the windowsill was Allison. Sonny's
death had interrupted her life in Minnesota and
brought her to Philly. She sat there with the Goodman family, people she knew only from the stories
Sonny told. She had come because she thought it
was the right thing to do. She had one main recurring
thought: he had no business being in that house. Suddenly it didn't matter that she had been nearly ready
to end their relationship. Suddenly she missed him.

And then she turned to Absalom, who was still
alive. She could see in Absalom's contorted face the
love and pain that had brought Sonny back home.

And yes, Absalom was still there, though he was

fitful. The doctor, who had visited less than an hour earlier, had said that Absalom was tired, and much weaker. Who wouldn't be tired? Fighting death as a way of surviving. As the only survival. Normal life was a dream. Could he hope to wake up in the morning and put on his clothes and go out to work again? He held his thoughts like delicate porcelain.

But more than anything he wanted Rainy to know that he didn't blame her. She still had time to change her life. To remake the Goodman future.

"Remember, Rainy, we have to keep breathing to make the song. Don't you go giving up. You got to go back to that house and set things right. I want the same for you that I wanted for Sonny. If you stay on Whither you got to fight for it just like I did. No two ways about it, if you live you got to struggle. And if you struggle, sometimes you get hurt. But let me tell you, baby girl, if you ever stop working for something and start trying to scheme your way through, you're asking for trouble. They got you then. They got you then." Absalom stopped talking to her and opened his eyes. Everyone in the room felt them open—Allison, Gwen, Rainy—they all stared at him. He stared back.

"It's a song. It's a struggle to sing it, but it surely is a song. Somehow, we have to make the singing mean something." The perfume of his voice needled its way into Rainy, allowing her a thin, transparent sigh. Their stricken, expectant eyes lay upon him like down. His eyelids slowly closed. Still they stared.

Rainy heard him. Felt him pushing her. Maybe he wouldn't die. Maybe her mother was right, maybe he would rise from his deathbed after all. Absalom's strength was incalculable and, being a black man, he knew how to suffer in grace and with hope.

But whether he rose or not, she would sing for him. She would practice the choir, lead it, if that's what it took. She would sing from now until her last breath, until the sound of her voice was Absalom's hope.

And then, unknowing, there was Selma Mae, crashing through the heavy brush of bruised life. "Come on everybody. Is that all you all gonna do is sit around here crying and looking sad? Sonny wouldn't want it to be like this."

Selma Mae stood at the door with Austin behind her. His hat was missing and Allison could see the thin gray hair smiling from the top of his head. "I've already taken care of services for Sonny, bless his heart." She wasn't smiling; her voice was modulated, tuned in to the suffering. Yet, there was a distance. Somehow, she had already dealt with Sonny's death. She had faced the body. The arrangements. She had internalized the tragedy. It was her business to move everyone forward.

She looked around the room. Gwen looked up at her, and for the first time in a long time she loved her sister. Now a teacup smile slowly materialized on Selma Mae's face. Her round cheeks grew. She felt like singing a spiritual. Instead, she walked over to Absalom, bent down and brushed his forehead with her cranberry lips.

BEBE MOORE CAMPBELL

SINGING in the COMEBACK CHOIR

Putnam